THE
PIGSKIN
RABBI

THE PIGSKIN RABBI

willard manus

BREAKAWAY BOOKS
HALCOTTSVILLE, NY
2000

The Pigskin Rabbi
Copyright © 1999 by Willard Manus
First paperback edition: October 2000

ISBN: 1-891369-23-7
Library of Congress Control Number: 00-133189

Published by Breakaway Books
P.O. Box 24
Halcottsville, NY 12438
(800) 548-4348
www.breakawaybooks.com

Distributed to the trade by
Consortium Book Sales & Distribution

FIRST PAPERBACK EDITION

This book is for Al & Betty Bodian,
Joe Kierland & Estelle Galeano,
Bob & Fran Riche,
and Tom Migliore

THE
PIGSKIN
RABBI

1

SEE SHRDLU. SEE SHRDLU RUN. SEE ETOAIN SHRDLU, THE Albanian placekicker, boot a fifty-four-yarder and win the game in the last three seconds.

See Homer Bloetcher, the sixty-four-year-old, 267-pound scout for the New York Giants, nearly go bananas.

Homer had journeyed all the way to Holland to look Shrdlu over. That's Holland the country, not the tunnel. Homer had flown across the ocean to a foreign country in search of a kicker with a name like a Transylvanian curse word, an unknown kid whose background was equally bizarre. He was rumored to have snuck out of Albania and reached Amsterdam by clinging to the underbelly of a freight car for seventy-two hours. After they thawed him out and hosed him down, the Dutch police asked him his name.

"Etoain Shrdlu," he replied, adding: "I keek, I keek."

I Keek had been given asylum and a tryout with the Amsterdam Canallers of the new Intercontinental Football League, who discovered that he could indeed kick. He was able to punt and placekick with equal skill, driving the ball downfield with homing-pigeon accuracy. News of his golden toe had reached the Giants' head office and Homer was dispatched to find out if the stories were for real.

Homer had bitched mightily about the assignment, feeling it was a wild-goose chase, but the club was desperate for a kicker, having lost their number one man, an Argentinian, to a groin pull (too much *concha*), and numbers two and three to cocaine and shotgun wounds, respectively. The Giants had tried out just about every available kicker in the country: prospects cut by other teams, former players now selling computers or tending bar. The club had even given a prisoner on Ryker's Island a try, a safecracker whose warden was willing to let him out on weekends.

None of these free agents could hack it, though, and the club had lost its first three games because of fickle feet. Homer had been ordered to find a kicker fast, no matter what his story was or how he spelled his name.

Homer was an ex-kicker himself, the last of the straight-ahead, American-style field-goal specialists. He had lasted sixteen seasons in the NFL, playing defensive tackle as well until that infamous day in Chicago when the Bears mousetrapped him ten straight times. It left him not only crippled but punchy, unable to remember the days of the week.

In light of his serious mental deficiencies, there was only one thing Homer could do: become a coach.

He'd soon be out on his ass, though, if he didn't find a kicker. The Swiss conglomerate HEN (Helvetia Enterprises Network), which had bought the Giants from the Mara family in the early part of the twenty-first century for a ton of francs, despite the team's four straight losing seasons, did not have much patience with failure. The Gnomes of Zurich expected the franchise to start winning and winning big or everyone running the show would have to go.

Homer thought it was kinda loony to pin your hopes on an Albanian placekicker playing in Holland for four hundred guilders a week and all the herring he could eat. The big man's spirits sank even farther when he got to the Canallers' ballpark, a shabby stadium with open seats on the outskirts of Amsterdam. Back home in Oklahoma they had high school fields that were nicer spreads than this one.

Homer sighed plaintively as he limped his way to a seat, leaning on his hand-crutches as the warm September rain pelted down on the skimpy crowd. He sat under an umbrella, sipping Jack Daniels from a plastic cup as he watched a bush-league game played by U.S. Army boys and NFL rejects, guys who couldn't even make it in the Canadian league.

Then he saw the Albanian go into action. The kid not only kicked off, punted, and booted point-afters, but played quarterback as well, throwing passes with power and precision. Homer couldn't believe his eyes. The kid seemed like a natural —big, fast, and strong, moving with ease and grace, completely comfortable out there, in command of the game, unbothered by the rain, enjoying what he was doing.

Homer put the duty-free bottle away and leaned forward, studying the Albanian intently. He felt his skin tingle, his heart kick over like an old diesel engine. The kid was a magician. He threw bullets, kicked cloud-breakers, ran draws with sudden, explosive speed. And he was tough. The other team started pounding him, trying to hurt him, but he kept bouncing up, a big grin on his face, defiant and high-spirited as ever. It made his opponents angry and wild, weaknesses that he exploited time and time again with his devastating passes and runs.

Shrdlu was a one-man team. He was playing with a bunch of stiffs who ordinarily wouldn't have stood a chance against the other guys. But the Albanian kept them in contention, valiantly and skillfully. Where in hell had he learned to play quarterback like that? Homer sat there marveling, caught up in his spell.

Then came the last seconds of the game, the kick that made Homer go ballistic. With the Canallers two points down and half the field away from the goal line, Shrdlu stepped forward and calmly drilled the ball through the uprights. It wasn't just the distance that impressed Homer, or the fact that the game was on the line. What really got him was the way the ball was kicked, with the clean, sweet, authoritative sound that only true kickers, born kickers, got.

Homer leapt up as soon as he heard it, watching transfixed as the football took off over the outstretched arms of the onrushing linemen and soared high in the sky, describing a long, graceful arc as it carried toward the far end of the field, splitting the goalposts perfectly.

"You like football more'n you like sex," Homer's late wife Myrna had once said. "You make more noise watchin' somebody kick a field goal than you do when we're makin' love."

It wasn't quite true. Homer did not get that excited over any old field goal, just one that was kicked with that clean, sweet sound, the sound of perfection.

In celebration, he pulled his cowboy hat off and swung it around overhead, yelling "Yee-haaah!" and "Soo-weee!" at the top of his lungs.

The Dutchmen in the stands gaped at him.

Homer cornered Shrdlu right after the game, surprised once again at the kid's size. Most kickers today were runty things with potbellies and wishbone legs, but this one was about six four and 240, with dark, curly hair and striking good looks. He had a Mona Lisa–type smile, as if he never ceased to find life faintly ridiculous.

Homer introduced himself and made his pitch.

"The Giants are lookin' for a kicker and I think you might be it," he said. "But I'm supposed to have you take this test before I make a firm offer."

"Test?"

Homer dumped a pocketful of small blocks and plastic shapes on the locker room table. He also dangled a beanbag and a pair of goggles before Shrdlu.

"Some damn fool sold the team on the idea that you can measure a prospective player's capabilities off the field, the old hand-eye coordination thing. Do you know what I'm talkin' about?"

Shrdlu shook his head.

"Good, 'cause neither do I!" Homer swept the blocks away with a contemptuous wave of his hand.

"I know you can kick, son, I know it in my heart. But the

team ain't gonna give you a contract on my say-so. You're gonna have to go to New York for a three-day tryout. No pay, but a per diem. If you pass muster, you'll get a one-game contract," he explained. "Basically you're gettin' one shot at succeedin' in the NFL. Make it and they'll sign you for the rest of the season. Blow it and you'll be back here playin' in the boonies again."

Homer peered at Shrudlu. "Did you understand what I said?" he asked. "Do you speak English or just Albanese?"

"Albanian."

"Whatever."

Shrdlu, who appeared to be about twenty-three or twenty-four, smiled his enigmatic smile again.

Homer nervously pulled out a plug of tobacco and bit off a chaw.

"Hell, you must speak English; you were callin' signals out there. How'd you learn to play quarterback in Albania, son?"

"From library book," Shrdlu replied. *"Sid Luckman: My Life Story."*

"What? You learned to play quarterback from a book? You amaze me, boy, you just knock me out. Are there any more like you back home?"

"No ca'peesh. Understand only leetle English."

"Never mind, it ain't important. We don't need you to play quarterback, just kick."

"I keek, I keek!" the kid suddenly shouted.

"I know you keek. I'm a keeker myself—takes one to know one."

Homer put his arms out wide and flapped them up and

down. "Will you fly to New York and try kickin' for us?"

Shrdlu made like a bird in return.

"Fly in sky?"

"Yeah, to New York."

"Big city. Too many people," Shrdlu grumbled.

"Pay much money, though, if you keek. If you make it," Homer pointed out.

"Make what?"

"Make keek," the big man on crutches pantomimed. "Make field goal."

"I make keek today," the Albino crowed.

"I saw. But what about New York? Can you make it there?"

Shrdlu suddenly dropped his eyes and contemplated his shoes, frowning.

Seconds passed.

He's scared, Homer realized. The kid is scared shitless to try his luck in the U.S. of A.

It was true. Shrdlu was scared, but not for the reason Homer assumed. Other factors were involved. His name was not Shrdlu. He was not an Albanian.

His name was Ezekiel Cantor, known to his friends as Ziggy, and he was an American, from the Bronx. And he was a rabbi.

2

ZIGGY TOOK THE TRAIN FROM THE STADIUM AND GOT OFF AT
Central Station, pausing before he crossed the Amstel to buy
flowers for Rachel from the stall by the side of the bridge. The
rain had stopped, leaving puddles of sweet-smelling water
underfoot. It was evening, almost eight o'clock, but the north-
ern light made it look like late afternoon, something he still
couldn't get used to, even after four months in Holland.

The square was full of people: homeless, dope peddlers,
travelers rushing to their trains, backpackers exchanging
information about cheap pensions and restaurants, street
musicians singing for their supper. Ziggy headed left, toward
the big office building with the neon sign atop it announcing
GOD ROEPT U—God loves you.

God roepts u very much, he said to himself, feeling pretty
good, tired and sore but victorious, as he turned the corner.
The street lights along Binnenkant were on and their pale yellow glow reflected on the ink-black surface of the canal water.
He stood for a time on the bank of the canal, watching a barge
chug by, leaving a long, low wake that gently rocked the

houseboats anchored here, chimneys leaking dinner smells, laundry hanging from lines and railings. He felt deeply attached to this cozy, liquid city.

"It's going to be hard to leave Amsterdam, even for a few days," he said to Rachel after having told her about the offer from the Giants.

"Don't leave, then. Stay here," she said.

"How can I pass up a chance at kicking in the NFL? You know what kind of money I'll make if they offer me a contract? We could get married, stop living in sin."

"I like living in sin. It's delicious."

Ziggy knew she wasn't just being frivolous. Rachel had grown up in an Orthodox Jewish family in the Bronx, not far from his home. She had been pressured all her life to behave like a good Jewish girl, which meant, among other things, that sex was permissible only within marriage and should never be enjoyed for itself, only in connection with procreation.

Now here she was, living with her lover in a one-room flat in Amsterdam whose only piece of furniture, except for a wobbly table and chairs, was an enormous double bed. It was wicked how much time they spent in bed, thought Ziggy as he snuggled against her, naked, his legs entwined with hers.

"I have to go," he said, "if only to see my father. This way I can do it on their money."

She pointed out that his father had already recovered successfully from his heart surgery, and that lots of people were looking after him.

"What are you saying—that I should turn the Giants down?"

Rachel frowned, knowing she'd been backed into a corner.

"Please understand, Ziggy. I'm not really trying to stand in your way. It's just that we've been so happy here—I don't want it to end."

"It doesn't have to. Chances are I won't make the team and'll be back in a week."

"You'll make the team. You're a wonderful player. How could the Giants not recognize that?"

"Okay, let's say you're right and a miracle happens. That doesn't mean we'll be apart. You can join me in New York." Even as he said it, he knew she would never agree to it; Amsterdam meant too much to her. "I don't want to hurt you—and I certainly don't want to lose you."

"Same here. But maybe life isn't going to let us stay together. Maybe our affair has to end. It's been a romantic dream, something that can't last."

Ziggy felt a stab of anxiety. "That does it," he said. "I definitely won't go."

Rachel wouldn't hear of it, explaining that if he didn't go he'd only resent her for having kept him back in life. It would spoil everything between them in an even worse way.

Ziggy's anxiety boiled over into anger. "I'm damned if I do and damned if I don't. Give me a break, for God's sake!"

She sighed heavily and put her cheek against his chest.

"I'm being a pain in the ass, aren't I?"

He stroked her hair. "I haven't even made the Giants and you're getting all worked up."

She got up and put on a Grateful Dead tape. "What will you tell your father?"

Ziggy shrugged his shoulders. "If I make the team, I guess

I'll have to level with him."

"I'll believe that when I see it."

Ziggy reminded her that he had stood up to him when he graduated from Yeshiveh, telling him to his face that he was dropping out as a rabbi and going to Holland instead.

That was different, though. The whole story hadn't come out; playing football had never been mentioned. "He thought you were going to Holland to study Spinoza and wrestle with your troubled Jewish conscience."

"He hates football."

"Ziggy," she said, "you're just afraid of him."

"No I'm not. . . . What my father doesn't know won't hurt him."

"What'll you do if he forbids you to play for the Giants?"

"I'll defy him."

"Defying your family is nearly impossible. I'm not going back to what I was. I will never again let them brainwash me with that religious bullshit."

"Don't call it bullshit."

"You see? You're still a believer at heart. You haven't really cut the umbilical cord—just stretched it a bit."

He wondered about that. Rachel had only her family and its orthodoxy to cope with, but he had centuries of history and tradition as well. Not only was his father a rabbi, but his father's father before him, and so on. The rabbinical line stretched way back in time, connecting him to the shtetls of Eastern Europe and to the renowned Yeshiveh in Dvinsk, Russia, where the patriarch of the family, Reb Joseph Kantorwicz, had headed the faculty and published forty books on Jewish history, theology, and literature.

But that line was also a wall that encircled him. It had always been expected of him—demanded—that he become a rabbi too. Ziggy had gone along with it, attending one religious school after another, studying Deuteronomy and Torah and the other books of Mosaic law. But by the time he graduated from Yeshiveh University and was ordained as a rabbi, he no longer wanted to be one. He had too many doubts about Judaism and Orthodox values to put himself forward as a leader of other Jews.

He'd cut off his forelocks and beard—a shocking transformation—and gone off to Holland with Rachel. He spent his time exploring Amsterdam, reading Spinoza, playing football, and eating unkosher food for the first time in his life. He'd felt himself a renegade, and loved it. Now here he was, ready to give it all up and return to New York for the lure of making it in the big leagues. He wondered if Rachel was right—was he still caught in his father's grip?

How can we understand life if we cannot understand ourselves? the Torah had asked.

Ziggy couldn't answer that. All he knew was that he loved football and had taken to it from the start; it was as simple and easy for him as breathing. The first time he picked up a ball he'd fired a pass at his friend Hook with such force that it knocked him flat. Ziggy was only six at the time.

The game got easier and more enjoyable as he grew older and stronger. Football was his joy, his pride, his salvation. When he was pursuing his religious studies, poring over books all day, analyzing minute points of philosophy, arguing complex passages of Jewish law, always indoors, always hunched over a lesson in some dim, cold classroom, struggling to learn Hebrew and Yiddish as well—what a relief it was to go from that to the football field, all sunlight, bright grass, and openness. It was like entering another world, a brighter, simpler, more agreeable one.

He loved everything about the game—calling plays, kicking and throwing the ball, and, yes, the primal satisfaction of banging heads with another man.

He'd been injured over the years, had cracked his ribs, strained his back, been knocked cold a couple of times, but it had never spoiled his zest for the game. Every time he stepped on a field he felt a feeling of pure, warm pleasure flooding through him, an indescribable happiness. He always felt like laughing when he played and many times he did, out of sheer good spirits.

His father didn't understand any of that. He hated football, thought it was all nonsense and goyisher *mishegass*. He tolerated it, though, when Ziggy's mother was alive, because she stuck up for her son, insisting there was nothing in the Torah that prevented a Jew from playing ball. But when she died, the Reb's heart had hardened and he forbade Ziggy from going out for the team in high school, using the excuse that the games were almost always played on Saturday. It was unthinkable, he said, that a rabbi's son should violate the Sabbath.

Out of respect, Ziggy obeyed his father. He gave up all chances of playing organized football, but he didn't give up the game altogether. He joined a sandlot team, one that played on Sunday—no violation of the Sabbath there. The same held true for the Hoboken Wharf Rats, a semipro team in the Hudson Valley League for whom he began playing when he was eighteen and just starting at Yeshiveh University.

The Wharf Rats played their games on Sunday afternoons. Ziggy got forty bucks a game as quarterback. He stayed with the Rats for five years, leading them to a championship each year. He also kept improving his skills as a player, becoming so good that everyone in the league—coaches and players alike—kept urging him to try out for the NFL. But by then he was deep into his rabbinical studies, closing in on graduation. He still thought he might become a rabbi; difficult and suffocating as his studies were, who could not be humbled by the wisdom of the Torah or touched by the profundities of Judaism's moral code?

So he didn't try out for the pros. Nor did he come out of the football closet, not even when he took off for Holland with Rachel to play in the brand-new Intercontinental Football League. He couldn't see the point in telling his father, making him even more unhappy about his defection from the rabbinate. He dreamed up a fictional character for himself—Etoain Shrdlu, the Albanian placekicker.

Now his little joke, his bad joke, was backfiring on him. The NFL was beckoning. If he flubbed the trial, he could still be Shrdlu. But if he passed it and signed to kick for the Giants, he'd have to reveal his true identity. Embarrassment all around —especially for his father. The Reb would be deeply hurt by his dishonesty and deceit.

Ziggy felt like hell. Football—his pride and joy—was exacting a price from him. His beloved game was giving him nothing but *tsurris* now. He almost wished he'd fail the tryout. That way he wouldn't have to confront his father or risk losing Rachel.

That was cowardly thinking, though—the same kind of cowardly thinking that had made him back off from being honest with the Reb. Enough of that weaseling around, he decided. It was time to meet the world head-on, be what he was meant to be. If that turned out to be a football player, then he'd be one—openly and proudly.

But he didn't want to lose Rachel. He loved her.

He looked at her. Her heart-shaped, lovely face was twisted up with pain.

"Come with me," he begged her once again. "You can stay with me. Your family doesn't even have to know you're back in New York."

"Are you kidding? How could I ever get away with it if you make the Giants? They'll find out and come after me, inviting me to dinner and all that."

"Is that so terrible?"

"Look, I managed to break away from them once, but I might not be able to do it a second time. They'll go to work on me, Ziggy, hit me with everything they've got. You know how Jewish families do it—with the warmth, the closeness, the concern. And then, wham, when you're feeling vulnerable, flattered, wanted—they lay that guilt trip on you and the next thing you know, you're ready to rejoin the cult."

"Don't call Judaism a cult."

"It is, especially for an Orthodox Jewish woman. Your whole life is programmed—they tell you how to eat and dress, what to think and feel. You're sent to the back of the bus, made to feel an inferior creature because you're a woman, an unclean, unwanted, second-class citizen."

"You're exaggerating. You're turning the religion into a caricature."

"That's how I felt. No matter what I did, how good my marks were in school, I was told it meant nothing, that I should just think of marrying and having children. It was so demeaning!"

"That's changing."

"No it isn't and you know it. Did they let you read or discuss Spinoza?"

Ziggy had no comeback on this point. Orthodox students were expected to parrot what their teachers taught, nothing of which ever conflicted with biblical belief. Traditional subjects prevailed. Dissent and doubt were discouraged.

It wasn't until he came to Amsterdam that he felt liberated enough to read Spinoza. It was a heady if shocking experience—the philosopher not only didn't believe in the Chosen Race but was close to being an anti-Semite, the worst kind too, a Jewish anti-Semite.

Still, Spinoza ought to be read by every Jew, especially in light of what had happened in Israel in the last fifty years or so, where Jewish compassion and decency had been brutalized by the wars against the Arabs and turned into behavior that at times was reprehensible, even frightening.

He was glad, then, that he had opened Spinoza's books and read them in the very city where they had been written five centuries ago, when Spinoza was twenty-four—exactly Ziggy's age.

Interestingly, for all his youthful, renegade ideas, Spinoza had never renounced his faith. He'd remained a Jew even when the tribe cast him out and he'd turned to Christianity, only to find fault with much of the New Testament, too. His courage and independence never ceased to amaze Ziggy.

"Go to New York, then," she said, "and try to decide once and for all who you really are—Ziggy Cantor, rabbi, or Ziggy Cantor, football player."

"Why can't I just be Ziggy Cantor, nobody? Ziggy Cantor, nebbish?"

"I don't think you could be a nobody. Certainly not a nebbish. Maybe a nudnik, though," she grinned.

Ziggy embraced her. "Rachel," he asked, his voice tightening, "what's going to happen to us?"

"I wish I knew."

They held on to each other for a long time, as if it were the last time.

3

So Etoain Shrdlu was escorted onto the field at Giants Stadium by Homer Bloetcher, who was even more nervous than his protégé. Also, Homer's hip and knee implants were hobbling him a bit more than usual, owing to all the damp weather he'd experienced in Holland.

"I'll call Coach Schimpf when you're ready. Ca'peesh?"

"I keek, I keek," Ziggy babbled, hoping to forestall any further unnecessary conversation. He liked Homer, but the man had a tongue that flapped like a flag in a windstorm.

Ziggy jogged down the field in his sweats, raising a quick sweat on the humid day, passing little knots of players working on their specialties under the stern, watchful eyes of their coaches. There seemed to be as many coaches as players. Nobody was laughing or even saying very much. The atmosphere made him think of a prison yard, with the players as cons, the coaches their guards.

At the center of the field, standing atop a portable steel scaffold with a bullhorn in his hands, was the warden, the Giants' head coach, Gus Schimpf, Ret. Col., U.S. Army.

"Armstrong, get your butt down . . . Watson, make that cut off your right foot, not your left, you dummy!"

Schimpf didn't need the bullhorn, so loud and rasping was his voice. He never shut up, either, just kept needling the players: "Amen, stop using your arms to block, you're supposed to be a man, not an ape . . . Pewter, how many balls are you going to drop today? Did your hands turn to shit last night?"

Ziggy's spirits sank even farther when a little guy in street clothes cupped his hands and shouted at him from the sidelines, *"Chinga tu madre, maricon!"*

This could only be Jesus Maria Gonzalez, the injured Argentinian placekicker for whose job Ziggy was competing.

"I hope you break your fooking leg, *hijo de puta!*" Jesus snarled.

His name *would* have to be Jesus, was Ziggy's first thought.

Then he tried to stop thinking and concentrated on limbering up for his kicking test. He took the bag of balls Homer had brought him and started practicing punts. He was still a little jet-lagged—on Dutch time it was something like two in the morning—and it took him much longer than usual to get his rhythm and timing back.

Finally, he looked over at Homer and said, "Okay, I keek, I keek."

Homer in turn waved one of his hand-crutches at Schimpf, who climbed down the scaffolding and came striding over, a scowling, flat-topped, malevolent-looking man.

Homer had prepared Ziggy for Schimpf as best he could. "The guy's all-army, if you know what I mean. War hero in Panama and Grenada. Played five years of pro ball as a 190-

pound linebacker. Eats nails for breakfast and barbed wire for dinner, but don't let none of that bother you."

"So you're Shitloaf," Schimpf said. "The Albino kicker."

"Shrdlu," Ziggy corrected.

"That's what I said—Shitloaf!" Schimpf said, eying Ziggy distastefully. "Get something straight. I don't like third-worlders. My son was killed in Desert Storm and I'll never forgive any of you Arabs for it, and don't give me any now-we're-capitalists bullshit!"

"Me escape Albania, love Amerika," Ziggy said.

"That's a lot of crap, you fucking Albino!" Schimpf shot back. "You're probably ex-KGB or whatever it is you called them in your cockamamie country. You've got one chance only to make my team. I don't give a goddamn what Homer said about you. Today's your only shot at kicking and if you fuck it up, you're outta here, you can go back to Albania, you ratfink commie creep!"

Stunned by this outburst, Ziggy stared at Schimpf, not wanting to believe what he'd heard. But Schimpf meant it; his hatred was as palpable as the sweat on his brow.

Ziggy walked away and tried to settle down. His heart was kicking away like baby feet in his chest.

First they wanted him to show what his kickoffs looked like. Schimpf brought a stopwatch out, to measure hang time. His helpers were ready to measure distance.

Ziggy set a ball up on its plastic tee and stared down at it. The baby feet thumped away and he felt short of breath.

Feeling nervous on a football field was a new sensation for him. But then again, this wasn't a football field; it was the exercise yard at Fort Leavenworth.

Ziggy took a couple of deep breaths and eyed the ball, which had suddenly become Schimpf's head.

"I keek, I keek!"

Laughter bubbled up in him. He felt like himself again, the mad Albanian comsymp, Etoain Shrdlu. He ran up and blasted the ball, put his foot into Schimpf's face.

The ball flew high up over the field, catching a faint breeze and soaring all the way to the end zone and beyond it, almost to the stands.

"Sweet heavenly Padre!" the ecstatic Homer cried out, "thank Thee for Thy generous help!"

Schimpf said nothing, just stared in disbelief at his stopwatch. Jesus screamed from the sidelines, "You lucky that time, meng—you jes lucky that fooking weend come up!"

Ziggy kicked off another time, then another. After the third try, Schimpf put his watch away and stared at Ziggy with new, appraising eyes.

But Ziggy was no longer aware of Schimpf or Jesus or anyone else. He was just playing football and enjoying it. In all, he kicked off a dozen times from the forty-yard line, putting each and every ball out of the end zone.

Schimpf called over a couple of his assistants to help put Ziggy through his paces. They had him kick field goals for the next half hour, first from close in, then farther out, making every angle a tough one, backing him up to the fifty-yard line. Ziggy kept kicking straight and true, just as he had done all his life, and the more he kicked the stronger he felt, the more confident.

"I keek," he shouted triumphantly at Schimpf, "I keek!"

Before long all the coaches on the field and a goodly number of the players had gathered on the sidelines to watch Ziggy's performance. He was punting the ball now, first from the goal line, then from midfield, with Schimpf calling each shot like a pool player: "Go for the five-yard line . . . the ten . . . kick left, kick right . . . put it up there for three seconds, four seconds. . . . "

Ziggy delivered each and every time, smiling his Mona Lisa smile all the while, and each time he put his foot into a ball and drove it skyward with that clean, sweet sound, that sound of perfection, Homer felt such a hot rush of pleasure that he almost messed his pants.

Schimpf's gimlet eyes never left Ziggy, not for a minute, but when the tryout ended all he said was, "Okay, you can kick for us on Sunday. But if you miss a field goal or shank a punt—just one, mind you—you can pack your bags and go back to Albania, you big, scuzzy ball of commie slime!"

4

Because Schimpf went around the rest of the week telling everyone that Ziggy was an ex-KGB man, no one on the team deigned to speak to him, except for two players, both of whom were involved with his efforts as placekicker: Sam Robespierre, the second-string quarterback, who had the responsibility of holding for him, and Buford Sifton, the 278-pound snapper, better known as Siffie.

Robespierre was in his seventh year in the league and with his fifth team, a man whose superior talents had been undermined by drugs. Ziggy quickly came to dislike him, not because of the drugs, but because of the sloppy way he spotted the ball for him.

"Laces out," Ziggy said—begged, really. "I like see whole ball when I keek, not white."

"Yeah, yeah, I hear you," Robespierre would mutter, only to screw up the very next hold.

In contrast, Siffie was a man-mountain of reliability and steadfastness. Every snap came at the same speed, allowing holder and kicker to get their timing down and develop a rhythm. Off the field, he had an easygoing, friendly way and was the kind of guy who talked at great length about anything and everything. He even tracked Ziggy down after their first practice session together, finding him in the maintenance closet Schimpf had assigned to him as a locker. The coach had also given orders for Ziggy to be issued jersey number double zero.

"The man really has it in for you, doesn't he," Siffie said, a look of commiseration on his round, black, cherubic face. Then he went directly to the question on his mind.

"I majored in European history at the University of Pittsburgh and have visited every country on the Continent except your birthplace. Can you tell me a little about Albania, its major exports and its present administration?"

Ziggy, guilty enough at playing the imposter, tried to get out of the conversation by playing the idiot, as usual.

"I keek, I keek!" he shouted.

"Shit, man, I know that," Siffie said calmly, even pedantically. "I've seen you kick and have every confidence that come Sunday you will excel at your specialty. Meanwhile, I would like to discuss Balkan politics with you, particularly in light of the never-ending problems in the former Yugoslavia and all that. I would also like to try and get to know you as a person, Shitloaf—"

"Shrdlu."

"Shredlow. You see, I also minored in psychology at Pitt and am interested in what makes people tick."

Ziggy couldn't resist. "It's their wristwatches," he said, but under his breath.

"What was that? I didn't catch your gist, Shreckload. You're gonna have to improve your English, bro."

"I keek, I keek!" Ziggy babbled, grabbing a towel and rushing off to the shower room.

It took Robespierre till Sunday to say anything personal to him. A slender, fair-haired chap with badly bloodshot eyes, he sidled over to Ziggy while they were waiting in the training room to have their ankles taped and said, out of the corner of his mouth, "Anything I can help you with, Shitloaf? Need a little pick-me-up, son? I'm in possession of some wonderful uppers. This is primo shit, made by the company that owns the team, guaranteed to make you feel like a tiger, without any side effects, no dry mouth or nuthin'."

Ziggy made a face.

Robespierre misread its meaning, though. "Okay, I understand," he said, with a conspiratorial wink. "You're already holding. You kickers have got your own potions, right? You guys are built different from us."

"I keek, I keek," was all Ziggy said.

"Well keek good, man, because if you don't Schimpf will nail your ass to the wall. He's on the last year of a three-year contract and hasn't had a winning season yet. You heard about his son, I guess, but what most people don't know is that his wife committed suicide, too. Because of all that, the man is terminally insane."

The insanity charge could be leveled at several other people around here, especially the injured placekicker Jesus. Ziggy had tried all week to befriend the man, make him see there was nothing personal in their rivalry, but Jesus remained implacably hostile and resentful.

Now he came over and stood in front of the seminaked Ziggy. Without warning, he raised his stiletto-heeled boot and brought it down with all his might on Ziggy's right foot. "Nobody takes my job, meng! I'm feeding a family back home."

Ziggy's reaction was instinctive. He lashed out with his fist, decking Jesus with a hard shot to the jaw.

An uproar followed. Players rushed over, yelling; coaches and trainers as well. An early-bird sportswriter named Dora Glick caught the whole thing on her vidcam.

"What's the matter, you trying to cause dissension on my team, you red bastard," Schimpf screamed in Ziggy's face.

"He hurt me goot," Ziggy explained, pointing to his inflamed right instep.

"I know how you people operate. I know your tricks," Schimpf went on. "You goddamn terrorist, you're probably planning to blow up Giants Stadium!"

"I no terrorist, I keek, I keek!" Ziggy cried.

"No keek on my team," Schimpf shot back. "Not after today and that's no sheet, you crazy fucking Albino!"

To calm himself down, Ziggy took himself off to his broom closet and sat down on the floor, putting his head against the wall. He could hear, over the heavy throbbing of the next-door boilers, the people pouring into the stands overhead. The Giants, despite their many losing seasons, still sold out every home game. Seventy thousand spectators would soon be watching him kick.

In his last game in Amsterdam, Ziggy had performed before seven hundred people.

He was hit with a bad case of the jitters. His right foot not only ached but was swelling. Maybe he should have taken up Robespierre on that offer of those pills. He needed strength, sustenance.

He soon found it. But not in a chemical. He found it by standing, draping a towel over his head, like a tallis, and beginning to pray. He hadn't prayed in a long time, not since he'd asked God to help his father survive open-heart surgery. This wasn't as important, it wasn't life or death, but he said a Krias Shema anyway, swaying back and forth as he did, if only to calm himself down, forget Schimpf and Jesus and the seventy thousand people upstairs.

Somebody appeared in the doorway—the reporter from the *New York Post*, Dora Glick. She stared at Ziggy, a small, bulky, black-garbed woman who hovered over the Giants like a crow, always looking, always ready to pounce.

"What are you doing?" she asked. "What's your story, Shrdlu?"

"No spik Englitz."

"Don't give me that bullshit," she said, glaring at him from behind her thick, black-rimmed spectacles.

"Albanian people Muslims. Must to wear hat when praying. Is sign of respect for Allah."

"You believe in Allah?"

He nodded. "Allah the merciful. Allah the compassionate." Then he pushed past her and headed down the tunnel toward the Giants' dressing room.

She rushed after him, shouting, "Who are you? I called the Albanian Embassy this week. They never heard of you. What is your story, Shrdlu?"

"I keek," he threw back over his shoulder, "I keek!"

An hour later he was doing just that, kicking off before all those screaming fans in Giants Stadium. He'd never heard noise like it before or felt such pressure. His ears rang and he couldn't breathe as he eyed the ball on its tee, but he did remember the mantra that had always got him over difficult moments like this: *one foot, one ball.*

One foot, one ball.

That's all kicking came down to, no matter where you were, in sandlot, semipro, or the NFL. One foot, one ball. What could be simpler, more clean-cut than that? Besides, Schimpf had told him he was finished no matter what happened today, good performance or not. One game and out, the short happy life of Etoain Shrdlu, the phantom Albino placekicker.

Smiling a little, ol' double zero, twice nothing, ran up and kicked off, putting foot into ball with oomph and skying it high and deep over the receiving team. The ball, spinning end over end in the bright fall sunshine, carried all the way to the Redskins' end zone, where a prudent return specialist touched it down.

"Way ta go!" yelled Siffie as Ziggy came off the field, head ringing with the fans' cheers. "Nice goin', kid."

"Keep it up," was Schimpf's only comment. "Keep it up or I'll rip your fucking balls off."

Ziggy did as told. He kept kicking the ball steadily and reliably all through the first half, chalking up one punt of fifty-five yards and another unreturnable kickoff. No field goals, though. Schimpf didn't trust him, not even when the situation called for a three-point try. Instead the coach kept ordering his quarterback, Fred Walston, to go for the yardage. The strategy hurt the Giants, because when they came up short it left the Redskins in excellent field position.

The fans started booing Schimpf but that only served to make him more determined. Before coming to the Giants, Schimpf had coached at Mississippi Military Academy, where nobody—not even the folks in the stands—would dare criticize him. Now he was taking shit from all manner of rabble, all these loudmouthed, obnoxious New Yorkers. It was enough to drive an old colonel crazy. If he had his way, he'd have every one of them court-martialed. Even better, shot at dawn.

Ziggy was just as upset as the fans were, but for different reasons. If he couldn't kick a field goal, he wouldn't be able to prove himself. Punting didn't put points on the board and neither did kicking off. He had to get some treys if he was going to make it in this league, shed the anonymity of Etoain Shrdlu for his own name. And a real number.

He finally got his chance, at the end of the first half. The Giants behind Walston had driven down to the Skins' thirty, where the defense held, even pushed the Giants back a bit. So on fourth and long, with just two seconds left on the clock, not enough to throw anything but a desperation pass, Schimpf turned to Ziggy.

"All right, Albino. Here's your first and only chance in the NFL."

Nothing like playing for a confidence-builder, Ziggy thought as he jogged onto the field.

"Miss it!" Jesus screamed from the sidelines. *"No lo hogas!"*

It wasn't a difficult kick: the ball sat right in front of the goalposts, forty-three yards away, with a fair breeze behind him. But when Siffie's snap came, Robespierre, high on cocaine, juggled the ball momentarily and slapped it down with the laces facing in, naturally.

Pissed, Ziggy hit this one poorly. The ball barely got up over the defense and wobbled in flight like Daffy Duck, clearing the crossbar by a fraction of an inch.

"That was a piece-of-shit kick," Schimpf complained as they trudged to the locker room. "It was the worst kick I've ever seen, a real KGB three points."

But the harried coach had to go to Ziggy one more time that day. It happened late in the game, the last minute to be exact, at the tail end of a horrendous second half for the Giants. They had blown a fourteen-point lead, seen the score draw even, then go against them. They were down by two, but Walston pushed them up the field with his mathematical passes until he got sacked and went down with a hyper-extended left knee.

Robespierre, still stoned, came in and overthrew his receivers, not once but twice.

Fourth and twenty on the forty-yard line. It was either throw a Hail Mary or go to the Albino.

"Go ahead, prickface," screamed Schimpf at Ziggy. "Humiliate me! Cost me my job!"

"Choke, choke, choke," chanted Jesus from the bench.

Up in the scouting booth, high above the playing field, Homer took off his headset. His heart was pounding, his palms sweating. His lungs felt all squeezed in, like a deep-sea diver's.

Ziggy's foot hurt, but he felt calm. He was a man with nothing to lose. A man on the way out. Nobody expected him to make a fifty-two-yarder, least of all his own teammates. In the huddle they looked as dour and depressed as undertakers.

"Siffie, just give me a good snap," Ziggy begged, with a terse aside to Robespierre, "and put the ball down right, with the laces out for once."

Robespierre, snot dripping from his nose, eyes blinking like a stop signal, sniffed hard and nodded his head.

"Give me two seconds," Ziggy begged his linemen, who were so punchy they didn't realize he was speaking perfect English. "Give me everything you've got, guys."

Siffie's snap was good, the line held—only Robespierre, old ironhands himself, faltered, slapping the ball down all wrong.

Putz, Ziggy thought as he kicked. Useless fucking putz.

Somehow, though, he managed to kick the ball cleanly. And hard. He could hear the contact, feel it shoot up through his leg, along his spine, like good sex.

The ball sailed toward the goal on target, carrying . . . carrying. . . . It hit the crossbar, bounced up, fell, teetered on the bar for an instant, then toppled over on the far side.

Pandemonium.

So, Ziggy thought, casting his eyes up to the heavens gratefully. Maybe You really do exist.

5

"I'LL KEEP YOU FOR TWO MORE GAMES," SCHIMPF SAID AS THEY ran off the field together after Ziggy's winning kick. "But that's all, got it? Don't send your laundry out just yet."

To escape the ensuing media uproar, Ziggy skipped showering and slipped the back way out of the stadium and caught a cab across the river to New York.

"Hey, you're da guy dat kicked dat field goal!" the cabbie crowed, looking back at the happy, sweating Ziggy. "Dat was some kick, man. I saw it on TV and won fifty bucks on dah game. Shlomo Volokh at your service!"

Shlomo told Ziggy his life story during the drive home, how he'd emigrated from Russia thirty years ago and was proud to be an American. To prove it, he overcharged Ziggy by forty dollars.

There was a message waiting for him at the hotel, a phone number, nothing else. Ziggy showered and dressed before calling it.

"Glick," a woman's voice said. Then: "I spent the entire game on the telephone and have discovered who you are. My story will be in the paper tomorrow. Why don't you drop the disguise and start talking to me, Rabbi—"

Ziggy hung up and called the operator, instructing her to hold all calls. Then he called his father. The Reb's housekeeper, Mrs. Karp, answered and said he was spending the day at Bubbe's and could be reached there. "By the way," Mrs. Karp said, "a reporter from the *Post* called, an obnoxious lady whose name I didn't get. She asked me lot of questions about you and the Reb. I didn't give anything away, of course. She cursed me out—you can't imagine the language! What's going on, Ziggy?"

Ziggy had hoped for a few more days' grace before having to confront his father. But with Glick bird-dogging him, he had no choice but to speed things up. It was important that the Reb hear the news from him, before he read about it in the *Post*.

Gathering the presents he'd brought from Amsterdam, Ziggy caught another cab and rode uptown to his grandmother Rose's small apartment on West Eighty-Seventh, between Columbus and Amsterdam.

Bubbe greeted him at the door, flying into his arms and smothering him with hugs and kisses. *"Chukkeleh!"* she cried, tears of joy in her eyes, "why didn't you tell us you were arriving, I would've prepared something special."

His father, more reserved, conscious of his dignity, hung back a little, but was smiling. Then he too hugged Ziggy, squeezing him with his powerful arms. Ziggy got his size and strength from him, Reb David Saul Cantor, whose name in Hebrew was Dov Aryeh, the lion. With his tall, powerful build and head of hair and full, luxuriant beard, Reb David was an imposing presence made even more arresting by his magnetic personality and bright brown eyes. Years of overwork and stress, compounded by the slow, horrible death of Ziggy's mother, and by his recent heart operation, had taken their toll, left him gaunter and grayer and more lined than he should have been at sixty, but he still radiated vigor and keen intelligence. And he still dressed immaculately, tonight in a tailored dark blue suit and vest with matching velvet skullcap.

He welcomed Ziggy, thanking the Supreme Master for returning his son safely. Then he put an arm through Ziggy's and led him to the dining room table, where Bubbe began to bring out the food she had prepared. Her Sunday night dinners were legendary—soup, *cholent,* pickles, two different kinds of potatoes, roast chicken, brisket, fresh carrots and peas, pungent-smelling black pumpernickel, kosher red wine from Israel. As Ziggy tore happily into the meal, his father brought him up to date on all his activities.

Reb David's intellect and erudition were keen, but he was mostly known as a people's rabbi, one who was completely involved in the human side of the rabbinate. He not only held court twice a week for his congregation, receiving anyone who wanted to see him and discuss a problem, but he went from house to house counseling the bereaved, dealing with adolescents, trying to shore up sagging marriages. He was also active on the community and city levels, meeting with politicians, Christian clergymen, black activists, and cooperating with them in various programs aimed at alleviating social tensions. When he wasn't attending a meeting or talking on the phone, he was writing letters, drafting petitions, rushing up to Sing Sing to hold special services for the Jews incarcerated there.

"You've got to slow down," Ziggy warned him, "you know what the doctor told you. You can't be all things to all people anymore."

"What can I do?" the Reb said. "I'm a warrior for God and Torah. I can't afford to slow down, anyway. Do you know what's happening in the neighborhood, Ezekiel?" he asked, using his son's formal name, as always. "The drug dealers are coming in, especially around the shul. They're selling stuff right on the streets, to people who drive in off the expressway, make their buys, and drive off again. The housing project is overrun with these bums and people who've lived there all their lives are terrified to go outside, even during the daytime. I'm chasing after the borough president, the mayor, the police chief, so how can I take it easy? We don't want Pelham Parkway to become a war zone like other parts of the Bronx."

"Fighting the drug-dealers is one thing, but going without sleep is ridiculous. You've got to learn to pace yourself, Reb," Bubbe said. "What good will it do your congregation and the neighborhood if you have another heart attack?"

She wasn't afraid to stand up to him. Bubbe was a petite woman, but a dynamo in her own right. Widowed herself for ten years, she had survived on her own by starting a dress shop downtown and turning it into a success. It was nothing new for her; she'd always been good at business. It came as easily to her as cooking did, though she loved food more than she did money. Her bookshelves were packed tight with nearly every cookbook ever published. She was a longtime subscriber to *Gourmet* and had a Cordon Bleu diploma on the wall. But in deference to the Reb, her son-in-law, she kept a kosher house and cooked only traditional food for him when he came over, even though she herself no longer followed Orthodox ways. She belonged to a Reform temple on the West Side and ate what she wanted outside of the house.

She was very much her own woman, his Bubbe, and Ziggy loved her unrestrainedly—the sight of her nut-brown, wrinkled but sweet face making his heart warm and bringing a smile to his lips.

"Eat, eat, *chukkeleh*," she said, heaping his plate again and again. Usually Ziggy protested, but not tonight. He hadn't tasted soul food since going to Holland.

He ate and ate, making Bubbe happy, asking his father question after question, putting off any inquiries about Amsterdam as best he could. But finally it came time, he couldn't stall any longer. Over lemon tea and pound cake, he told the Reb everything, told him all about his secret life as a football player, beginning when he was a kid and going on to the Hoboken Wharf Rats and then the Amsterdam Canallers. And now to the Giants, the New York Giants, who had offered him a two-game contract.

When Ziggy got done talking, a silence followed. His father just sat staring at him, plucking distractedly at his beard.

Bubbe said nothing either.

The silence became oppressive.

Finally the Reb found his voice. "So what does this triumph of yours today mean in practical terms?"

"The coach, who thinks I belong to the Albanian KGB,

agreed to keep me on the team for the next few weeks."

"But it could be longer than that."

"It could."

"That takes you into October—the High Holidays. You'd be expected to play then?"

"Yes."

"And Yom Kippur? If a game fell on that date, would you be expected to participate?"

"I'm ahead of you on that one. The Giants have a game scheduled then, but it's a night game. Technically the holiday would be over."

The Reb nodded, his mouth a grim, unhappy line. "This football," he sighed. "This foolishness. I thought we were done with it once and for all. You were supposed to be studying, rethinking your commitment to Judaism."

"I was doing that, too."

"But mostly you were running around like a lunatic, knocking heads with ruffians for no good reason. It's not the life I envisioned for you."

"I'm sorry to disappoint you, but it's my life to live."

"There's no talking to you," the Reb said, his voice rising. "You've always been a fool where football is concerned."

"And you've always dismissed it out of hand, simply because you don't like it."

"Only morons could like it. Only hoodlums play it."

"Reb David, don't exaggerate," Bubbe said. "He's not robbing banks, you know, just playing a game of ball."

"But he lied about playing—and you know what the Torah says about a son who'd lie to his father."

"Forgive me, but Ziggy never lied," Rose argued. "He didn't say he wasn't playing football, he just didn't talk about it. It was a lie of ommission, not commission, if you will."

"I'm sorry I had to do that," Ziggy said to his father. "But you've bullied me on this issue all my life, simply on emotional grounds."

"I don't deny that I've opposed you. But with good reason. It's not just a game, it's something demonic, a force from the Other Side."

"That's ridiculous," Ziggy argued. "It's a rough sport, admittedly, but it's still a sport, a game men play."

"For money. In front of millions of drunken, screaming bums."

"Again with the exaggeration," Bubbe complained. "I've watched Ziggy play many times, and enjoyed it. Though every time the other boys jumped on top of you, I died a little," she admitted with a rueful smile.

"You could end up a cripple, you said it yourself," the Reb reminded, still attacking relentlessly.

"Nobody could hurt my *chukkeleh*," Bubbe said. "I wouldn't let them. Look at him," she crowed, "he's strong and handsome as a movie star!"

"Now you're talking like a fool," the Reb said, annoyedly. *"Farmach dos moyl!"*

"No, I won't shut up," she shot back. "You should be the one to keep quiet, with your endless complaints. You criticize him because he's your son. If it was any other Jewish boy playing for the Giants, you'd be walking around beaming, saying how good it was for the tribe that a Jew was succeeding at a gentile sport, becoming famous at it."

"Hold on now," Ziggy said. "Nobody's becoming famous. When the Giants' regular kicker comes back, I'll be dropped from the team."

"They won't drop you," Bubbe said confidently. "Not my Ziggy, not my *chukkeleh*."

"One mistake and I'm out, Bubbe."

"So you won't make a mistake, darling. You'll be perfect, just like you've always been."

Reb David cut in, trying to keep his anger in check. "Do me this favor, since whatever I say will evidently have no bearing on your decision. At least try to conduct yourself like a good Jew—sensitive to the reputation and standing of your family."

"I'm not a good Jew," Ziggy told him. "But I'll try to do the best I can. The last thing in the world I want is to hurt or embarrass you. That's why I played under another name—to spare you all this."

The Reb massaged his throbbing temples before embarking on a long speech about the history of the Cantor family. He reminded Ziggy that they had descended from the ancient Judeans who, unlike the Israelites who emphasized integration with the Canaanites and lost their religion, went into the wilderness instead. "They resisted intermarriage and outside ideas," the Reb reminded him. "They endured great hardship because of this clinging to principle—hunger, exile, death. But their ideals kept the faith alive, kept them intact as a people, and eventually when they were allowed to return to Judah, they gave their name to a people that has survived to this day. That's still the only way the Jews can survive—by living by the book, the old laws."

It was a terrible struggle to keep fighting this fight, the Reb admitted. "The odds are against us and our enemies are many, even among other Jews," he said. "I have soldiered on for many years now, but I can't go on forever. I look to you for help, Ezekiel. I raised you to stand by my side and then take over from me when my time on earth is up. That's why I don't want you to play football, because you're needed for more important things. You're needed to serve God, serve your people, make this world a better place to live!"

Later, after the Reb had been picked up by his driver and returned to the Bronx, Bubbe drew Ziggy close and said, "Give him time, maybe he'll come round. He does love you, you know that."

Ziggy shook his head and told her that the Reb would never change his ideas about football, any more than he would about Reform Judaism or Israel or anything else. He was locked into a set of rigid, dogmatic views and that was that.

"We'll see about that," was all she said. Then her face brightened as she suggested that they have a nice little songfest, the way they used to every Sunday night when his mother was still alive.

Bubbe went to her piano and brought out her musical scores. She played skillfully and had once studied to be a concert pianist, until her father objected and persuaded her to marry instead. "What shall it be?" Bubbe asked. *"Hello, Dolly* or *Fiddler on the Roof?"*

"In light of tonight's discussion, we'd better make it *Fiddler,"* answered Ziggy, smiling.

"A wonderful choice," Bubbe agreed. Spreading the score

out, she began playing and singing the show's music.

> Matchmaker, Matchmaker,
> Make me a match . . .

Soon Ziggy joined in and the two of them began harmonizing as of old, having a wonderful time.

> Matchmaker, Matchmaker,
> Find me a find,
> Catch me a catch . . .

Midway through the song, Bubbe broke off and looked sideways at Ziggy. "I knew the whole time that you were playing football in Holland. Rachel told me, but I never let on, darling, because whatever you want to do with your life is fine with me. You should only be happy and well!" she said.

Ziggy bent over and kissed her on the cheek. "The same goes for you, Bubbe."

They picked up the song again, singing their hearts out in unison:

> Matchmaker, Matchmaker,
> Look through your book
> And make me a perfect match . . .

6

Dora Glick's scoop hit the newstands the next morning under a banner headline: SHRDLU UNMASKED—THE TOE IS A REB FROM THE BRONX!

Dora had discovered his true identity by phoning one of his teammates on the Amsterdam Canallers and by tracking down his old coach from the Wharf Rats, Duffy McGurk, now in the alcoholic ward at Bellevue Hospital.

The news turned New York upside down. The press got after Ziggy in full force, with researchers digging into his past and hordes of reporters clamoring to interview him. On advice from Russell Hogarth, general manager of the Giants and the man who reported directly to the Gnomes of Zurich, Ziggy scheduled a press conference at the club's midtown office late that afternoon.

When Gus Schimpf heard the news, he rushed from his tract house in the Meadowlands to Manhattan and burst in on Hogarth, annoyed to find Homer already there before him.

"What's going on? What are you people doing to me? Why in hell didn't you tell me who this damn kid was?"

"Nobody knew a thing about him, Gus."

"An officer is only as good as his intelligence."

"This ain't the army, remember? It's a football team."

"No, it's not, it's a joke, we're the laughingstock of the nation now. Can't you just hear the Letterman wisecracks tonight?"

"Fuck Letterman. This could be a wonderful thing for us," Hogarth insisted.

"Wonderful? Are you crazy?" Schimpf's voice was rising, taking on emotion. "How can I turn out a winner with a rabbi kicking for me?"

"Rabbi or not, the kid can kick," Homer said, chewing on his cud nervously. "He's a natural."

"He's a fucking Albino commie creep!" Schimpf shrieked, losing it.

"Shut up!" Hogarth shouted back. "You moron, stop babbling about Albinos and commies! The kid's from New York."

"They're all Albinos and commies here. The whole town oughta be put under house arrest."

"If you'd won a few more football games, you wouldn't feel the way you do about New York, and vice versa."

"Too many Jews, Latinos, blacks, and other leftists, that's the problem with this city. You know that, everybody knows it. And that's why I don't want him on my team. He must be cut from the squad immediately."

"I give the orders around here," Hogarth reminded him sharply. He was half Schimpf's size and wore horn-rims and bow ties and was bald at thirty-five, but he feared no man. Guys like Schimpf were mooches in his eyes, guys you got fat off.

Hogarth would never think of saying that about the

Gnomes. They were smart. They were winners. They were Swiss. They never made mistakes, never lost money or fought wars.

Hogarth was proud to work for such wise men, such great captains of industry. He would never dream of disobeying their advice, even if they had never even seen a game of American football and thought a forward pass had something to do with feeling up a woman. They'd bought the Giants to add to their leisure-field portfolio, which included movie studios, TV stations, record companies and roller-skating rinks. Software, that's all pro football was. Entertainment software.

Schimpf didn't understand that; his tiny military mind couldn't cope with these complex new realities. He knew that football was a business, but had no idea just how big it was. The Gnomes' projection was that in just a few short years, when they fully controlled America's cable systems, the seasonal take would be in the billions of dollars, right up there with motion pictures and rock music. No difference between the three endeavors. They all came under the category of show business and worked the same way—on star power.

Ziggy had copped some print for the Giants. He'd put them on the front page, where they hadn't been for years. No doubt the kid was a three-day wonder, a fluke, a joke. But he was giving the Giants what they sorely needed, product recognition. The Gnomes had pointed that out. Ziggy was good public relations, and he was not to be dropped from the team, not right now anyway, no matter what coach Schimpf felt or how loud he screamed.

Try reasoning with Schimpf, though. The man was pure

cement between the ears and kept bitching about interference from above and how he couldn't do his job because of it. "It's bad enough having to coach a bunch of multimillionaires and dope fiends, how am I gonna cope with a rabbi? What in hell do Jews want with football, anyway? It's *our* game, dammit!" he shouted.

"You fool, this is New York. If he makes it, he'll be more popular than chopped liver! He could save your job, dummy—mine too, because we'll both be out on the street if something doesn't happen to turn this season around."

"I never thought I'd hear you sticking up for a Jew, Hogarth. Isn't your father a big honcho in the KKK?"

"Leave my father out of this!" Hogarth snapped. "I'm not responsible for his life and he's not responsible for mine. I work for the Gnomes and so do you, and don't you forget it! Now, they want us to bend over backward to make Ziggy shine," he continued. "Did you hear that, you two punch-drunk old pugs?"

"Shoot, I don't need no proddin'," Homer replied testily. "I'm the guy that discovered him, remember? I think the kid could be somethin' really special."

"A kid who never played high school ball, not to speak of college? Come on, Homer," Schimpf protested, "you've gotta be kidding."

"Remember an old-time quarterback named Johnny Unitas? He went from sandlot to the pros to the Hall of Fame."

"This guy's no Unitas."

"Maybe not, but the boy can kick with the best of them. I know it in my bones. He won us a game yesterday, didn't he?"

"By an inch, a cunt-hair. He lucked out and now every-body's supposed to go gaga over him, just because he's a god-damn Hebe."

"You should thank your lucky stars that he is," Hogarth shot back. "You should get down on your knees and give praise to God, you shell-shocked shithead!"

To be humiliated in front of one of his own assistants was too much. Schimpf stormed out of Hogarth's office, dodged the press people gathering for the conference, and rode two flights down in a private elevator to his personal padded cell, built for him in the middle of last year's seven-game losing streak. He locked the door behind him, removed his wrist-watch and upper bridge, and ran full speed into the wall facing him, screaming at the top of his lungs. The impact knocked him over, but he got up and threw himself headlong at another wall, then another, bashing away with all his might until he finally succeeded in knocking himself into unconsciousness.

The next day Schimpf, smiling benignly like a Buddha, approached Ziggy before practice and said, "I'd like to apolo-gize for the names I called you." Then he broke off, frowning a little. "Would you like me to put my hat on?"

"What for?"

"Out of respect for your religion."

"That won't be necessary, Coach."

"Thank you," Schimpf said, flashing his false smile again. "You must understand that I do have a thing about commu-nists and you did say you were an Albanian. Of course, now that I know you're a Jew, it's a whole other thing, though even you will admit, I think, that many of your people are of the left-liberal persuasion."

Ziggy said nothing, so Schimpf plunged on.

"It's going to be different between us from now on, but at the same time, please understand that Gonzalez is still my number one kicker."

"I know that, coach."

"You can't expect me to drop a man who's won a lot of games for me over the years."

"But you've only won five games in the last three years," Ziggy pointed out.

Schimpf scowled.

"I'll do what I can for you," Ziggy promised.

"Jesus's groin still hasn't healed, so it looks as if you'll be kicking again this Sunday. Show me something and I might keep you on the team for the rest of the season. Plenty of teams carry two kickers."

"If I'm going to be kicking this Sunday, I'll need something from you."

"What's that?"

"Get me The Hook."

"The hook? You want me to give you the hook?"

"No, *get* me The Hook. He's an old teammate of mine." Ziggy explained that he and The Hook had grown up together. His real name was Tommy DiVecchio but he'd always been called The Hook for a special reason and had always held for him on kicks. "He's also a great receiver," he told Schimpf, "but that's not what I'm concerned about—just getting a good spot on Sunday."

"What's the matter with Robespierre?"

"He has the hands of Venus de Milo. Besides, with Walston injured, Sam's going to be starting at quarterback for you, right? That means he'll be too busy to practice with me."

"I've got other people who can hold," Schimpf said, feeling his self-imposed benignity slipping away.

"If you want me to kick, get me The Hook," Ziggy insisted.

"Goddammit, what are you trying to do to me? Do you really think I'd hire another sandlot player?"

Ziggy picked up his warm-up jacket and started off the field.

"Wait a minute," Schimpf yelled, panicking. "Where are you going?"

"Home . . . and I won't be back, not unless you sign my friend."

"You son of a bitch!" Schimpf screamed. "I don't care how many TV shows you were on yesterday or how many reporters are interested in you. You can't push me around and get away with it."

"Have it your way, coach. I'm outta here," Ziggy said, heading toward the huge ring of media people gathered on the sideline.

Schimpf ran after him. "Where is this fucking Guinea?"

"He's still playing with the Hoboken Wharf Rats."

"The Hoboken—!" Schimpf broke off, fuming. "Jesus Christ, I'm going to be the laughingstock of the nation."

"I've got news for you," Ziggy said, putting his jacket down, "you already are."

7

THE HOOK LIVED ON MACDOUGAL STREET IN THE VILLAGE, IN an apartment that he had inherited from a relative and was still under rent control—World War II rent control. The low rent, forty dollars a month for a two-bedroom place, allowed him to survive without working much. He had a part-time job as the office manager of a well-known modeling agency, a position that allowed him to pursue his main interests in life: girls, food, and football, in that order.

The Hook had always been able to get girls, even in his pre-mustache years. Strong and handsome with dark, Italian good looks—long, black wavy hair, soulful brown eyes, petulant full lips—he seemed to have been born to stir women in their private places. He was not only a virile and insatiable lover, but had been fitted out for sex by nature in an astoundingly generous way.

Ziggy had known The Hook all his life, yet, up until recently, had never double-dated with him. Their values were too different: Ziggy had been brought up in a devoutly religious family with strict rules against licentiousness and immorality. He could meet girls, at social functions sponsored by his father's shul, but was not allowed to go out with them. Would-be rabbis were supposed to remain celibate until marriage.

The Hook, meanwhile, was chasing everything that moved. Ziggy didn't approve of such behavior but he did take vicarious pleasure in hearing about his friend's sexual exploits. It was, like watching the soaps, a form of cheap, sinful entertainment.

On his side, The Hook was just as amused by Ziggy. "My uptight friend, the last virgin in America," is how he used to introduce him. He found Ziggy, in his forelocks and beard, to be exotic and quaint—a relic from another age. Together they formed a symbiotic friendship: the Rabbi and the Rake.

Tonight was the first time Ziggy had ever gone to The Hook's place for dinner. It was also the first time he had allowed The Hook to fix him up with a blind date—with a non-Jewish girl, no less. It made for a bad case of nerves; by the time he reached MacDougal Street, he felt as anxious and unsure of himself as a teenager. Also weighing on him was the thought of Rachel, back in Amsterdam, the girl he had walked out on.

Over the years, The Hook had become a little more discriminating when it came to women. He now favored only the model and cheerleader types. They had to be between nineteen and twenty-three, perky and busty, with nice legs and thin ankles.

Thick ankles were a sign of water in the body, he believed. And girls with water in the body were not sexy.

Neither of tonight's girls had thick ankles. Devrah, The

Hook's date, was a small, lively, snub-nosed blonde: a central-casting cheerleader. Darcy, Ziggy's date, was in the super-model category: tall, slender, and exotically beautiful with long red hair and emerald-green eyes. But Ziggy didn't dwell on those physical qualities—just her incredible smile. It lit up the whole room like a dazzling chandelier.

She had a way of holding herself that enhanced her appeal as well. She didn't sit back the way many women did, passively, merely reacting. She sat right up at the edge of her seat, poised to pop, like a coiled spring. The look in her eyes was just as forthright and alive, brimming over with high spirits and humor.

The three of them had already gone through a bottle of wine and were a bit tipsy when Ziggy arrived, especially Devrah. Her inhibitions down, she was giggling and talking nonstop about The Hook's infamous sexual equipment.

"You know what my nickname is for him," she said to Darcy. "Attila the Hung."

Darcy let out a shriek of laughter but said, "Come on. All men are pretty much equal in an aroused state."

"Not The Hook. He's in a class by himself—the dreadnought class." She looked to Ziggy for corroboration.

"The Hook certainly is a very unique individual," Ziggy said carefully.

"You should've been a politician instead of a rabbi."

"I still say the whole subject is overrated," Darcy insisted. "Once you've seen one prick, you've seen 'em all."

"Honey, you're just gonna have to play show-and-tell with her," said Devrah to The Hook.

The latter professed indignation. "What do you think I am, some kind of circus freak? I don't go around exhibiting myself in public."

"Now don't get all huffy. You're among friends, cupcake. And you know you really do love that thing of yours. You're always boasting about it."

"I've never boasted about it," The Hook replied. "It's no big deal, really, just an accident of nature."

"Like Mount Everest."

"Cut it out, Devrah, you're really upsetting me," The Hook warned.

"Just give her a teensy-weensy peek. Come on, baby," she cooed, "stop playing hard to get."

"But we're having a dinner party."

"All the more reason to let your hair down. You're among friends."

"What do you think?" The Hook asked Ziggy.

"I think that, in light of the serious controversy taking place, you should heed her request."

"All right," The Hook said with an exaggerated sigh of surrender. He stood up and began to unbutton his tight, fashionably modish slacks.

The girls watched breathlessly, eyes fixed on his fly.

The Hook, lips curling back in a sneer, tore the zipper open and shoved his pants down to his thighs. He was wearing black bikini briefs.

Slowly, tantalizingly, he took hold of his briefs and began to lower them, stopping at the very last moment.

"Aw, c'mon," Devrah begged, "take it off!"

Finally, The Hook's namesake was unveiled in all its glory.

It hung down like a boa constrictor from the branch of a tree—long, thick, and powerful-looking, with a fiendishly curved, fiery red tip.

"Good God!" Darcy cried, recoiling.

"Didn't I tell you," Devrah said proudly. "That is some dingus, is it not?"

They all, The Hook included, stared down at the dingus, admiring it.

"Interesting," Darcy said, "very interesting."

"Now can I put the pasta on?" The Hook asked.

It wasn't until they had reached dessert—chocolate- and almond-filled figs, one of The Hook's specialties—that Ziggy told him about the Giants' offer: a two-game contract, at minimum wage, to hold for him on point-afters and field goals. If Ziggy was cut when Jesus came back, The Hook would be dropped as well. Conversely, if Ziggy made the roster, The Hook'd be brought along for the ride too.

"Is that all I get to do?" his friend asked. "Hold for kicks? My mother could do that."

"Nobody holds for me the way you do," Ziggy replied. "Besides, the pay is pretty good—three hundred and fifty K for the remainder of the season."

"That's great!" Devrah cried. "Three hundred and fifty thousand just to hold for kicks!"

"I don't need their money," The Hook growled. "If I'm going to be on a team and practice and all that bullshit, I expect to play."

"First you make the team, then you get to play," Ziggy said.

"That's right, who knows what could happen," Darcy added. "They have all those special teams and stuff, right?"

"You've signed?" The Hook asked.

"Not yet," Ziggy replied. "I held out so I could get you in the door. We might surprise 'em with a thing or three."

"You'll surprise 'em, all right," Devrah said to The Hook, "especially when they see you in the shower."

"Don't be such a wiseass," The Hook grumbled. "I've got a lot more to offer the Giants than they realize. I'm a damn good wide receiver, y'know."

"The best, Hook, the very best. Maybe the Giants'll come to realize that," Ziggy said.

"If they don't, they're a bunch of *shtummies* and *paskudnyaks*," The Hook said hotly.

"Say what?" Darcy cried, taken aback. "Where'd you learn to speak Yiddish like that? I thought you were Italian."

"Everybody in New York is Jewish, even the Italians," The Hook explained.

"What about me?" Devrah asked.

The Hook looked her over, taking in her white-blond hair, pale blue eyes, and lightly freckled skin, and said, "Aliens from another planet don't count."

"How does it feel to be famous?" Darcy asked Ziggy as they rode uptown in a cab driven by Shlomo Volokh, who kept turning up in Ziggy's life wherever he went, like an omen.

"Get outta here with your famous," Ziggy said.

She sat turned toward him, smiling that smile of hers. Another thing he liked about her was the way she flicked her hair back before speaking, as if wanting to give you the unconcealed truth.

"C'mon, you were all over the TV today. The whole town's talking about you."

"He's a hero—a Jewish hero!" Shlomo yelled from behind the wheel. "He also won me fifty bucks last week."

"I'm not a Jewish hero," Ziggy argued. "I'm just a guy that kicked a lucky field goal."

"Sixty-one yards is luck? There are guys making a million bucks a year that couldn't kick sixty yards unless they had a hurricane behind them. And none of those guys are rabbis, either."

"I'm a rabbi on paper only."

"How come you never used your credentials?" Darcy asked.

"It's a long story."

She sat back and stared out the window as they headed up Avenue of the Americas under a moonlit sky. Suddenly she began to giggle.

"What's funny?"

"I just remembered something Devrah said about The Hook." She quoted her friend's remark: "The thing I like about doing it with him is that you don't just get screwed, you get screwed to the *earth!*"

They both laughed over that.

"The Hook does make his mark with women. Sometimes I envy him that," Ziggy allowed.

"Relax. Despite what men think, women don't really care about a man's size," Darcy said.

"Oh, yeah? Then how come your eyes bugged out when you looked at him?"

"Well, what the hell—that thing of his is the eighth wonder of the world. But that doesn't mean I want to sleep with him."

"I'll bet you do. I'll bet you'd like to have one night with The Hook, small *h*, that is."

"There is *nothing* small about The Hook," she laughed. And took his hand and said, "I'd rather have one night with you."

"Nothing shy or devious about you, is there?"

"Look, I grew up in California. It's a very free, open kind of place. We didn't have to play games with each other."

"You're lucky. I grew up in an environment where there were rules for everything." He studied her. "What religion are you—Catholic, I'd guess."

"My father's background is Irish, my mother's Scottish. But they never went to church and hardly ever talked religion. There were no demands on me whatsoever. I know it sounds Pollyannaish, but I never had any big fights or problems with my parents. I had a ridiculously happy and carefree childhood."

"So that's why you have that incredible smile."

"I've been lucky, Ziggy. I've got these perfect parents, grew up in a beautiful house, have nice friends. I even had a great time in high school."

"Nobody has a great time in high school!" Shlomo yelled. "It's not humanly possible."

Ziggy closed the glass panel on him.

"This interests me," he said. "Surely something went

wrong in your life—you can't be completely happy. Didn't you ever have an unhappy love affair or lose a friend to death?"

"It hasn't happened yet. It's disgusting, I know, but only trivially bad things have ever happened to me, like somebody spilling wine on a party dress. Otherwise I've been lucky—even in looks. I didn't ask to be born pretty, didn't deserve it, but here I am, on my way to making a fortune for just smiling, something I do anyway."

"No guilt, no hang-ups, no problems—you're definitely not Jewish," Ziggy said.

"Is that a problem for you, being out with a—what was that word The Hook used?"

"*Shiksa.* I cannot tell a lie, Darcy. You're my first."

"Is that exciting for you?"

He took her hand. It was soft, smooth, and warm.

"I like you. But you must understand—I'm in love with someone else."

He told her all about Rachel.

"I see," Darcy said. "She seems like a fine person—a real woman, I guess, compared to a kid like me. But I can learn, Ziggy. I'm only nineteen, you know. Give me a chance."

"I will," he said. "But I'm not like The Hook, I can't go from one woman to another, just like that."

"Does that mean you don't want to come up?" she asked as the cab drew up beside her building on the East Side, just off the river.

"I'm afraid not."

"Holy shit," Darcy cried with disbelief. "I've spent most of my life being hit on by guys. Now, for the first time, I do the hitting—and the guy turns me down. It's not fair—it's just not fair!"

"Welcome to the club," Ziggy said.

At the entrance, Darcy turned her face to him, brushing her her hair back. She smelled of some exotic essence, tantalizing. Her mouth was equally provocative and sweet.

He kissed her a little longer and harder than he meant to because it was difficult to stop. That gave enough time for someone in a car to pull up at the curb, jump out, and fire off a flashbulb twice at him.

Ziggy wheeled and caught sight of Dora Glick as the car roared away.

8

By THE TIME SUNDAY CAME, ZIGGY WAS A MEDIA STAR IN NEW York—the Kicking Rabbi. The papers and airwaves not only ran endless stories about him and Darcy, but about The Hook. In detailing the latter's sexual exploits, Dora Glick dubbed him a "Casanova on Cleats." It was the first time a kicker and holder had ever captured the public's fancy like this, to such an extent that on Sunday morning approximately ten thousand fans turned up early at Giants Stadium just to watch them warm up.

Ziggy and The Hook put on a good show. It was a show they'd performed many times before, but only for their own amusement when they were kids and practicing at French Charlie's in Bronx Park or on the hot sands of Orchard Beach. The Hook used to start running pass routes downfield. But instead of throwing him the ball, Ziggy would kick it to him, timing it so that his partner could spear it without breaking stride.

Today, just for the hell of it, Ziggy tied a hankie over his eyes and tried to deliver ball blindly, going on instinct and timing alone. When he dropped three out of four long punts into The Hook's hands, the fans went crazy.

When Schimpf saw what was happening, he nearly lost it. He hated it when guys clowned around during practice. He believed in tight, rigidly prescribed workouts—a time and a place for everything. Football, like the army—like life itself—had to be ruled from the top by a strong, capable, ruthless leader.

"Just what in damnation do you think you're doing?" Schimpf demanded of the young upstarts from the Bronx. "You trying to make a fool of me?"

"Just having a few laughs, Coach."

"Laughs? I'll give you something to laugh at!"

Just as Schimpf was about to shred them, he felt a restraining hand on him. Homer Bloetcher, chomping on his tobacco a mile a minute, looked at him and said quietly but firmly, "Leave 'em be, Gus. You gotta remember that these boys have just come out of semipro. They're used to a lot looser lead round their necks."

Schimpf made it clear that he could not have them breaking the rules, lest it lead to chaos and anarchy.

Maybe a little of that wouldn't hurt, Homer suggested. "Bein' dead serious hasn't got us very far in the last few years."

"What is this? You taking their side against me? I'll have all three of you shipped out if you're not careful."

"Like hell you will!" came another angry voice. Russell Hogarth came up all out of breath and sweating from his busy morning of coping with the extra crush of press who'd showed up to cover the Ziggy and Hook story. "I told you to shut your mouth, Schimpf, and keep it shut, especially where Ziggy is concerned."

"What is this? Am I the coach or aren't I?"

"You're a horse's ass, that's what you are—and an extremely expendable one."

"What's that mean—if I don't let Ziggy walk all over me, I lose my job?"

"Nobody's walking all over you. Your trouble is, you've got a Napoleonic complex."

"Look who's talking, a shrimp who wears platform shoes!"

"I should fire you for that remark."

"And I should kick your ass."

Schimpf felt Homer's huge paw tightening around his wrist again, pulling him away.

"Cool it, old hoss," Homer counseled. "No use gettin' yourself all riled up."

"They're trying to cut my balls off, dammit, and you tell me not to scream."

"Gus, wake up. Ziggy's a New Yorker. The fans around here haven't had one of their own to cheer in a long time. You'd be a whole lot better off worryin' about Robespierre. He's down in the locker room heavin' his guts out."

Schimpf couldn't understand this kind of talk. Defying authority was at the root of the world's ills; it was rebellion against the natural order of things, against God's will itself.

The undermining process had been set in motion, that much was clear; a palace revolution was under way to topple him from his throne, all because of a Jew placekicker from the

Bronx. Schimpf went off fuming.

Sam Robespierre, meanwhile, was trying to calm his nervous stomach. He was doing it with the help of modern chemistry, in the form of a steroid gas derived from adrenal tissue. The stoners on the team had sardonically bestowed the name of "laughing gas" on the stuff, which came bottled in twin metal cylinders like oxygen tanks and stood in a tiny chamber behind the main locker room, access to which was controlled by the coaches. The gas, which gave one a feeling of strength and invincibility, had originally been invented by a Prussian scientist during World War I, on orders from the Kaiser, who wanted a stimulant that would induce his soldiers to consent to insane, suicidal bayonet charges. HEN developed it commercially, first as an anesthetic, then as a bracing and legal energizer for reluctant athletes. The stuff was particularly effective with injured players, of whom there were many now that the league played an eighteen-game season, not including exhibitions and postseason tournaments. There were only a couple of minor side effects to beware of: kidney failure and cardiac arrest.

One or two whiffs did the trick for Robespierre. He felt fine now—steady, calm, strong. He had a lot riding on this game, which was his first start as a pro after all these years in the league. If he shone out there, he could take the number one spot away from the injured Walston, who was thirty-four, a borderline age for a quarterback. Walston was also in the last year of a three-year contract with the Giants, every one of which had been a losing year. Thirty-four-year-old losers did not get renewed—not when their subs stepped in and excelled.

Robespierre cringed when he thought of the shit money he was making as a backup QB—a mere two million dollars a year. Fucking waterboys made that much in this league. It was an outrage, a disgrace, especially when he'd been a two-time college All-American and a high school All-American before that, on the cover of *Sports Illustrated* with his blond, surfer-boy looks. He'd made a hundred and fifty thousand bucks under the table just to sign with a Big Ten school, the most it had ever paid to a player. By all rights he should've been a multimillionaire now, up in the highest tax bracket with the real winners, except that he couldn't budge Walston from the starting team.

He looked over at Walston, who had a Mohawk, a gang tattoo on his cheek, and a small gold ring in his nose. He'd never made All-American. He'd never even played Big Ten ball, having been arrested in his last year of high school for assault with a deadly weapon. That was followed by two years of reform school, more trouble with the law culminating in a long prison sentence. While inside Walston had become the leader of a gang called the White Fangs which ran the drug trade. What saved him from becoming a career criminal was his prowess as a football player. Schimpf had happened to see him scrimmage against a junior-college team he was scouting, and liked the way he played. Walston was tough, mean, and angry—his kind of man. And he had a rifle for an arm.

Schimpf pulled strings to get him into Mississippi Military Academy, where Walston excelled as a quarterback and tried to control his antisocial behavior. Schimpf took him with him when he got the job with the Giants. Walston had done well as a pro, though you never knew what might happen when he lost his temper. Once he shot holes in the side of the team bus for being late. He often decked receivers for dropping one of his passes.

Schimpf kept Walston as his starting quarterback, even though he was considered a crazy, hostile son of a bitch who only looked out for himself. But he was effective in a steady, relentless kind of way, and Schimpf loved him, if only because they were two of a kind.

Robespierre hadn't been able to break up the marriage, no matter what he did. Walston never got hurt, either—the fuck-er was made of Teflon or something. Last week had changed all that, though. Walston had finally gone down and if Robespierre had his way, he was going to make sure he stayed down.

To make the real bread, the long bread, you had to be num-ber one. You had to run the show, get the ink, cop the air-waves. The killer was, now that Robespierre was finally get-ting his big chance, what happens—a fucking nobody comes along, a Jewish kid from the Bronx, and steals the limelight from him!

Not a single reporter had come to interview him all week. They'd all followed Ziggy around, like dogs after a meat wagon, clamoring for his attention. And when they were done with him, they turned to his buddy Hook, the Don Juan with a boomerang for a dick.

Robespierre glanced over at the nearby Walston, wanting to blurt it out, tell him what an outrage it was that a couple of rookies were taking the play away from them. But Walston, in black street clothes, just sat with his arms folded over his chest, stony-faced and tight-lipped as ever. Nobody knew what was going on inside that lone wolf's head—and nobody dared ask.

Robespierre knew better than to expect any help from Walston today. As if to emphasize the point, Walston put on a pair of black aviator shades and stuck Walkman 'phones in his ears.

Well, fuck him, Robespierre thought defiantly. I don't need him, I am the master of my own fate. He looked up to discover Ferdinand Daniels, the team's third-string quarterback, checking him out. Ferdinand was cocoa-colored, plump, and goateed, a little toy duck of a man.

Sorry to disappoint you, Robespierre mused, I'm fine now. Just stay where you are, fat man.

Ferdinand had once been a terror in the NFL, having broken all rookie passing records in his first year in San Diego. But a punctured spleen, two knee operations, and a couple of ruptured discs had taken their toll, relegating him to permanent third-string status.

Ferdinand, who'd majored in economics at Princeton, had invested wisely in the stock market and branched out into venture capitalism. He did a little arbitrage on the side and was the only player in the league who served on the president's economic council.

Ferdinand hadn't taken a single game snap in two years. His waist was the size of a truck wheel. But if you gave him time in the pocket, protected him like a newborn babe, he could still zip the ball downfield with the best of them.

Ferdinand got to prove it against the St. Louis Rams that day. The butterball stockbroker was pressed into action in the second quarter in what would later be called one of the most memorable games of the century. The four announcers working the telecast—the usual two ex-players, the obligatory woman, and the data freak, the man responsible for filling every millisecond of silence with some kind of chatter—outdid each other in their descriptions of the contest.

The game didn't start out auspiciously. It was a real snoozer for the first quarter. The Giants, behind the well-meaning but ineffectual Sam Robespierre, saw the Rams go up by two touchdowns. Robespierre started throwing the ball more but, unfortunately, usually to the wrong team. On the last interception, he was so angry with himself that he tried to tackle the runner, a 245-pound linebacker and Thai kick-boxing champ named Aloysius McCarver. Aloysius hit Robespierre head-on and knocked him straight into cuckooland.

Schimpf screamed for Ferdinand to take over. The number three QB sucked his gut up and trotted out and coolly threw two touchdown passes in the second quarter, tying things up. But in the third period, the Rams really worked the preppie over, going for his mushy middle time and time again. Ferdinand tried to avoid those killer rushes, but it was like a parrot fish trying to avoid a pack of sharks. They caught up with him finally and decked him hard, dislocating his right shoulder.

Schimpf went back to Robespierre, who, thanks to the Swiss laughing gas, had recovered most, if not all, of his marbles during the halftime break. The frantic coach grabbed him by the shoulder pads and shook him like a dirty rug in front of the Giants' bench.

"Don't fuck up again," the great motivator shouted, "because if you do I'm going to ram my fist right up your ass until it opens a sunroof in your head!"

Robespierre did his best. He got off some deft passes and called a few audibles, which sprang Amen Armstrong, the Giants' main runner, free for long gains. But Robespierre's old problem—inconsistency—came back to haunt him and the Giants' attack began to sputter.

The Rams, meanwhile, kept rolling along smoothly. By the end of the third quarter they were back on top by two TDs and a field goal. Robespierre took over thinking *bomb*, thinking *six*, but the Rams were on the same wavelength and came on an all-out blitz. There was a loud, sickening *thwack* and Robespierre went down with a scream.

"Mincemeat," was the team doctor's verdict when he took a look at the injured knee. "Sprinkle a little lemon juice on it and serve it on a cracker."

Schimpf blew a fuse. He pulled off his headphones and stomped on them with both feet. Then he looked around for somebody to punch, anybody. He'd lost three out of three quarterbacks and somebody had to pay for it. The team doctor got it first, a shot right in the kisser, then a photographer from *Gay Pride* magazine.

Schimpf's tantrum was so bad and so prolonged that BBU (a wholly owned HEN subsidiary), the pay channel televising the game, ordered the officials to call a timeout. It would not do for the youth of the nation to see an ex–war hero turning into a serial killer.

With six gargantuan linemen holding him down, Schimpf was given a tranquilizing injection by the trainer. That calmed him sufficiently for him to confer with Homer again, up in the team skybox.

"What am I gonna do?" he wailed.

"You got no choice, Gus. Put Ziggy in."

"What? What was that?" Schimpf asked thickly, head all fuzzed up by the depressant.

"Let the kid play QB. I've seen him in action. Take my word for it, he knows what he's doin'."

"You gotta be kidding. Do you think I'd let a KGB ratfink rabbi run a team of mine?"

Homer pointed out calmly, "Who else do you have? We're all out of players at that position."

"I'll play Amen there—anybody but the Jew."

"You will not!" Homer said bluntly. "You will put Ziggy in. That's an order, soldier!" he yelled.

The coach's spine snapped straight; his hand flew up in a salute. "Yes, sir!"

But that was only a reflex reaction. His senses returned to him in a moment or two, just as Ziggy was strapping on his helmet to go on the field.

"Look, rabbi, don't get any ideas, hear? All we're going to do is run the ball for the rest of the game. Just give it to Amen and get out of the fucking way! Try a pass or anything fancy and I'll have you gang-raped!"

The fans in Giants Stadium cheered when they saw double zero come in, only to fall uncomprehendingly silent when he lined up to take a snap, not attempt a long field goal. They weren't prepared for this; no one except Homer knew that he could play quarterback.

Schimpf, scowling like a parched camel, signaled a play from the sidelines—Amen up the middle.

It was ridiculous. Everybody on the Rams was expecting a run; what else would a brand-new, bush-league, scared-Jew quarterback do but hand off and get out of the way? So Ziggy changed the play at the line of scrimmage, audibilizing that he'd be faking the ball to Amen and throwing a pass—a long pass—to the tight end Cannonball Murphy.

"Huuuhh?"

He could hear his own team react with disbelief as he called the play. But they were real pros, trained to obey and deliver on demand.

And deliver they did, executing the fake run beautifully. Amen grabbed at Ziggy's nonexistent handoff and leapt into the air, as if hurdling for a few yards. Everyone, including the Rams' secondary, went for him gleefully, ready to rack him up.

It left Cannonball wide open. The 275-pound end had never been this free in his life. It was too good to be true, he thought as he rumbled down the sideline. Something's gonna go wrong.

But when he looked over his shoulder for the ball, there it was, coming right at him, big as the moon. He was so surprised—overjoyed—that he bit right through his heavy-duty plastic mouthpiece.

Murphy was not called Cannonball for nothing. His immense, powerful hands not only caught the ball, they crunched it.

Tucking the pass under his arm, Cannonball took off for the distant goal line. It had been many years since he had run so far. The Rams' safety, a gold-medal-winning sprinter at the Bangladesh Olympics, managed to catch up with him at the ten. Murph might have been slow, but he wasn't weak: he carried the track star on his back all the way into the end zone.

Everybody in the ballpark went crazy—everybody except Gus Schimpf.

He stood stunned. Numb with cold fury.

"I thought I told you to run the ball," he confronted Ziggy as he came off the field.

"It was a dumb call, coach. Why call a play that everyone expects?"

"Because I told you to," Schimpf said. "Because I'm your coach."

Ziggy tried to make him understand. In sandlot he had done his own play calling. In semipro his coach was a guy named Duffy McGurk whose only words of advice to the team were, "Let's kick ass out there." Duffy also drank during the game and was usually half in the bag by the second quarter. In short, he'd always been on his own as a quarterback.

"I couldn't care less. You'll either take orders from me or—"

"Or what? I'm not trying to defy you—it's the only way I can play," Ziggy explained.

Schimpf's mouth fell open. This was it, the culmination of something that had been building ever since Ziggy had joined the team. Rebellion had raised its filthy head. Bolshevism was taking over. But what could he do about it? Right now Ziggy had Hogarth and the Gnomes and thirteen million New York

Jews behind him.

As if he could read Schimpf's mind—what was left of it—Ziggy said quickly, "On the next set of downs I want The Hook in there as wide receiver."

Schimpf said nothing, just turned and walked to the Giants bench, where he sat down, put his head in his hands, and groaned piteously.

Ziggy went to The Hook, who was sitting at the far end of the bench, schmoozing with the Giants' cheerleaders. "Get ready. You're going in."

"It's about fucking time," The Hook muttered. "I've been bored out of my *kugel* sitting around like this."

A few moments later, after the Giants' defense held off the Rams, up in the stands Devrah let out a shriek when she spotted The Hook entering the game. "That's him," she shouted, poking Darcy in the ribs and pointing.

"Oh God, this is so exciting," Darcy cried. "Our guys are actually in there together!"

"C'mon, Ziggy!" Devrah yelled through cupped hands. "Do it again!"

That's exactly what the Rams were thinking when Ziggy started his next sequence of plays, that he would try to show them up with another pass. They dropped back into a prevent defense, only to react with dismay when Ziggy, his football instincts working perfectly, faked throwing the ball and slipped it into the waiting Amen's gut. The Giants' fullback, five six but 240 pounds of solid, steroidical muscle, a cement sack with legs, looked for an opening, found it, and knifed right through the line, finding nothing but daylight. Seconds later, he picked up his interference and followed them downfield, dodging one defensive back after another. Then he was gone, long gone.

Two plays, two touchdowns.

Giants Stadium became a sea of white noise. Pandemonium everywhere, even up in the broadcast booth, where all four announcers shouted into their mikes at once, each trying to drown the other out. Next door, Homer Bloetcher removed his headset, clasped his hands before him, and said a few words of thanks to the Almighty. Unlike his daddy, who was a deacon in the Baptist church back home, Homer had never been a religious man. But he knew a sign from God when he saw one. Ziggy was surely heaven-sent, there could be no doubt about that. The boy was no mere mortal, not the way he kicked and threw, so easy and perfect-like. Look at the name he bore. With his religious background and upbringing, he just had to be a reincarnation of Ezekiel or one of them other priestly fellows. Homer might have been a little weak on his theology, but he sure as hell knew an angel when he saw one. Quickly, he left the coaching box and headed downstairs, to get in on the miracle.

Angel or no, Ziggy found himself in a tough football game. The Rams, smarting at having given up those two quick scores, came back clawing. They went right after him as he kicked off, putting two of their hatchetmen on him. Ziggy dodged one, but the other guy caught him in the midriff with his helmet. Ziggy went down hard, a wave of nausea hitting him and almost making him puke. He had to be helped off the field.

The trainers gave him a whiff of oxygen and waved powerful chemicals under his nose. It didn't help much; he still felt mashed up inside, ready to toss his cookies.

Someone tapped him on the shoulder. Ziggy turned and was stunned to see the tiny, wrinkled face of his grandmother.

"*Chukkeleh*," she cried, "are you all right, darling?"

"Bubbe, how did you get down here?" Ziggy asked.

"It was easy. I told the guard I was your grandmother and had some food for you. He was a nice Jewish boy and understood."

Bubbe set a picnic basket down on the ground and began unpacking plates and pots.

"Here," she said, handing him a cup. "Have a little chicken soup. I made it special for you this morning."

"Bubbe, I don't think I should."

"Have a sip, *chukkeleh*. It can't hurt you, you know."

Ziggy obeyed. He had always loved his grandmother's chicken soup. Today she had outdone even herself—it was bracing and rich, redolent of spices and goodness. He drank the cup down, then had another, feeling better, much better.

"Who's this? What's going on?"

"This is my grandmother," Ziggy explained. "Bubbe, meet Coach Gus Schimpf."

"The pleasure is all mine," she said. "I brought him a little chicken soup; why don't you have a cup, too. You look like you could use it."

"Chicken soup? Chicken soup?"

Schimpf kept repeating the words, as if his mind had got stuck.

"I also brought a nice little piece of gefilte fish."

"What? What's that you're saying?"

"Try a piece. It's good on pumpernickel."

Schimpf just shook his head and walked away, without a word. He was dreaming it all. He would soon wake up and none of this would be real—that he was coaching a team with a rabbinical student for a quarterback and a little old Jewish lady dishing out chicken soup on the sidelines. It could not be, it just wasn't possible, so what was the point of getting excited? Soon his eyes would open and it would be Sunday morning and he'd get out of bed and drive out to the park for the game.

Meanwhile, Ziggy, joined by The Hook, was feasting on his grandmother's food. She'd brought some homemade horse-radish—the red, fiery kind—to go with the fishballs.

"*Geshmakt!*" The Hook pronounced. "*A meichel fur dem beichel!* It's the best gefilte fish I've had in years." He gave Bubbe a hug. "I've really missed your *shabbes* meals."

"And I've missed having you over," she said in return. "Now that Ziggy's back from Europe and you two are teamed up again, maybe we can get together, like in the old days."

Somebody else came up. It was Homer, leaning on his crutches, looking puzzled.

"This is my grandmother; Bubbe, this is Homer. I told you about him."

"The man who discovered you. How nice. Have some chicken soup."

"Chicken soup?" Homer was taken aback. But then he sniffed the soup's strong, rich smell, and smiled. "Ah never met a plate of food ah didn't like," he drawled.

As she poured him a cup, making sure he got plenty of noodles and his own matzoh ball, he asked, "How'd you get the name of Bubba? Back home, that's a boy's name."

"It's not Bubba, it's *Bubbe,*" Ziggy emphasized. "It's Yiddish for grandmother."

"I see," Homer said, sipping. His eyes widened. "This is the best damn soup I've ever had!"

"Why thank you," Bubbe said in a pleased voice. "I cook it with the chicken feet in, you see. The gelatin makes all the difference in the taste and consistency."

"Any other specialties?" he inquired.

"You can find out for yourself, if you like," she replied, smiling at the big Okie. "Come to dinner next Friday night. We call it *shabbes.*"

"Shop us?"

"Sha," she corrected, "sha-bus."

"Shawpuss," he offered, trying hard.

"I can see we're going to have to work on your Yiddish," she said. "You'd better give the coach a little coaching of his own," she advised Ziggy and The Hook.

"Your grandson is the best thing that's ever happened to me, Bubba," Homer said sincerely. "I love him as if he were kin."

"*Richtiker chaifetz!*" Bubbe cried.

"What's that mean?"

"She thinks you're the real McCoy, coach," said The Hook, strapping on his helmet. The Giants had gotten the ball back. "Come on," he said to Ziggy, "let's show these *grobber kops* what we can do."

Ziggy nodded and as he leaned over to buss his grandmother on the cheek, Dora Glick, the Black Crow herself, shot the photograph that made her famous, the one the *Post* sold to thousands of newspapers around the world.

Later there would be those who attributed her good fortune to luck, a case of being in the right place at the right time. Not true, though. Luck did not figure in Dora's life, only a drive to succeed and a dedication bordering on fanaticism. She had dogged Ziggy closely ever since discovering his true identity, but it wasn't until a little while ago, when he had rung up those two quick touchdowns, that her gut feeling about him had blossomed into a true epiphany.

Seeing him noshing on the sidelines with his Jewish grandmother had clinched it. Ziggy's story was the big one for her. It could do for her what the Dreyfus case had done for Zola, what Watergate had done for Bernstein and Woodward.

That Ziggy didn't like her and had declined to give her an interview didn't matter. Dora thrived on rejection; intransigence turned her on. She'd done her best work writing about people who hated her. That kind of reaction was normal, she expected it. She was a reporter, not a social worker.

And what a story she had now.

Here was his Bubbe bringing him chicken soup in the middle of the game. Unfuckingbelievable! And she had the roll of film to prove it. Her exclusive photos were already on their way to the *Post*.

This was just the start of it, though. From now on, she was going to devote her life to Ziggy. Wherever he went, so too would Dora Glick. She'd only sleep when he did, eat when he ate, shit when he shat. She was going to make him her property, her creation, her Frankenstein. And she was going to get fat on him, put the name of Dora Glick on the journalistic map. As he rose to fame—or at least notoriety—so would she. Maybe he'd turn out to be a flash in the pan, a ten-minute celebrity. Didn't matter. By then she'd have established herself, gone from a fourth-string sportswriter to a hot-shot columnist.

Dora knew how she was going to do it; it all became clear as she watched Ziggy's amazing debut from the sidelines. She was going to sell him to the women, move his story from the Sports section to the Style pages. That was the key to success in this country, selling your stuff to the women, the smart sex. The men still made the money, but the women determined how it was to be spent—what clothes were to be bought, what TV shows would be watched, which books would be read.

If you couldn't find acceptance with women, you were up shit's creek. That's why Dora didn't fear the competition from the many other sportswriters present today. They were going to write lots about Ziggy too, but it was all going to be aimed at the men. Their jive was going to run on the Sports pages, as it always did. Which is why they were such a bunch of losers, hired hands working for Guild scale, because women didn't pay them any mind. Sportswriters were stuck for life in the back pages, but not Dora. She was heading for page three, with Ziggy in tow. And if he didn't like it, he could go take a flying fuck.

Ignoring the game, exciting as it was, Dora concentrated on the human-interest angle: JEWISH GRANNIE'S CHICKEN SOUP SAVES DAY FOR GIANTS. She moved over and introduced herself to Bubbe, grilling her while the Giants had the ball. It wasn't easy; the old biddy was caught up in the excitement Ziggy was generating with his rifle-shot passes to The Hook. She lived and died with everything her grandson did, screaming like a teenager when he completed a pass, hiding her eyes and mumbling a prayer in Yiddish every time the Rams gang-tackled him.

She understood some of the things Bubbe was saying. Dora had been born a Jew but didn't consider herself Jewish; the whole thing was a crock, like all religions. However, she tried hard to dredge up the few Yiddish words she'd suppressed all these years, in order to get on Bubbe's good side.

Dora was dying to find out more about Ziggy's father, his dead mother, the whole family shmeer. But all Bubbe did was keep refilling her cup with chicken soup, urging her to, "Eat, eat, darling, it's good for you."

Normally Dora wouldn't be caught dead eating chicken soup and gefilte fish. Only a mockie ate that Old World salty shit. But now she scarfed it down as if her life depended on it.

Which it did. Because as Bubbe, Ziggy, The Hook, and the rest of the Giant-Jewish connection went, so went Dora Glick. The girl who'd started off at the very bottom of the journalistic world, checking facts at *The New Yorker,* who'd then served for five years on the Devil's Island that was the *Time* magazine research department and another five in the gulag of the *New York Times'* Entertainment section, meant to have the last laugh on all her old bosses and colleagues—the big laugh, the fuck-you laugh.

Dora didn't let Bubbe's rejection throw her. She stayed by the woman's side and tried to ingratiate herself with her all through the remainder of the game. It was some game too;

even Dora, who was only mildly interested in football, had to admit it. It stayed a hard-fought, close match to the very end. The fans were up on their feet most of the time, screaming their lungs out.

There was something astounding, even miraculous about the way Ziggy and The Hook worked together. Like just-severed Siamese twins, each seemed to know exactly what the other was doing at all times, and where. Ziggy would drop back deep in the pocket, only to be rushed hard by five or six behemoths. Dodging, ducking, he'd get turned around, twisted up, only to suddenly break free and fire the ball through a maze of defensive players, right into The Hook's strong, sure hands.

Everyone knew he was going to throw to The Hook. The Rams put two men on the line of scrimmage to try and knock him down, but the slim-hipped receiver had more steps than a Cuban dance instructor and was able to shake free and get into the secondary. If the defensive backs played him loose, he'd stop short and curl in, or fake deep and cut to the side-line, giving Ziggy a perfect angle to throw to. When the backs got mad and tried to take away the short pass, The Hook would fake them out with another mambo move and take off downfield with surprising speed, putting himself in line for one of Ziggy's long, perfect spirals.

Working together was second nature to them. Communication was instant, brief—a cock of the head, a hand sign, a spoken word. In a way, they had an unfair advantage over everyone else on the field, most of whom had played together for five or six years at most. But Ziggy and The Hook's symbiotic relationship went back decades, all the way back to French Charlie's and Orchard Beach and the Senrabs (Barnes Avenue spelled backward) and the Hoboken Wharf Rats. It was no big deal, what they were doing today, because they had done it all their lives, on one field or the other. The only difference was, a lot more people were watching.

The lead seesawed back and forth. When it came down to the last minute of play, the Rams were ahead by two and trying to hold the home team off. Everyone in Giants Stadium had long ago gone berserk. People were standing and screaming hoarsely and desperately for a score, photographers were firing off flashbulbs like strobe lights in a disco, the TV commentators' booth was a miniature Tower of Babel, reporters were pounding away at their computers as if they were creaky old Underwood uprights. And from on high in the plush-lined duplex skybox perched atop the stadium, Russell Hogarth, collar opened, bow tie cast aside, was shouting into a transatlantic telephone as he described the game's finish in pidgin German to the Gnomes of Zurich:

" . . . der Juden is dropping back . . . er warft der ball . . . it goes gannz weit down the fielt to the Italiener, Hook . . . who catches it undt er ist knocked down bei un grosse shvartzer of der Rams!"

The Giants got to their own forty, where, with everyone thinking *pass*, Ziggy ran a quarterback draw, right up the center of the field to the Rams' twenty-five, only to have the whole thing called back because Siffie was caught holding. "I'll have you sent to the stockade in the morning!" Schimpf screamed at his deeply chagrined and remorseful center.

Ziggy, face bloodied from the hits he'd taken from the Rams' linemen, mouth sucking wind, uniform covered with dirt and snot and soaked through with sweat, dropped back and fired a quick bullet to the equally soiled Hook, who juked and jostled his way to the Rams' forty.

Four seconds left. Schimpf, collar ripped open, eyes bulging, frenziedly signaled for a timeout. Over the tumultuous roar of the crowd, he screamed at Ziggy, "Kick it, go for three!"

"Hold on now," Homer shouted, pushing between them on the sideline. "The goddamn wind's come up!"

They looked up at the flags on the roof of the stadium, all of which were blowing hard—and the wrong way.

"Fuck the wind! Keek, keek, you fucking Albino," the demented head coach shrieked.

"Here, *chukkeleh*." It was Bubbe again, pressing a hot cup of soup into Ziggy's hand. He gulped it down quickly, feeling, as before, the strength and warmth spreading through him.

He turned and walked back slowly to the huddle. The wind—almost gale force now—had brought new smells to the field, smells that went back to the days when the land around here was occupied by pig farmers. He could also detect the odor of the old Secaucus marshes. The Mafia used to dump the bodies of their victims here. Somebody was trying to tell him something. If not the ghosts of murdered Mafia victims, if not the wind itself, then his own football instinct, his heart of hearts. He had to go with it, had to believe in what he believed, or else he wasn't a man but a robot. And robots didn't win football games, men did.

Ziggy didn't let on in the huddle, didn't say anything special other than: "Field goal try, on three. Hold 'em, guys."

This way nobody could tip the play, if only because they didn't know it was coming. And it was only now that he looked at The Hook and whispered, "Let's go with our old trick play, the one we used against the Fordham Guineas that time. Remember it?"

"Are you crazy?" The Hook asked.

"No, I'm not crazy. Just do it!"

The Hook knelt on one knee, ready to take Siffie's snap. But when it came he turned and flipped his backpedaling buddy the ball and took off, fighting through the onrushing Rams and slipping past the startled safety and racing straight down the center of the field. The only thing close to him when he finally turned to look back was the ball itself, which Ziggy had laid up there for him, so perfectly that The Hook caught it without breaking stride and was able to continue at full speed into the end zone.

The press could not remember the last time the team had been so happy. From the way the Giants celebrated, you'd think they had just won the Super Bowl, prancing around in their jockstraps and spraying everyone with soda pop and Gatorade. The high jinks were attributed to the dick-daring victory, but that was only superficially correct. It wasn't just that the team had won, it was the way they had done it—with a Mickey Mouse play that connected them by sweet nostalgia to their own sandlot days, when they were kids and had no coaches, game films, or game plans to worry about. It was the last time any of them had played football just for the sheer hell of it.

Although they themselves didn't realize it and certainly couldn't articulate it, Ziggy had allowed them to be young again. Long ago the adults had grabbed hold of them because of their natural abilities and had pushed them into the system: Pop Warner, high school, college, and now pro ball. They'd been highly trained and disciplined, taught to be aggressive and violent, made to pump iron, ordered to play with pain and endure injuries, filled with painkillers and steroids.

The system had rewarded them handsomely, made them rich and famous, but it had taken the fun out of the game and turned it into a business instead—until Ziggy showed up and worked his crazy magic. The whole thing just tickled them to death, made them want to laugh and shout and grab ass and spit water all over each other.

What they loved even more was hearing about Bubbe from Homer, how she'd snuck down out of the stands with this soup and fish for Ziggy, and what a great little old lady she was. Ziggy brought her to the locker room, where she was cheered and hugged and carried around on shoulders. She was everybody's grandmother, not just Ziggy's—a repository of overflowing maternal love, warmth, and homeyness. They thanked her for reviving Ziggy and for bringing them luck, begged her for a cup of that chicken soup and gerfluckter fish or whatever the fuck it was called.

The only man in the Giants' locker room who was not celebrating was Fred Walston. He knew better than anyone that he was no longer number one. His knee was healing, but even if it were a hundred percent by the end of next week, he wouldn't be starting, not after Ziggy's performance today. How could the Giants not promote the kid, a Jewish quarterback in a Jewish city?

Could be Ziggy had been lucky today, had played way over his head. But Walston's gut told him otherwise. The motherfucker knew what he was doing; despite his lack of experience and his off-the-wall attitude toward the game he'd moved the team and put a W on the board. And Ws were what it was all about, not only in the NFL, but in the other league out there, the big one they called the United States of America.

Walston slipped on his black-leather jacket and took off fast, dodging the media folk who came his way. Those who continued to follow him he led on a merry chase through the basement to the side door where his Harley-Davidson was parked.

He waited until he was a good distance down the turnpike to pull into a gas station and find a pay phone.

The man at the other end listened silently as Walston made his pitch. Then, finally: "Hey, Fred, do you really care if this guy takes your job away? You've been in the NFL a while now. You must have enough salted away to live off for the rest of your life."

"That's where you're wrong, Jake. I put a lot of money into a drug deal that went wrong."

"That's tough, Freddy. But shame on you for takin' such a big chance."

"I was a sucker, all right, but I ain't gonna be one again. I need you to get rid of the competition for me. I need three more years in the league to get well again."

"You're asking a lot. The eyes of the world are on this guy."

"That's why I'm calling you, Jake. You're the best at what you do."

"How much are you offering?"

"Fifty K."

"No way."

"Come on, Jake. I remember when you used to ice people just for the joy of it."

"That's when I was young and crazy," Jake reminded him. "But I'm all grown up now. I need a whole lot more than fifty thousand bucks for a job like this."

Walston tried to bargain, but Jake wasn't buying any of it. He was just out of jail and needed a big score to get straight with the world.

Walston finally caved in and offered to pay seventy-five thousand.

"Make it an even hundred," Jake said. "But I want it all up front."

"C.O.D., man."

"Fuck that."

"What's the matter, don't you trust me? We used to be cell-mates."

They argued some more before coming to an agreement: half down now, the balance on completion.

There'll be no more direct calls after this, Walston instruct-ed. "I'll communicate with you through third parties only. You know which ones."

"Hey, not to worry," Jake said reassuringly. "I'll do your dirty work and I won't blow your cover, either." His voice took on a mocking edge. "You'll be able to walk away from the mess smelling like roses."

Z IGGYMANIA.

New York took Ziggy to its heart. He was one of their own and a hero and a winner and they loved him with a spontaneous outpouring of affection and adulation. The Big Apple hadn't seen anything like it in a long, long time. People just couldn't stop talking about him, treating him like a major deity.

When the Rams game ended, some five thousand fans waited for an hour outside Giants Stadium, just to catch a glimpse of Ziggy. Wherever he went that next week, whether to a restaurant or just for a walk around town, people screamed at the sight of him and flocked around, begging for an autograph, a word, a touch. Women he had never met before, complete strangers and not all of them young, sent letters to him, enclosing their phone numbers and photographs, in varying degrees of nudity. Others hung around his hotel day and night, trying different ways to sneak past the security guards and knock on his door.

Ziggymania took on even greater proportions after the

team's next game, against Tampa Bay. It was Ziggy's first start against a capable opponent playing at home; a lot of people (Schimpf included) expected him to screw it up. But Ziggy fooled everyone by turning in a solid, steady performance, throwing two touchdowns to The Hook and running up thirty-five points in all, more than enough to win the ballgame.

Fifteen thousand fans were on hand to greet Ziggy at JFK when the team returned home that night. Many wore Ziggy T-shirts and caps, chanted "Zig-geee, Zig-geee!" and tried to rip the clothes off his back. One teenage girl fainted at the sight of him.

To shield Ziggy from all this hysteria and also to reward him for his excellent performances, the Gnomes of Zurich instructed Russell Hogarth to move the young quarterback into the penthouse of the hundred-story condominum HEN owned at Fifty-Ninth and Fifth, on the site of the old Plaza Hotel.

The penthouse had fourteen rooms, five marble bathrooms, an indoor swimming pool, sauna, and a master bedroom with a gilt-edged mirror in the ceiling.

"That'll be my room!" The Hook cried, having been invited by Ziggy to join him. "This is where I'm going to do the best shtupping of my life."

The Hook had never been so happy. Gone was every vestige of Mediterranean melancholy from his visage. He was a man on the verge of self-fulfillment, a man about to live out his most improbable but deep-rooted fantasies.

"I intend to make it with every girl on the Giants' cheer-leading squad," he announced as he paced round the room, testing the king-sized waterbed, smoothing the satin sheets, checking himself out in the overhead mirror. "I'm going to do the nasty with them right here, one by one, until I've gone through the whole bunch."

"Come on, Hook, don't talk like that."

"What's the matter, think I'm not capable of it? There are twelve girls on the squad and an equal number of games left in the season. That works out to a girl a week."

"I'm not doubting your sexual prowess, just the morality of it."

"Don't give me any of that rabbinical crap. Shtupping is what I do."

"I thought you were a football player."

"Football is for now; sex is forever."

Ziggy tried a more pragmatic argument. "What about the new diseases?"

"I'm always careful."

Ziggy cautioned him not to mistake the way he conducted his sex life with normal behavior.

"Look who's talking about sex," The Hook scoffed. "If you hadn't gone off to Amsterdam with Rachel, you'd still be a virgin. Shit, you won't even shtup Darcy even though she's crazy about you and wants to be your love slave."

"Don't be crude. She's an incredibly sweet girl."

"They're all sweet girls! So what? They want it more than we do, Reb. I've been trying to teach you that all your life."

Ziggy's voice rose. "I'm not a rabbi," he reminded The Hook, "I'm a football player. And I can't sleep with Darcy just like that, not while I'm still involved with Rachel."

"Rachel is history," The Hook shot back. "Why can't you

accept it? She gave you the message in Amsterdam and again on the phone last week."

"If we were together right now, she'd change her mind."

"Well you're not together. She's in Amsterdam and you're in New York. She won't come here and you can't go there. Finita la musica, my friend."

Ziggy pointed out that even if that were true, he still couldn't sleep with a girl he didn't love. The Hook scoffed at that notion. In his view love was the death of sex. It was all religion's fault, he charged, with its emphasis on procreation and holiness. It was just a ploy on the part of a bunch of overweight monks to gain control over the human race.

Ziggy blew up at that. He couldn't stand the way The Hook dismissed spiritual values and felt so casually toward the powerful and profound force of sex.

The Hook came back at him just as forthrightly, accusing him of being afraid of sex.

"That's your problem, Ziggy. You've got balls on the gridiron, but when it comes to women you're a wuss."

"Get off my back! I've got enough going on in my life without having to worry about Darcy. Among other things, we've got the Bears on Sunday, remember? I've got a tremendous amount of preparing to do."

"The Bears!" The Hook said derisively. "Who the hell are the Bears—just another football team. Stop worrying, Ziggy. Just remember Duffy McGurk's advice—just kick ass out there. That's all football is—not game plans and films and charts, just kicking butt. The more butt you kick, the more games you win."

It was all well and good for The Hook to believe that, but he only had to catch passes and hold for kicks, while Ziggy had to run the team, throw and kick the ball, handle the press and the fans—and take hits from the Bears. The Bears were murder on quarterbacks, always had been, always would be. Owned by a consortium of retired CIA officers, they had the meanest defensive line in the business, four headhunters led by a seven-foot-tall, 350-pound ex–pro wrestler named Mad Dog Marlboro whose contract provided a seventy-five-thousand-dollar bonus every time he sacked a quarterback.

"We ain't gonna let no bush-league boy from the Bronx beat us," Mad Dog was quoted in the press.

Homer told Ziggy that what Mad Dog had really said, before the Bear's PR man cleaned up the statement, was "we ain't gonna let no goddamn Jewboy from the Bronx beat us."

Ironic that a Bear player should talk like that, Ziggy thought, when it was in Chicago that the only other Jewish quarterback in league history, Sid Luckman, had rung up such an illustrious career. Luckman had played before Ziggy's time, way back when the players still wore leather helmets, but Ziggy had read about him and kept his picture tacked over his bed, a kid from Brooklyn's Erasmus Hall who went on to play at Columbia and then become the first T-formation quarterback in the pro game. In those days, quarterbacks played defense as well; Luckman excelled in both departments to such an extent that he was elected to the Football Hall of Fame shortly after retiring.

Luckman had showed that a Jew could not only play football but eventually make everyone forget his religion and accept him for what he was, a football player. That's all Ziggy wanted—to live up to Luckman's standards. Football on this level was tough enough without religion coming into it.

That's why he avoided getting into a spitting match with Mad Dog all week and why he downplayed his Jewishness as well. He even tried to dissuade Bubbe from accompanying the team to Chicago. What would Sid Luckman have accomplished if he had his Jewish grandmother standing on the sidelines, calling him *"chukkeleh"* and "bubbeleh" all the time?

Surprisingly, the team wouldn't stand for the idea of leaving Bubbe behind. As Cannonball Murphy put it, "She brought us good luck three games in a row and she'll bring us good luck again. Ain't no way we'll go anywhere without her now."

There was a pragmatic as well as a superstitious side to Cannonball's position: "We need her chicken soup, too," he pointed out. "It's keeping us healthy. Injuries have been way down lately." The team was even attributing miraculous powers to Bubbe's chicken soup. Last Sunday, for example, Homer Bloetcher, after gulping down three straight bowls during the halftime break, had suddenly flung away his hand-crutches, crying, "Look, everybody, look! I can walk again!"

MIRACLE IN THE MEADOWLANDS was the headline over Dora Glick's column the next day. Dora's profile of Bubbe and her magically potent chicken soup clinched it for Russell Hogarth, who signed her to an exclusive personal services contract. HEN bought out her dress shop and placed her on salary so that she could devote herself full time to cooking for the team. From now on, Bubbe's chicken soup, gefilte fish, and other savory dishes would be available not only during games but at practice sessions as well.

Hogarth, on behalf of the Gnomes, also made an offer to Ziggy's father to become the team chaplain—two good-luck charms were better than one, no? But the Reb declined. He hadn't softened his stand against the game one bit. If anything, Ziggymania had soured him even more. He was not amused by the phone calls he got from abrasive reporters like Dora Glick, or by the groupies who hung around his shul, hoping to catch a glimpse of Ziggy.

Ziggy did his best to blot out his father's disapproving voice and concentrate on Sunday's game. There was much to do. He had the Giants' playbook down pat now, had memorized the scouting report on the Bears, and had watched so much film his eyeballs hurt. He was even getting to know how his teammates played the game—which blocks his linemen could make and which they couldn't, how his receivers ran their routes, what he could expect from his running backs, and so on. A good quarterback carried around all these details in his head.

He was also beginning to make some friends on the team. The close ones included the runner Amen Armstrong; Cannonball Murphy, the freckle-faced, pug-nosed tight end with the mashing-device hands; Buford Sifton, the rock-of-ages, history-major center; and Ferdinand Daniels, the now fourth-string quarterback. Ferdinand was still recovering from his knee injury but took advantage of the layoff to concentrate on the stock market. He'd tipped Ziggy off to a swift-rising Taiwanese genetics stock and made him a quick four thousand dollars in the last two days, on a five-hundred-dollar investment. "This is just the beginning," he promised. "I'm going to make you so much money that you'll be able to reforest all of the Golan Heights."

Cannonball Ziggy admired and liked for several reasons. The guy was always good fun and a prankster, even though he and his wife, Lynne, had a serious problem at home, with one of their four kids being retarded. Cannonball also had a strongly spiritual side and was a devout Catholic who tried to lead an exemplary Christian life, except when he was on the football field and turned into a complete Neanderthal.

Siffie was also an awesome hitter and brawler in action but a pacifist and a scholar the rest of the time, one of those rare jocks who liked to read and study and discuss world events in minute detail. Ziggy understood his split personality because it mirrored his own—the Yeshiveh *bocher* who loved knocking heads with 250-pound linebackers.

Ziggy even made an effort to reach out to Jesus Maria Gonzalez and Fred Walston, taking counsel from the Torah: "The true hero is one who converts an enemy to a friend." No luck. Jesus's anger was long-lived, and Walston wouldn't stop sulking and smoldering either. Ziggy finally gave up trying with them, if only because he was worn out from the effort of coping with his main adversary, Gus Schimpf.

"I've let you have your way these past three weeks, but no more," the coach said in a private meeting. "You've had a chance to learn my system, so from now on you can forget about improvising and calling your own plays. I'm taking over again, goddammit, and I don't care what Hogarth says!"

"Sorry, Coach. I just feel your system is all wrong. It's too regimented and controlled. It just doesn't work," Ziggy argued.

"You know better than me, thanks to your one month in the league," Schimpf sneered. "What an arrogant son of a bitch you are."

Ziggy tried to make him see that he wasn't being arrogant, just realistic. Schimpf was locked into an old way of looking at the game and that's why he hadn't won very often, despite all the talent the team had. Defenses were so complicated today, so quick to change and attack that you just couldn't play in a structured way against them; you needed to be as quick and adaptable as they were. That meant no more coaching from the sidelines, no hand and radio signals. They didn't even need huddles anymore but should call plays from the line of scrimmage, not allowing the defense to substitute and adjust.

"In other words, you'd like to do away with me completely," Schimpf said, unrelentingly.

"We'll have plenty of time to talk during timeouts. You can give me all the advice you want then."

"Advice? I don't give advice, I give orders!" Schimpf thundered, blood pressure making the veins in his forehead bulge like cables. "Either you obey them or I'll bench you."

"Go ahead, then, do it," Ziggy said, just as hotly.

Tossing his helmet aside, he strode off the field and into the locker room. Schimpf followed after him, screaming, "Communist, anarchist, you'll be sorry for this, I'll have you kicked off the team!" Then the red-faced, pop-eyed coach turned and gestured wildly to Walston on the sidelines.

"Get out here and take over!"

Walston, in his motorcyle gear, just looked perplexedly at Schimpf and pointed to his bum knee.

"All right, then you!" Schimpf spat at Sam Robespierre.

Robespierre was willing but unable, having inhaled a little too much laughing gas before practice. He got up from the bench, took one wobbly step, and collapsed in a heap, big goofy smile on his face.

"Fucking dope fiend!" Schimpf yelled. He turned. "Where the hell is Ferdinand?"

"Down in the locker room."

"What the hell's he doing?"

"The market's up, coach."

Schimpf flung his baseball cap away, then his whistle, even his sweatshirt, and took off for the basement of Giants Stadium and the sanctuary of his padded cell. He began to hammer himself against the walls with such force that he opened huge gashes in his head and was soon covered in blood and slime, like roadkill.

That's how Ziggy found him, sitting dazedly against the far wall of the cell, mumbling to himself.

"God, look at you," Ziggy cried, horrified. "Why do you do these things to yourself, Coach?"

"Your fault," Schimpf got out. "Have you court-martialed, soldier."

"I'm sorry, I shouldn't have defied you like that. It's just that we see the game differently. And I guess you take football a whole lot more seriously than I do."

"Football's all I have. Lost my son . . . wife, too. She was only forty-three, just snapped when we got that call from the

Defense Department," Schimpf recalled, voice choked into a whimper by pain and sorrow. "Good woman . . . I miss her."

Ziggy found himself talking about the death of his own mother, also at a young age, and how it had affected him, left him so desolate and lonely, so angry at God and religion and life itself. "I think that's when I really decided in my heart that I didn't want to become a rabbi, even though it wasn't until years later that I did anything about it."

As they both went on talking about their losses, Ziggy found himself warming toward Schimpf. They didn't exactly become friends but they did manage to listen to each other for the first time and to come to an understanding. Schimpf would let him go on running the offense in his way, winging it, until such time as Ziggy started losing games.

"When that happens, you're outta there, understand?" Schimpf said. "Walston takes over again and you go to the bench, no matter what Hogarth or the Gnomes or anyone else says."

"Coach, if I can't cut it, I don't want to be out there," Ziggy replied. "I'd ask to be dropped from the team."

"Say that again," Schimpf said with disbelief.

"If I'm not good enough to start and win I shouldn't be playing football. I'd only be wasting my time."

"You could still kick for us."

"You don't really need me to kick anymore. Jesus can do that."

"You'd really give up everything if I don't play you—your salary, the penthouse, all the goodies that are beginning to come your way?"

"Coach, that's not why I play football. I do it for the fun of it. Without that, there's no reason for me to bother."

Schimpf sat back, studying Ziggy with new eyes. "You know what," he said finally, "I've heard lots of players claim they don't do it for the bucks, but you're the only one I've ever believed. You got depths, kid. You're complicated—maybe too complicated to be a success at the game."

"Why do you say that?"

"You think too much, and that's probably what'll screw you up. In the long run, the guys that really succeed in football are the well-meaning dummies like me." He paused a moment. "I'd like to start over with you, Ziggy."

"Until I start losing games, right?"

"Right," Schimpf nodded, smiling thinly, "until you start losing games."

ON SUNDAY THE BEARS GAVE ZIGGY HIS SEVEREST TEST. NOT only did they have one of the finest teams in the AFC, rivaled only by the Laredo Lariats, the Mitsubishi-bankrolled expansion team, but they played an exceptionally bruising game built around putting all-out pressure on the opposing quarterback. Doubly determined not to let this upstart get the better of them, they went after Ziggy with all the muscle and violence they possessed, rushing five, six, or more men on every play, hitting him time and time again, some times legally, other times illegally. It cost them over two hundred yards in penalties during the first half alone, but it was a price they were willing to pay, figuring that if they pounded Ziggy long and hard enough they'd either unhinge him or drive him out of the game.

The worst offender was Mad Dog Marlboro, the Bears' designated pass rusher. A one-time inmate of the North Dakota Hospital for the Criminally Insane, the psychotic Mad Dog kept coming at Ziggy with a vengeance, screaming each time he knocked him down or speared him with his helmet,

"Howdja like it, rabbi? Think chicken soup is gonna protect you now?"

The Giants tried to stop Mad Dog by double-teaming him, but he was so hyped up on chemicals and hate that he kept crashing through and clobbering Ziggy.

Soon Ziggy's head began to spin, blood leaked out of his nose, and his ribs throbbed with pain so intense that every breath felt like a knife stab. In the midst of it, though, he remembered a line from the Bible: "He who endures to the end will be saved." What also helped keep him going were the bracing cups of Bubbe's chicken soup that he gulped down on the sidelines.

Calling on all his strength and wiles, he did what he could to duck and dodge the head-hunting Bears, rolling out to the left, then the right, calling draw plays and screen passes, trying to simultaneously stay alive and move his team down the field. He also tried to keep his cool with Mad Dog, knowing the thug would love it if he took a swing at him and got kicked out of the game.

Who is a hero? He who controls his passions. The Torah this time. But how much could a man take, particularly when his enemy not only played dirty but kept making jeering anti-semitic remarks after each hit: "Howdja like that one, Jewboy? That'll teach you, you fucking Hebe."

Most football players forgot race and religion once the game began. But every so often a Nazi came along and made trouble, particularly in Ziggy's sandlot and semipro days when he still wore a beard and forelocks. Generally his teammates managed to control the guy by threatening to break his legs if he didn't shut up, or by high-lowing him a couple of times. Here in the big top, though, things were different. Guys like Mad Dog were either too big or crazy (or stoned) to be frightened off. Nothing to do but let Ziggy take his licks and pray Bubbe's chicken soup got him through.

The Giants began to get physical too as the day wore on. Tempers heated up, aggressions were unleashed, people began to hit with vengeance, turning the game into a donnybrook. Backs had to claw for every yard they gained, receivers took backbreaking shots, special teams gave their bodies up like kamikaze pilots. Ziggy kept pleading with his boys to give him a little extra effort, which they did, yet he still found it hard to move the ball.

It was maddening, mystifying. Every big gain was followed by two losses. Ziggy kicked some long field goals to keep them in contention, but otherwise they couldn't get on the board. The Bears seemed able to anticipate every move they made, stop them cold each time they finally got something going.

By the time the first half was drawing to a close, the Giants were down by sixteen points. That's when The Hook made his big discovery. He had split out wide left, on the far side of the field, in front of the Bears' bench, when he heard a little bald-headed guy in thick glasses call to the Bears' defensive captain, "Look out!" On the next play, a run, he yelled, "Look sharp, Larry." Then, on third down, "Look out again."

"They're stealing our plays," The Hook informed Ziggy, when they were heading off the field together. "That's why we can't move the ball—they know what's coming each time."

It figured. The ex-spooks who owned the team had obviously put their expertise in spying and surveillance techniques to good use. Somehow they were able to eavesdrop on the Giants' huddles, maybe even decipher the audibles Ziggy called.

"That little putz in glasses is the mastermind," The Hook said. "He probably teaches code breaking at Langley."

"Would they go to all that trouble to win a lousy football game?"

"Hell, yes. It's like Schimpf said—football isn't like war, it is war."

Ziggy tested it. He called a run, only to hear four-eyes shout "Look sharp!" as he went into his snap cadence. "Larry" was used for left, "Ray" for right. "Look out" meant pass.

The bastards. Ziggy felt sick; worse than hurt. Wasn't there anything like sportsmanship or ethics left in the NFL? Had everybody been corrupted by the money, the mania to win?

"We're screwed," he said as they came off the field again, on the heels of another aborted march. "We can't beat their dirty tricks."

"The hell we can't," The Hook said, reminding him of the old days in the Bronx, when they used to horse around in pickup games with seven or eight on a side.

They'd give their teams self-mocking names: Super Jews versus the Golden Goys, Mockies versus the Yoshkies. The fun came in the exaggerated way they played out the team's identity, turned the make-believe into caricature.

"Are you really suggesting what I think you are?" Ziggy asked incredulously.

"Let's fuck the CIA where they breathe," was The Hook's reply.

Ziggy laughed for the first time that day and decided to employ the new strategy on the Giants' first possession of the second half. Ordering The Hook to set up wide, he then yelled to him in Yiddish, *"Du mach zich vee du gaist rechts, uber emes vestu links! V'shtai?"*

It was a command to fake right, then go left.

The Hook confirmed his approval: *"Dos gefelt mir."*

Ziggy could see the look of consternation on the defensive captain's face. The poor, confused guy shot a pleading look for help at four-eyes, but the code breaker was just as befuddled as he was. While the Bears were trying to figure out what in hell was happening, Ziggy began to complete one pass after another to The Hook.

It was indeed like old times, with the two of them chattering away in Yiddish before each play.

"Zoll ich gayn vyter?" The Hook would ask. (Should I go far?)

"Vart dorten by der dreizig," Ziggy would reply. (Stop at the thirty-yard line.)

Then he'd add, *"Loz nit op dem boll, shmuck!"* (Don't drop the ball, prick.)

"What kinda signals are you guys using?" inquired Cannonball Murphy as the offensive team gathered on the sidelines.

Ziggy's answer brought huge, raucous whoops of laughter from his teammates, who then demanded to be taught a few key words so that they too could get in on the action.

Quickly, Ziggy taught them how to count up to five in Yiddish. When it came time to take the field again, the Giants charged out and took their stances, choking back giggles like schoolkids as Ziggy barked, *"Gibbem* a good *knok,* guys! *Gibbem a zetz* they'll never forget! Go on *feer."*

He'd start the cadence chant: *"Einz . . . tzvei . . . drei . . . feer"* and they'd come off the ball with fiendish glee, huge shoulders shaking with mirth as they blasted into the nonplussed Bears and indeed did give them a *zetz* that sent them flying everywhichway, like tenpins.

They were able to score two quick touchdowns using this Semitic code, both on Ziggy-to-Hook combinations, and went into the fourth quarter tied with the Bears.

Ziggy kept calling the signals in a mixture of English and Yiddish and the Giants continued to move the ball easily, scoring again, this time on a short pass to Cannonball Murphy. The Yiddish lessons continued when the offensive team regrouped on the sideline, so that by the time the guys took the field again, most of them could count up to ten. Ziggy was thus able to call audibles by using numbers, even as he and The Hook continued to converse in the Ashkenazic vernacular of his ancestors.

"Voss zollen mir ton?" The Hook would ask. (What do we do now?)

"Loif glaich in mitn feld," Ziggy would reply. (Let's run right up the middle of the field.)

Soon the Bears became thoroughly bamboozled. Not only had they been deprived of their secret weapon, the Giants were deploying one of their own, communicating in a weird tongue that was impossible to comprehend. In a panic, the Bears sought in vain a Yiddish speaker among them. The

Giants, all loosey-goosey and confident now, kept rolling all over them. The game, which had begun as a grim, bloody battle to the death, turned into a romp instead. The Giants ran off twenty straight points and, as Cannonball Murphy shouted in the locker room afterward, *"shmeised the Bears but good!"*

The Giants' high spirits did not wane, with the celebrating continuing all through the flight back to New York that night. The team drank the plane dry, kept bantering roughly and good-naturedly with each other, shouting and laughing. They were only 4-3 on the season, but they had it together now and they knew it. Ziggy had not only turned them into a team, he'd turned football into a game again.

So like the goofy, overgrown kids they were, the Giants whooped it up as the airliner flew through the night toward home, the high point coming when Bubbe got up at Ziggy's request and taught the team her favorite song from *Fiddler on the Roof*:

> To life, to life!
> L'Chayim, L'Chayim . . .

Watching her as she skipped up and down the aisle singing and dancing, her brown eyes gleaming with happiness, Homer Bloetcher suddenly realized just what a great woman Bubbe was and how much he liked her. She was something else, that little one, and she looked so handsome too in her tailored suit and upswept gray hair, so sophisticated and polished.

Homer felt his heart going out to her; felt, for the first time in too long, something akin to love. It made him feel shaky and scared—what the hell was an old Baptist redneck like him doing falling for an ultrasmart Jewish grandmother? But falling he was. Nothing to do but sing along with the others:

> We'll raise a glass and drink a schnappes
> To life, to life!
> *L'Chayim!*

IT WAS TWO IN THE MORNING WHEN THE GIANTS' PLANE LANDED at JFK but thousands of highly excited fans were on hand to greet the team at the arrival gate. Some in the crowd carried signs and banners reading: WE LOVE ZIGGY . . . ZIG WITH ME, ZIGGY . . . THAT'S OUR BOYCHIK . . . BUBBE'S BRIGADE.

There were reporters and sports-anchors, a woman from the mayor's office, people from the Swiss Embassy (sent by the Gnomes), various honchos from the NFL, a couple of soap opera stars . . . and Darcy Dalton.

"Can I have your autograph?" she asked as she hugged Ziggy and helped him fight through the swarms of well-wishers and hangers-on, the bright lights of the TV cameras almost blinding them.

"It'll cost you five hundred bucks."

"Will you take it in trade?" When Ziggy's laugh died down, she asked, "How's it feel to be the talk of the town?"

"Scary. Let's get out of here," he said, waving off a heavily made-up woman with a mike in her hand who wanted to take a thirty-second sound bite out of him.

The New York press was not so easily put off, though. They soon corralled Ziggy and ran him through his paces, asking endless questions about the game and how and why the Giants had used Yiddish to win it. The Hook was also getting his share of attention and was had fun explaining how he came to know the language so well. ("My first girlfriend was studying to be a cantor.") Bubbe was not being ignored either and with only a little prompting regaled everyone with a few verses from *Fiddler* again. Homer, Amen, and Cannonball joined in lustily. The whole city buzzed about the Giants all week.

When they were finally alone and heading toward Manhattan in Darcy's convertible, Ziggy sat back with a sigh of relief. "Whew. Can you believe everything that's happening?"

"You must be flying high. Do you want to go somewhere and celebrate?"

"Great idea. Any suggestions?"

This was what Darcy was good at, finding romantic things to do. She put her car into overdrive and they sped all the way down to the lowest point of Manhattan and caught the ferry across to Staten Island. They sat up top with a blanket wrapped around them and cuddled as they watched the receding city skyline and the Statue of Liberty, with a swarm of seagulls circling and crying overhead. Then they went to an all-night Greek diner and had breakfast, or at least Ziggy did ("I don't eat much because of my bella figura problem," Darcy explained). After that, they found their way to a beach and walked for a while at the edge of the surf, hand in hand, stopping finally for a kiss.

Flash.

It was the Black Crow herself, Dora Glick, with camera in hand.

"Are you two lovebirds having fun?" she asked.

"For God's sake, Dora, have you been following us all the while?"

"Just doing my job."

"Your job is a disgrace. You ought to get another one," Darcy said.

"Who asked you, little Miss Hotpants?"

"Beat it, Dora, will you?" Ziggy said angrily.

"Hey, why don't you just wise up and start cooperating with me? I could make you the biggest name in America."

"No thanks."

"It's going to happen anyway. Tomorrow I start a new column, on the woman's page: 'Ziggy's Day.' With a little luck it could go into syndication."

"You're kidding."

"I kid you not. Play ball with me and I'll turn you into an icon."

"No thanks one more time."

"I could help you, Ziggy, keep you from making the kind of mistakes you made today."

"What kind of mistakes?"

"Using Yiddish out there. Wrong move, pal. Sure, New York got a kick out of it. But the rest of the country's going to hate you for it."

"We were only clowning around."

"Clown around in some other language, pig latin or something. Americans don't like Jews. I'm talking about the real

Americans, the people who live in swamps and mining towns, the rubes, the shitkickers, the desert people. When they hear Yiddish they reach for their revolvers."

"The guys on the team loved the idea."

"That's because they're on your side, same as everybody else in New York. But out there," waving to the other side of the bay, "things are a whole lot different. This is an anti-Semitic country. You're going to bring all the poison and shit out by flaunting your Jewishness."

"I'm not flaunting anything. We just called a few audibles in Yiddish."

"Yeah, and drank chicken soup on the sidelines and sang *Fiddler* all the way home. That's what I call asking for it."

"The team needed a little loosening up."

"If you're smart you'll drop the tribal stuff and act like a goy. Then all of America will take you to its bosom."

"I can only be myself."

"That's a crock. You dropped out of the religion, didn't you? It shows that you yourself think it's a crock."

"I dropped out of the rabbinate, not the religion. And if Judaism's a crock, how come it's survived for thousands of years?"

"So has Christianity. Smart money says you should go with the flow."

Ziggy made a sour face.

"Okay, I know you disapprove of me, think I'm a pushy broad and all that. But I know how things work in America. If you made friends instead of enemies with the rednecks, you could become president one day. All you have to do is join

'Jews for Jesus.'"

"What is this? What are we talking about? Jews for Jesus, becoming president one day! For God's sake, I'm only a rookie quarterback."

"You've become the celebrity of the month and it's going to snowball from here, you'll see. People like me are going to make you the hottest thing since Elvis. But whether you become famous or infamous is strictly up to you. You'd do well to remember the old saying, 'Think Yiddish, dress British.' That's the ticket to success, not the other way around."

With that, Dora was gone, crossing the beach to a waiting taxi. She was nowhere to be found on the ferry back to the city, which made Ziggy and Darcy think they had finally gotten rid of her for a time. What they didn't know, however, was that Dora had taken a helicopter to her new apartment, in a high-rise in view of Ziggy's penthouse. The place had just a few sticks of furniture, but she equipped it with such state-of-the-art surveillance devices as night-vision telescopes, infra-red cameras, laser listening devices, phone bugs, and zoom-lens vidcams. Compared to her James Bond was a hayseed.

Dora was in place, tucked into the window seat of her pad, when Ziggy and Darcy got home. Training her high-powered binoculars on them, camera at the ready, Dora peered through the early-morning light (and through the open French doors of the penthouse) and watched Ziggy make up the couch into a bed for Darcy. Voyeuristic anticipation turned to rage when she realized Darcy was going to sleep alone on the couch.

The redheaded cocktease, what was wrong with her? Why wouldn't she go to bed with Ziggy? And why hadn't he booted her out for not coming across? Dora was puzzled by those two. She had been expecting sexual fireworks, enough hot pictures to break the bank at *Playboy*. Instead all she captured was Darcy in a negligee combing out her hair before curling up for some z's. As for Ziggy, she couldn't even see him behind his bedroom blinds. What was he doing for kicks, watching the Nature Channel?

The only one doing anything in bed was The Hook, who had brought home one of the secretaries from the Swiss Embassy he'd met at the airport. But The Hook's bedroom was on the wrong side of the building and all Dora got out of the wiretap was a lot of heavy breathing and the girl crying, "*Ach, mein gott,* how big you are, how *fantastiche!*"

What a bummer. One guy ends up with a Kraut, the other with Mr. Fist and His Five Daughters. That Ziggy was too much, a romantic washout if there ever was one. Look at the ditzes he was hooked up with. The first, Rachel, didn't even have the smarts to leave her dunghole in Amsterdam and rejoin him. She sits a million miles away twiddling her thumbs while he makes it big and runs around with another broad.

As for Darcy, she didn't even have brains enough to stop playing hard to get. An army of dames had the hots for Ziggy, and she sends him off to his room alone. What an iceberg. Dora hated her, the California moonbeam. She was all wrong for him.

What he needed was a woman like herself. That much was clear now. He needed an Amazon who would take him in hand and make him better than he was, the way Evita did with Perón.

Dora made up her mind. Writing about Ziggy was not enough; she needed to become an active participant in his life. Needed to become his lover, not his observer. Control him from the inside, not the outside.

To do it, she'd have to get her own shit together, improve her looks. Starting tomorrow she'd start rehabilitating herself, losing weight, building up her body, getting back to her old self.

Nobody would believe it but once upon a time she had been a decent-looking broad. Not as professionally beautiful as Darcy, but certainly on a par with Rachel. That was before she'd had the first of her nervous breakdowns, brought on by all the amphetamines she'd popped while working days at the *New Yorker* and trying to write a novel at night. The combination of shit job, shit book, and too many bennies had done her in.

The second breakdown came when she left *Time* and worked for a while as a fourth-string theater critic for the *New York Times*. Having to sit through all those gloomy off-off-Broadway plays from Poland and France, all that East Village performance art with one egomaniac after another babbling away about their unhappy childhoods, finally snapped her nerves. Everybody had a bad childhood—the very expression was a redundancy.

Dora knew whereof she spoke. She'd experienced it all as a kid—but what was the point of getting up on stage and whining about it? Having a bad childhood was a common, everyday thing, something you had to grin and bear and get over, the way she had. Shut up with your fucking complaints already.

Anyway, perfomance art had brought on her second breakdown. And mimes. It got so that if she saw one more guy in whiteface, pretending to walk in slow motion, she'd scream. Harmonica players did that to her as well.

By the time she recovered from breakdown two, she'd put on seventy-five pounds and looked like a leftover Thanksgiving turkey.

Now she was going to change all that. Diet, liposuction, exercise—she'd do whatever it took to whittle herself down, make herself attractive to Ziggy. She'd even walk around swilling that designer water, the way models like Darcy did. She'd go the whole nine yards to get her looks back, harden up her ass again. Then she'd make her move with Ziggy, fuck him dizzy. That's all it took to make a man happy; the size of their egos ran in inverse proportion to the tininess of their brains. And once she had him, she'd do for Ziggy what nobody else could. She'd parlay his football career into politics and steer him right into the White House.

That's right, the White House. If she could only convince him to convert to Christianity and maybe even become born again, she would steer him all the way to the top, the highest peak. She'd become the First Lady, make the cover of *Time,* the very magazine she used to slave for.

Dora Glick Cantor, Woman of the Year—make that Woman of the Century—the richest, bitchiest, most hated woman since Jezebel, daughter of the king of Tyre.

Dora had it wrong, of course. It wasn't Darcy who was holding out on Ziggy but the other way around. Much as he liked the blithe-spirited young model, Ziggy still wasn't ready to become intimate with her, not while he continued to have Rachel on his mind.

Ziggy's stubborn, old-fashioned attitude toward love irked The Hook no end. "What the hell's the matter with you," he railed the next day, while preparing supper. "The girl's crazy about you but you keep singing the blues for some cooz who walked all over you."

"Don't call Rachel a cooz. And she didn't walk all over me—we simply split up."

"If she really loved you, she'd be here right now."

"I told you why she's afraid to come back."

"I know all about her Orthodox hang-ups. But if she's so frightened and unsure of herself, how comes she keeps calling you?"

"She called only once, to congratulate me."

"She called to manipulate you, keep you on the hook. You

don't see that, of course. But that's because you're still naive where women are concerned. You don't know a damn thing about the way they work."

"I'd rather be naive than cynical."

"What's that mean?"

"All they are is sex objects to you. You sleep with them just to carve another notch in your gun."

"I sleep with them because it gives me pleasure. And I give them pleasure in return, tremendous pleasure. It's a natural state of affairs that you unfortunately can't accept on account of the brainwashing you got in Yeshiveh. They've got you believing sex is wrong and dirty."

"Nonsense."

"The Torah calls it 'the evil impulse,' right? And what was that passage you once read to me, the one warning of the dangers of sexual intercourse?"

"I don't remember."

"Bullshit. I'll recite it back to you." The Hook closed his eyes and screwed his face up as he tried to retrieve the passage. "'He who indulges in having intercourse, ages. Quickly, his strength ebbs, his eyes grow dim, his breath becomes foul, the hair of his head, eyelashes and brows fall out, the hair of his beard, armpits and feet curl up, his teeth fall out, and many other aches beside these befall him.'"

The Hook let out a scornful snort of laughter. "'Many other aches beside these befall him.' What a bunch of puritanical, woman-hating vipers those old Jews were. No wonder you've got all these complexes about sex."

"I don't have any complexes."

"Don't give me that. You were also taught that an Orthodox Jew is never supposed to see his wife undressed or to have intercourse by light."

"Is that true, Ziggy?" asked Devrah, who had just come in the door from a shoot.

"Not only that, while having intercourse you're supposed to have 'pure thoughts,'" The Hook went on, relishing making Ziggy squirm. "You're supposed to think of some passage from the Torah or another sacred subject—anything but enjoy what you're doing."

"That is, like, weird," Devrah cried.

"Dammit, stop ganging up on me," Ziggy said hotly. "Although I did grow up learning things like that, I liberated myself in Amsterdam with Rachel."

"Then what's the problem? Why won't you shtup Darcy?"

"Because I can't be like you two. I can't disconnect sex from love. You think I'm straitlaced and peculiar for that—but I find you just as weird.

"Think of it. A woman opens herself to you She invites you inside her. To be inside another human being—is there any act more personal, more holy than that? How can you treat it so casually? Don't you feel its power, its importance? Aren't you humbled by it? Sex does have to do with religion. It's not an evil impulse, though. It's exactly the opposite—a tremendously good thing, a force that comes from God and should be respected as such," Ziggy said.

There was silence after his outburst. Neither The Hook nor Devrah looked at him.

"I'm sorry," Ziggy apologized. "I've spoiled your evening,

haven't I? I've thrown a wet blanket over your little campfire."

"It's okay," Devrah said. "You've given us a lot to think about."

"It's not okay," The Hook groused. "Don't listen to him, Devrah. He's still a rabbi at heart, still trying to make us toe the line. Well, I'm not going to do it. I'm going to keep banging every girl I want, because sex is the only thing worth living for—the only thing that makes me feel alive!"

"What about money and fame?" Devrah asked.

"They don't mean a rat's ass to me. Pussy's my main and only game."

"That's disgusting, Hook. Women have a lot more to offer than just that, y'know," Devrah said indignantly.

"Yeah, well so do I—but all I'm ever seen as is a giant prick!"

"Well, that's just what you are," Devrah giggled. "A giant New York prick. A New York Giant prick. You can't escape your fate, Hook. You were born a prick and a prick you'll remain—and a big one, too."

"See?" The Hook appealed to Ziggy. "See what I have to live with? Is it any wonder why I've got sex on the brain?"

DORA WAS RIGHT ABOUT ONE THING, THOUGH: THAT THERE would be an anti-Semitic backlash to Ziggymania.

In the two weeks that followed, weeks in which the Giants won both their games and flaunted their use of Yiddish, thereby making even bigger media stars out of their rabbi quarterback and his chicken-soup grandmother (who now put *flanken* and *kugel* on the training table as well), Ziggy began to receive hate mail from around the country, containing such sentiments as:

> "Dear Jew,
>
> You hooknosed kike fuck youll be sorry you ever tried to play football because we intend to put you back in your place you ratshit scumbag sheenie.
>
> An American nazi and proud of it."

And:

> "Your life isnt worth shit if you use any more yidush in a game and let your granmother carrie on like that again.
>
> Pissed off in Milwaukee."

And:

> "Jew, if you know what's good for you, you'll quit now, because we ain't gonna stand for anybody like you making a fool out of our Christian country, the greatest country that ever lived.
>
> A militia patriot."

Ziggy was stunned by the number of these letters and appalled by their viciousness. His father chalked it up to football itself, which stirred up evil feelings in men. Again, the Reb urged him to stop playing ball. But Ziggy couldn't do it. He refused to believe that football was a force from the Other Side—not when it still brought him so much happiness. All he had to do was step on the field for his spirits to lift, a smile to come to his lips. He still loved the game, loved the way the sun hit his face, the grass felt under his feet, the heft of the ball in his hand. He loved to throw passes and feel the satisfaction that came when he was able to wing the ball into a speeding receiver's hands, creating a symmetrical connection with him. He loved to kick as well, thump a ball and watch it take off and soar far downfield, like a missile in flight. He loved to hear the linemen hitting, the guys yelling and joking as they worked out—in Yiddish now, as well as English. Thanks to the daily lessons he, The Hook, and Bubbe gave them, his teammates were becoming proficient in the language. The guys were forever coming up to him and asking him things like, "Ziggy, how do you say 'kiss my ass'?"

"Kiss mein tuchis."

"Kiss mein too-kas," was what came back.

"No, no—not too-kas, *tuchis.* Rhymes with *bubkes.*"

"With what?"

"*Bubkes*. Dogshit. Chicken feed."

"Got you now, podner. Great word. Wait'll I try it out on Cannonball!"

Yeah, that was part of his affection for the game—the camaraderie and rough male jokes and horsing around, all of which had replaced the prison atmosphere around here. Schimpf had even dismantled his scaffolding and given up his bullhorn. He didn't do much coaching any more, just hit the laughing gas a lot and walked around with a beatific smile on his puss, like a man with extensive rental property on the Upper East Side. As a result, practices were loose and lighthearted and full of laughs, especially when Bubbe trundled out a little *forshpeiz* for the team after the workouts were over—a pot of chopped liver to go with the soup, a few homemade *kichels* to leave a sweet taste in the mouth.

When Ziggy again suggested that maybe the Jewish thing was beginning to run away with itself, his teammates overrode his concern, so convinced were they that it was bringing them luck, putting them on the road to the Super Bowl and the fat financial rewards that came with it, the bonuses, product endorsements, and beer commercials. The Star of David was smiling down on them, like Lady Luck herself.

Ziggy knew that he was in deep, so deep that he couldn't get out if he wanted. Which he didn't. There was no way he could let the anti-Semites win. He was too much of a fighter for that; the side of him that had made him an athlete, a football player, prevailed now and wouldn't let him quit. He was a quarterback, after all—a leader, a scrapper, a competitor.

He also had an ego. How could he not when, wherever he went, people recognized him and called out to him, wishing him luck, begging him for an autograph. The notoriety and adulation couldn't help but puff him up, make him feel proud, like a king.

It was for all of these reasons that he continued to defy his father, even if his conscience did nag at him for it. He was convinced, though, that the Reb would finally come around and give him his blessings. Mainstay of orthodoxy that he was, he was also a compassionate and warmhearted man, a father who did not wish to alienate his only child.

Then came the sudden announcement about Saturday's game with the Eagles in Philadelphia. Word came down from BBU, the pay-TV company, that its starting time was being changed from 8 PM to 1 PM, owing to the intense national interest in the contest. The Eagles were undefeated on the season and in first place in the NFC, but with the Giants coming on strong thanks to Ziggy, the game had become a hot item and deserved a better time slot, one that would be accessible to a larger viewing audience.

Only trouble was (from Ziggy's viewpoint), Saturday was Yom Kippur. If he had to play before sundown, it would mean he was flaunting the highest of all Jewish holy days, the one on which a Jew was supposed to fast and pray and abstain from all worldly activities, in order that his conscience might be purified and his sins atoned for in the eyes of God.

Ziggy and many other Jews across the country complained to BBU, but the divinity of commerce prevailed over the word of God. The game would be played as scheduled.

The news prompted his father to call again. "This is very distressing," he said. "You assured me something like this would never happen, but now it has. What do you intend to do about it? You're not going to play, are you?"

"I don't know. I'm thinking about it."

Agonizing would be a better word. He was caught in a painful bind. If he played, his father (and many other Jews) would be horrified and accuse him of betraying his own faith and people. If he didn't play, he'd be letting down the team and all its fans.

His contract with the Giants also called for him to play. Russell Hogarth was quick to point this out in a meeting with Ziggy, reminding him too how generous the Gnomes had been with him. They'd not only given him a free place to live but ripped up his minimum-wage contract and given him an extra three hundred and fifty thousand dollars for the season, with more to come if he got them into the playoffs.

"We've treated you well," Hogarth said. "You owe us, son. You're being paid to perform and that's what we expect you to do."

Pulled this way by the secular world, that way by the spiritual realm, Ziggy spent a couple of sleepless nights. He kept seeing his father's pained face before him and hearing his distressed voice denouncing him for defiling the holiday and besmirching the family name. "It's bad enough that you didn't come to shul even once during the past days of penitence, but to consider playing on Yom Kippur is an outrage, a disgrace!

"Besides," the Reb continued, "there's your own soul to consider. God will judge you severely and cast your lot with

the wicked. Your future will not be happy—you'll be condemned to misery and maybe even death. Don't close the
gates on your fate, Ezekiel. Be a good Jew and don't deny
God's sovereignty."

That's what it came down to in the end, what kind of a Jew
he was. He'd been saying all along that he wasn't a good
Jew—and it was true, he realized, especially when judged
from the Orthodox position. Outside of Bubbe's food, he ate
treif (unkosher) meals. His whole world was *treif*, actually—
treif profession, *treif* girlfriend, *treif* roommate, and so on down
the line. He didn't go to shul, didn't wear his yarmelkeh, and
only prayed when desperate for help. He hadn't even cooperat-
ed when approached with a request to appear at a major UJA
fund-raising event. He has turned them down—not only them
but the numerous manufacturers of kosher food and beverages
as well, all of whom wanted him to endorse their products.

He'd declined because he didn't want to put himself up as a
spokesman for the religion, a flag-bearer of the faith. It would
be an act of rank hypocrisy. That the Giants loved to chatter in
Yiddish and scarf down chicken soup on the sidelines because
of him was another matter. It was a joke, a fluke, and Ziggy
knew that if the team went into a losing streak, all that stuff
would be quickly forgotten. He'd lose his job and Bubbe
would be sent back to her dress shop.

Nobody else on the team made an issue out of religion.
Many of the guys were devout Christians or Muslims but they
played on their holidays, no matter what, and settled up with
God privately. If it was good enough for them, it was good
enough for him.

When he finally did fall asleep the night before the game, he slept uneasily, dreaming that he was a child, in short pants, standing in front of a private house—the house they used to live in on Barnes Avenue. He was playing with some other kids. The play got rough and they fought, first with fists, then sticks, then stones.

Ziggy got hit on the side of the head with a jagged rock. He picked it up and ran after his attacker, drawing his hand back and letting fly with all his might. The other kid went down with a hurt cry. Blood shot out from where his head had split open. Ziggy's mother came rushing out of the house and knelt over the prostrate, bleeding boy. Suddenly she turned to him and cried, "You've killed him, you've killed him!"

And when Ziggy rushed over and looked down, he saw that it was his father lying there and looking up at him with white, lifeless eyes.

Ziggy's mind was filled with the dream when the game against the Eagles began. The strain weighed on him to such an extent that his performance was affected. He couldn't seem to get going, or to find his passing touch or kick with any accuracy.

He'd made the decision not to wave any Jewish flags today, it being the Day of Atonement and all. No signals in Yiddish. No joking around in the language with The Hook. In fact, no joking around at all. Ziggy played this one Schimpf's way, dead seriously, letting the coach run the game from the sidelines.

Schimpf was overjoyed to be back in command again, his rank and authority restored. He strutted around as of old, barking out orders, calling all the plays, waving his arms around. Ziggy said nothing, just functioned like a puppet, taking orders, executing on demand, never cracking a smile or raising an objection.

He was all business as well when he came off the field. Didn't talk to Bubbe or sample any of her wares. It wouldn't look right to be eating Jewish food on Yom Kippur. Or to be eating any food at all. The eyes of American Jewry were on him: better that he fasted, looked grave and repentant. Maybe then he could be forgiven his transgressions.

Only trouble was, he was incapable of playing football Schimpf's way. He just couldn't fit into a system, be docile and conformist. It was like asking one of the Grateful Dead to play in a string quartet; he felt choked, imprisoned. His game suffered because of it. He couldn't move the team; the harder he tried, the more he kept messing up. The smoothly functioning Eagles, buoyed up by the knowledge that Ziggy was having a lousy day, ran the score up to 21-3 by halftime.

The atmosphere in the Giants' locker room was as gloomy and depressed as the Roman catacombs. Nobody spoke above a whisper. The players sat with heads hanging down, expressions glum. Schimpf, shirt collar yanked open, eyes bulging and bloodshot, voice hoarse and hysterical, tried to rouse them with a pep talk. He reminded them of how much they were being paid to play, called on their pride and manhood, exhorted them to fight back, come from behind. When that didn't register, he began to shake his fist at them and call them names, threatening to trade every son of a bitch in the room unless they started to perform.

It didn't help. The Giants returned to the field and continued to misfire. It got so bad that Schimpf threw his clipboard in the air, ripped his earphones off, and tried to bite through their wires. When the Giants fell behind by another touchdown, The Hook cornered Ziggy on the sidelines and asked angrily, "What the hell's going on? You're playing like a real zombie today."

"I shouldn't be playing at all. This is my punishment for breaking the Mosaic code."

"Get off it! Stop with the goddamn Jewish guilt. What's happening today has nothing to do with anything spiritual. It's only a football game, not a test of faith, you *shtummie!*"

"It's a Yom Kippur Day football game."

"Yom Kippur *this!* Schimpf's on the verge of yanking you. And if he does, you may lose your number one spot once and for all."

"He should yank me. I'm stinking up the place."

"You're stinking things up because you're trying to be somebody you're not. It won't work, Ziggy. You can't be Fred Walston or Ferdinand Daniels, only yourself, Ziggy Cantor, the crazy Albino placekicker. So be him, dammit! Let's have some fun again!"

But Ziggy, still feeling the weight of four thousand years of Jewish history on him, still remembering the cautionary dream that had spoiled his night and stained his conscience, went out and stubbornly refused to heed The Hook.

He managed to throw one long pass for a touchdown and

kick another field goal, but it wasn't enough to bring the Giants to life. They were playing football the way they had played it before Ziggy had joined the team and it wasn't good enough, not against a top-notch squad like the Eagles. By the middle of the third quarter, the score stood 34-13, favor of the visitors.

Ziggy wrapped himself in a cloak when he came off the field and sat slouched over, feeling defeated and disheartened. When Bubbe saw him like that, her maternal heart was pierced with pain. Her little *chukkeleh* was desperately unhappy and there was nothing she could do about it. Or was there?

She knew her grandson, knew how he felt about football, a game he played out of love, out of childlike exuberance and joy. Take that away and there was no reason for him to play. It became drudgery or duty, like working on a construction gang.

She remembered that when Ziggy was small and went into a snit, all she had to do was tickle him, get him laughing, for him to come out of it. How to tickle him now?

It took her a few minutes to come up with an idea. By then the Eagles were driving downfield against the Giants again, moving the ball at will. With a TV timeout coming up, Bubbe went over to the Giants' cheerleaders and whispered animatedly to them. When the timeout was called, Bubbe grabbed the stadium announcer's microphone and called out to the seventy thousand people sitting in the stands:

"Here's a new cheer for you to learn, one that'll surely inspire our boys. It goes like this:

"Give 'em a *zetz*, give 'em a *whisk*

"Give 'em a *frosk in pisk!*

"Giants, Giants, Giants!"

When Ziggy heard Bubbe chanting in Yiddish for the Giants to give the Eagles a shot in the puss, he couldn't believe his ears. Neither could the New Yorkers in the stands. There was a collective intake of air, a collective "Wha'?" Then uproarious laughter went up as the entire Giant cheerleading squad gathered round Bubbe and took up the cry:

Give 'em a *zetz*, give 'em a *whisk*
Give 'em a *frosk in pisk!*
Giants, Giants, Giants!

Ziggy broke up, laughing so hard that his chest hurt.

Next time the Giants got the ball, he was ready and eager to return to action. Schimpf had beckoned to Walston and was just about to send him in when Ziggy pushed them apart and ran onto the field, saying, "Just one more shot, coach."

He made the most of it, doing without a huddle and lining the guys up with these words: *"Gib zich a shockel!* (Let's get a move on!) *Fangt un ain un tsvontsik.* (Go on the count of twenty-one.)" Then he turned to The Hook, indicating for him to split out wide right and asking, *"Voss ken men ton?"* (What should we do?)

"Varf vee vart un vee shtark du kunst," was The Hook's reply. (Throw it as far and hard as you can.)

By the time Ziggy began barking out the snap cadence, " . . . *achtsen . . . neintsen . . . tsvontsik . . . ,"* the Eagles were so unnerved that they hesitated on their rush, allowing Ziggy enough time to take a deep drop and The Hook to fight free of the line. Ziggy faked throwing to him on his first move to the outside, faked once more when he pretended to cut back to the inside, then was ready with the long ball when The Hook finally went for broke.

The ball carried fifty yards in the air before it dropped into The Hook's hands for the touchdown that put the Giants back in the game, 34-20. It was an electrifying play that charged Ziggy's teammates up. They gathered round him when he came off, pounding him on the back and yelling *"Mazel tov, mazel tov"* over and over again.

By the time the offense took the field again, they were loose and happy as monkeys. Ziggy was back—and they felt they couldn't lose with him.

Calling his signals in Yiddish, yelling at his line to give the Eagles *"a frosk in pisk,"* making up new plays during the time-outs, calling one trick play after another, Ziggy was able to forget all about Yom Kippur and his father and his other mental burdens. He had stopped thinking altogether now, except about football and having fun.

Within minutes he managed to drive the Giants to another touchdown. That score gave a lift to the defense as well, made them feel the momentum was shifting to their side. They held the Eagles on downs, forcing them to punt. Amen Armstrong, his short, chunky legs flailing, returned the ball the Giants' thirty-eight.

"Time to *shmeis* them again," Ziggy said as they huddled up. "It's a long pass to The Hook," he explained in Yiddish, adding, *"Oifn g'schrai zibetski."* (Go on the count of seventy.)

"Gut, gut!" they shouted back, clapping their hands and singing out as they ran to their positions. *"Mach es shnell!"*

Nothing fancy about this play. No juking by The Hook, or feinting on Ziggy's part. He just dropped back and threw the ball as long and high as he had ever thrown one before, straight down the center of the field, toward the distant goalposts. He didn't even look at The Hook, knowing that if he put it up high and deep enough, his sidekick would get there, somehow.

The safety had played The Hook well and had a shot at picking off the ball, down near the Eagle goal line. But what he didn't know was how a Ziggy long pass acted, how it always took a last-second little skip in the air that carried the ball an inch or two farther from where it was about to land. It was as if it had caught an updraft, an invisible current.

The Hook was ready for the skip and caught it in the fingertips of his outstretched hands, just over the desperate lunge of the defender, taking it in for the score.

Give 'em a *zetz*, give 'em a *whisk*
Give 'em a *frosk in pisk!*
Giants, Giants, Giants!

Spurred on by the tumultuous crowd, the Giants' cheerleaders did flips and handstands as the now tied game went into the last three minutes with the teams slugging it out hellaciously.

The Eagles started moving the ball, only to be shut down by the Giants, who forced them to kick from their own forty.

Ziggy, sensing that they'd be expecting him to pass with only a minute and a half left, went to the run instead, calling on Amen four straight times. The doughty, hard-driving fullback ripped through the line, following Siffie's blocks, picking up six, seven yards at a clip. But the Giants had started from their own twelve-yard line and the ground game ate up so much clock that there were only seconds left by the time they reached midfield.

A last timeout. With everyone up on their feet, not just the fans but the players on the sidelines, the coaches, trainers, and cheerleaders, even the groundskeepers and ushers, Ziggy ran over to the sidelines to consult with Schimpf.

"What do you want to do?" asked the hoarse, distraught coach.

"I'm going to kick it," Ziggy said. "I'm going to try for three points."

"It's over sixty yards, dammit."

"Not to worry, I'll make it." Ziggy said, lifting a cup of Bubbe's chicken soup and gulping it down ravenously.

It was a sixty-one-yard boot, to be exact. Ziggy had acted cocky on the sidelines, but inside he was apprehensive, as it was the longest field goal he'd ever attempted in a game. But he repeated his old mantra, over and over: *one foot, one ball, one foot, one ball. . . .*

When the snap came and The Hook placed it down, just perfectly, the way he liked it, with the laces out, Ziggy knew as soon as he hit the ball that he'd kicked it well. So did Homer up in the skybox. That clean, sweet sound again, that sound of perfection.

The ball not only carried to the goalposts and cleared them, but went another ten yards, dropping into the arms of an ecstatic bystander, Shlomo Volokh. Shlomo, watching the game as Ziggy's guest, thereupon sold the ball to the man standing next to him, making himself a quick five hundred dollars to go with the hundred and fifty dollars he'd already won on Ziggy's miraculous Yom Kippur Day field goal.

ZIGGYMANIA REACHED EPIDEMIC PITCH AFTER THE GIANTS'
victory over the first-place Eagles.

Sports Illustrated (now a HEN wholly owned subsidiary)
announced plans to do a cover story on Ziggy. Four women's
magazines followed suit and assigned their best staff writers
to try to interview him. All of the major TV and radio talk
shows around the country importuned him to come aboard
and answer questions. But Ziggy, still smarting from the
stinging criticism leveled at him by most of the Jewish press
for having violated the Day of Atonement, decided to keep a
low profile. Only Dora Glick seemed to be able to get to him,
as her daily columns were still filled with chunks of gossip
about his life—when he went out with Darcy, what he said to
Rachel on the telephone, that kind of thing. What no one
knew, though, was that even she was having problems getting
the goods on him, because the batteries on the bugs she'd had
planted in his penthouse were running down. But with Ziggy
being guarded by security forces because of the threatening
mail coming his way, it was impossible to get into his place

and replace the bugs, not unless she found somebody on the take, like a maid. To Dora, though, this was only a minor inconvenience. She could always invent stuff. In the meantime, she concentrated on writing about the people around Ziggy.

Her interview with Bubbe, for example, proved so popular that the *Reader's Digest* (also owned by the Gnomes) reprinted it and J. Walter Thompson signed Bubbe to appear in a TV commercial introducing a new cooking oil with a chicken-fat base.

All Bubbe had to do, after sampling the oil, was roll her eyes, smack her lips, and exclaim, "That's what I call *shmaltz!*"

Soon after, wherever Bubbe went, even in neighborhoods far away from the Upper West Side, strangers would imitate her, while laughing, "That's what I call *shmaltz!*"

The new product was a bodacious overnight success, prompting the Gnomes to instruct Hogarth to sign Bubbe as the spokesperson for a new line of kosher packaged foods to be sold under her name.

"We'll start with your chicken soup and go on from there," Hogarth enthused.

The deal called for her to be paid a quarter of a million dollars in cash and an equal amount of preferred stock in the new company. She would also be rewarded handsomely for each TV commercial she appeared in and for every personal appearance she made.

"In short, with one stroke of the pen, we're making you not only a household word but a millionaire," Hogarth said. Then, showing off the Yiddish he was studying (along with German) at Berlitz, he said, "Is that not a *mecheieh?*"

"A *shainen dank!*" she cried, planting a kiss on his cheek. "I'm the happiest woman in the world, not just because of the money but because I know people will be eating well and feeling healthy. My soup will always be cooked with the chicken feet in it—you can tell the Gnomes to put that in the advertising."

Bubbe then went out and bought a condominium in the same building where Ziggy and The Hook were living. This way she had a nice safe place to live and could cook dinner for her *chukkeleh* whenever he was free.

She celebrated her good fortune by putting together a Sabbath feast to which she invited not only Ziggy and The Hook (and their respective girlfriends) but the Giants' scout and special-teams coordinator, Homer Bloetcher.

Bubbe and Homer had been flirting over the past few weeks, exchanging coy looks and silly jokes whenever they were together, but now it was time to see if the attraction had roots. She went to Elizabeth Arden's on Fifth Avenue (another recent HEN acquisition) and had herself a three-hour beauty treatment to smooth the wrinkles out. Then she had her hair done, bought a new dress and accessories (wholesale, of course), and commenced preparing for the dinner itself. Since she was simultaneously unpacking the last of the household items that the movers had delivered from her old apartment, Bubbe had considerable work to get through. Fortunately, Darcy and Trish (The Hook's cheerleader-of-the-week) offered to help out.

They came over on both Wednesday and Thursday, got

Bubbe moved in and her house cleaned, returning Friday morning to go out shopping with her. It was their first Sabbath experience and they were amazed how much planning and labor went into the weekly Jewish ritual. A staggering amount of food had to be bought and prepared, all of it kosher of course, even though Jews would be outnumbered by gentiles two to four that night.

"As this is a learning experience for you, please ask all the questions you want," said Bubbe as they chopped fish and sculpted matzoh balls together. She told them about the Sabbaths of her youth, growing up in New Brunswick, New Jersey, in a comfortable, loving middle-class family. Her father, she recalled, was a quiet, gentle soul who spent most of his time in the synagogue, leaving most worldly affairs to her grandmother, Blanche, who was a beautiful and vivacious woman with a zest for life that Bubbe felt she had inherited.

"My grandmother was also a shrewd and successful businesswoman who opened the first movie house in New Brunswick and was the first woman to drive a car in that city, a great big open-topped Stanley Steamer," Bubbe said, her eyes misting over in remembrance. "We had such good times together, going out and visiting new places, trying on new clothes. Blanche was game for anything and always enjoyed herself, no matter what she did. When she walked into a room everyone's eyes went to her, she was so magnetic and gay. It was a terrible blow to me when she died suddenly, from a brain tumor."

Bubbe broke off preparing the chopped liver and gave a few sighs of pain for her grandmother and for Ziggy's mother, who had also died early. "Life can be wonderful, as they say, but it can also be a terrible and hurtful thing," she told them. "Grief makes you not only suffer but question the righteousness of God and life itself."

Both Darcy and Trish had come to love Bubbe by the time Friday sundown came. Her jokes and songs made the kitchen labor light, and they were enlightened by her explanation of Jewish ritual and beliefs. Darcy in particular wanted to learn everything she could about the religion.

"I really do care for Ziggy," she told Bubbe, "but I know we don't have as much in common as he does with Rachel. I don't even know what I'm supposed to do tonight, how I should handle myself."

"Not to worry," Bubbe comforted her. "These Sabbath dinners are meant as celebrations of the wonder of the world's creation and of the emancipation of the Jewish people, the escape from Egypt and slavery. They're a time for rejoicing and enjoyment, with lots of songs and storytelling."

"I can relate to that," said Trish, who was a Creole beauty from New Orleans, a pert, ponytailed girl with a voluptuous figure. She was known for her dazzling gymnastic abilities and had been a Giant cheerleaders for three years. "My people were slaves too."

"We'll drink a toast to them as well," Bubbe promised. "And if there's a gospel song of freedom you want to teach us, we'll sing that too, along with our own Sabbath songs."

Meanwhile, Bubbe taught them the Shehecheyanu prayer that the Jews recited when they were celebrating a new event in their lives. "This Sabbath is certainly a new experience for all of us," Bubbe pointed out, "and I'm sure it will be a wonderful one."

But as the time grew closer for Homer to arrive, Bubbe began to show more and more anxiety. She suddenly became concerned about her looks, whether her hair was right and was the dress the proper color and should she wear this pin or that one? She began to fret and fuss so much that Darcy finally cried out, "Bubbe, stop it! You look fine. You'll have Homer eating out of the palm of your hand."

"That's easy for you to say, Trish too. You're both young and gorgeous, you could walk through a hurricane and men would still want you. The rest of us mortals don't have that advantage."

"It should only be that easy," Darcy countered. "I still can't get anything more than a good-night kiss out of Ziggy."

"And I know The Hook wants me only 'cause I'm number five on his hit list," Trish pouted.

"You're number six, but who's counting," said Bubbe.

They laughed and made their last-minute touch-ups, waiting for the boys to arrive. They came just before sundown, laden with bunches of flowers, bottles of wine, and boxes of candy. Ziggy had even brought an extra yarmelkeh for Homer, which he fixed atop his head as Bubbe lit the Sabbath candles and said a prayer. Then they chatted for a while, awaiting six o'clock and the passing of the sun before finally taking their seats around the table. Ziggy and The Hook sang the traditional "Shalom Aleichem," with Homer joining in once he learned the words.

Ziggy was amused to see that Homer and his grandmother

had eyes only for each other. They were exchanging lovesick looks like teenagers. Ziggy watched them out of the corner of his eye as he said the *kiddush* for wine and removed the coverlet from the two home-baked challah breads, poured everyone some wine, lifted the breads, said another prayer, and cut off a chunk of bread for everyone at the table, showing them how to dip it in salt (symbolic of the salt used in the ancient Temple during ritual sacrifices). Homer and Bubbe never stopped gazing adoringly at each other.

Ziggy marveled even more when the food started to come out of the kitchen. There was chopped liver, chicken soup with matzoh balls, roast chicken, *flanken,* a *kugel,* a spinach and cauliflower casserole, an apple pie topped with nondairy whipped cream, a bowl of fresh-chopped fruit salad, all of it washed down with wine, soda, cordials, and a lemon tea.

Homer did Bubbe proud. He ate everything she put before him and then more, groaning with pleasure over every mouthful, bestowing on her enough praise to last a lifetime. He drank heartily as well and joined in all the *zemiros* that Ziggy sang, doing his best to handle the unfamiliar Hebrew. Homer's voice rang out, though, when he and Trish got together on some old Baptist gospel tunes. Bubbe was delighted to learn what a strong big voice he had and how transported he became when singing in praise of the Lord.

This was a man after her own heart. What he lacked in brains he made up in spirit—and he was a wonderful *fresser* to boot. Bubbe loved a man who ate well. Max, her late husband, *avah sholem,* was a skinny and sickly thing who always had to watch his diet. Not so Homer. He ate and drank like a man should, putting away one heaping plateful after another, enjoying every morsel of it.

He also looked the way a man should—big, round, and powerful. Her Max was the opposite, with his twenty-eight-inch waist and sunken shoulders and health foods. Fat lot of good being on a diet did him, though. He got run over by a car in the middle of the garment district and was dead by nightfall. His last words to her were, "I could have had that extra piece of *kugel* after all."

Homer wouldn't die with such a pathetic remark on his lips. He'd go down proud and happy with a full belly on him. Watching him eat like that, *kayn aynhoreh,* she felt a surge of warm desire. She hadn't felt this way in a long time, not since Max had died. She giggled guiltily, feeling like a young girl again—hot, ripe, eager for love.

Homer was feeling similarly. Bubbe was everything he craved in a woman—not just a good cook and wonderful hostess, but a high-spirited, lively person who was marvelous to be with. She was no skinny little toothpick, either, like the other two women at the table, Darcy and Trish. Okay, he knew they were models, young girls who had to take care of their shapes, but to him they were just skin-and-bones. Didn't they know that a man liked to feel something when he gave a woman a squeeze?

Homer sure felt like squeezing Bubbe. Uh-huh, he'd give anything to be able to wrap himself around her and love her to death. He wondered what it would be like. Real passionate, he was willing to bet. Any woman who cooked like that had to be good in bed, the two things always went together. Foreplay began in the kitchen.

Then he caught himself. Didn't make sense to get all het up over her, not with the difference in religion blocking the way.

His hard-shell Baptist daddy had taught him that only the people of Christ would be allowed into heaven. Old Ezra didn't have too much use for Jews and believed they'd be left behind when the ascension to the Pearly Gates began on Judgment Day. Homer didn't go for that stuff, though. He liked Jews and found his interest in Judaism growing, thanks to the way Ziggy had affected his life. He really did believe this boy was one of God's messengers. Even if he were wrong about that, Ziggy was still something special, a rare and remarkable human being.

But he was a rabbi and Bubbe was his grandmother. It wasn't likely that she'd ever agree to go out with a non-Jew, much less marry him. And that's what Homer had on his mind: not just a frivolous affair, like the kind The Hook was having with Trish, but the real thing, one that led to the altar. Homer was old and lonely and wanted companionship and good food and, yes, a little sex, at this late stage in life, the fourth quarter, as it were. Make that a lot of sex. And Bubbe was the woman he wanted it with, but he couldn't see her coming across, not to him, a man who hardly knew a *kugel* from a *kichel*.

Yet when they gathered round the piano for a songfest, she patted the seat beside her and snuggled right against him when he sat down, letting him feel the heat and heft of her thigh. And she leaned against him when they began to sing and put her cheek close to his so that their voices blended into one. She played all his favorites too, things like "That Old

Gang of Mine" and "I'll Be Seeing You," singing them just as spiritedly and sweetly as he did.

That did it. By the time it came time to have a nightcap before saying goodbye (a thimbleful of Cherry Heering for her, a shot of Jack Daniels for him), Homer Bloetcher and Rose "Bubbe" Diamond were firmly and dangerously in love.

T HANKS TO DORA GLICK, THE HOOK BECAME THE NEXT SUBJECT
of a heavy media blitz. She did several columns calling attention to his "fatal attraction to women" and his "incredible sexual appetite and remarkable physical attributes." Dora even
went so far as to interview the six Giants' cheerleaders he had
slept with since joining the team. Their candid comments on
his sexual prowess—"He goes where no man has gone before"
—set New York aboil.

Cosmopolitan jumped in with an offer for him to pose for
the monthly's first full-frontal centerfold. He turned them
down at first but when they upped the ante to a quarter of a
million dollars, he decided to take the money and run. The
photo session took place on a film studio set duplicating the
Giants' locker room and was noteworthy for the reaction of
the magazine's unperturbable, sex-savvy editor who, when
The Hook opened his bathrobe and revealed his namesake,
gave a strangled cry of "Holy shit!" and fainted dead away.

Numerous other photo offers followed, including several
from the gay press. The Hook was even offered the lead in an

adult male film tentatively titled *Heeere's Hookie!*

The Hook became incensed. "What are the gays trying to do, spoil my image? I'm one hundred percent straight, dammit."

"Certain people out there are insinuating that that's not true," Ziggy told him.

"What the hell do you mean?"

Ziggy reported what Russell Hogarth had told him after practice that day. Since physical intimidation hadn't worked against him, the Giants' next opponent, the Miami Dolphins, had decided to stop Ziggy by other, more subtle means. As the Dolphins were now owned by the TimeWarner conglomerate, they meant to use their expertise in propaganda to wage psychological warfare. According to Hogarth, the Dolphins had assembled a team of doctors, researchers, psychiatrists, and writers to compile a psychological portrait of him. The object was to pinpoint Ziggy's weak spots and exploit them in a disinformation campaign designed to embarrass him in public and cause him to play poorly on Monday night, enabling the Dolphins to come out on top.

The psychohistorian hired to whip the findings into shape —Bertie Briggs, a radical feminist whose book *The Male Animal: A Study in Five Thousand Years of Bestiality* had been on the nonfiction bestseller list for two years—focused on the death of Ziggy's mother and the impact it had on him as a young boy.

The study was leaked to the press over the next few days, with some of Bertie's key passages highlighted: "Deprived of love, gratification, dependence, and self-esteem, young Cantor soon developed a narcissistic personality disorder. His anger at his mother's death was turned inward and caused him to vent his rage on the football field, where his passes suggest an angry child hurling blows at a maternal substitute."

Bertie went on to state unequivocally that Ziggy was still living in the shadow of his mother's death and that "his character is a prime example of how deficient child-mother relationships render adults vulnerable to exhibitionistic perversions. In Cantor's case, this revolves around football. The ball itself can be seen as a penis-shaped bomb and his constant handling of this sex-substitute suggests a strong streak of homosexuality."

The study described Ziggy's powerful, domineering father, his education in the all-male Jewish parochial system ("our closest equivalent to a sexually suspect English-boarding school"), his puritanical upbringing, and also pointed out that his heterosexual experiences had been limited to a brief liaison in Amsterdam with a woman who later renounced him. In Bertie's view, Ziggy was clearly most happy in the company of men. His best friend was a "Don Juan who sublimates his hatred of women by seducing them. Cantor lives vicariously through this friend and quite possibly has had sexual relations with him, in light of the fact that they not only are roommates but have been inseparable since childhood."

IS ZIGGY GAY? screamed the headline in the *National Enquirer* that weekend. The tabloid's inside story insinuated that it was Ziggy's sexual ambivalence that had kept him from consummating his affair with Darcy Dalton, the luscious young model who was carrying the torch for him.

"We are good friends but that's not enough for me," the

Enquirer quoted Darcy as saying. "I want to live with him and be his woman in every sense of the word, but I guess he'd rather hang out with the boys."

Dora Glick jumped into the fray with a column conveying her views on the subject. "It's clear from the way football players throw themselves on each other all the time when tackling or blocking that this can be construed as homosexual behavior. Let's not forget the passion with which they embrace and fondle each other after a score or the way the quarterback always has his hands up against the center's buttocks. Does that mean a man like Ziggy is gay? I for one wouldn't be surprised."

When Jay Leno joined in with a full five minutes of whithering jokes about Ziggy's sexual orientation during his *Tonight Show* monologue, the whole nation roared with laughter and looked to Ziggy for some sort of response. Incredulous at the surreal, demeaning media circus camped out at his doorstep, he simply decided to keep silent.

Gus Schimpf awoke with a premonition that Monday morning, the morning of the game with the Dolphins. At first he thought it was a hangover or simply a headache that was bothering him. But he hadn't drunk much last night, nor had he needed to batter himself unconscious in one of his padded cells. He'd passed a pleasant, uneventful evening, so what was causing this sick, heavy feeling of dread?

It had to be the Dolphin game. Something was going to go terribly wrong tonight, on national TV no less. He tried to shake his gloom by taking a hit or two of laughing gas at the stadium, but the stuff didn't work. He kept moping around, chewing on his nails, feeling certain the Giants were going to disgrace themselves on the field. They simply could not go on winning with a rabbi at quarterback, a sex maniac at wide receiver, and a Yiddisher momma dishing out delicatessen on the sidelines.

Unlike most Americans, Schimpf was not an optimist. He did not believe that life worked out for the best, that problems could be solved, that man was inherently good. In his experience, the opposite was true. Life was a disaster, man a swine, hope a joke. Chaos threatened continually, the center would not hold, dystopia was a heartbeat away.

That's why leaders had to act like tyrants, had to bully, insult and horsewhip their subjects into order. Otherwise people would spend their time killing, raping, exploiting, and torturing each other—doing what comes naturally.

It was the same with a football team. Put twenty-two men on a field—twenty-two powerful brutes in an enclosed area— and they would soon tear each other limb from limb if there were no rules and rulers to impose restraints. The game, like life itself, cried out for a dictator to run things with a tight, strong hand.

Guys like Ziggy came along and insisted that democracy could work, that life could be run from the bottom, not the top. Ziggy'd had some success, no doubt about it, but Schimpf didn't believe it could last. The natural order of things would reassert itself; life would soon start fucking up.

Tonight could be the night. What was it the Germans called

the bill? *Die Rechuning*. How apt. Tonight was the reckoning, he felt—the time to pay for all the excesses, the crazy good luck, of the past seven weeks.

When the game began, Schimpf watched Ziggy closely from the bench, expecting him to snap at any moment. The kid could not keep standing up to the pressure, goddammit—he just had to collapse. The whole country was waiting for the fag in him to surface. They wanted to gloat over that and be reassured in their prejudices, just as he did. It was important that Ziggy should fail. It would mean that the traditional values of this Christian, conservative country had been restored, law and order upheld. Anarchy would be laid to rest once and for all.

However, the more Schimpf expected something to go wrong, the better Ziggy and the Giants played. The young quarterback trotted out with his usual cocky grin on his face and, seemingly unruffled by all the sexual innuendos of the past week, ran things in his own unique way. Dispensing with huddles, he called plays from the line of scrimmage, sometimes in English, mostly in Yiddish. The other players loved talking back to him in that ancient, colorful tongue. Tonight Ziggy switched to Hebrew for his snap counts, which served to further unnerve the flustered Dolphins and cause them to jump continually offside, giving away valuable penalty yards.

Because of their language advantage and no-huddle offense, the Giants kept outwitting the Dolphins' defense, forcing it to play warily and nervously. It meant that the Giants' line, fortified with belts of chicken soup and *gehakteh leber,* rocked them time and time again, opening up big holes for Amen Armstrong to barrel through. When the Dolphins began to gang together up forward, Ziggy would call loudly to his team, "They're all *farblondjet,* so let's go with a *langeh* ball, on *gimmel!*"

Obeying, The Hook would push and claw his way free of the line and take off downfield, looking as if he were running full out. But just as the corner or safety caught up, he'd cut loose with an extra burst of speed that only Ziggy knew was coming and put space between him and his man, leaving him free to nab his old *lantsman's* perfect spiral pass.

It went on like that all night long, with the Giants doing a demolition job on the Dolphins and the ecstatic hometown crowd roaring their approval:

Give 'em a *zetz,* give 'em a *whisk*
Give 'em a *frosk in pisk*
Giants, Giants, Giants!

Schimpf didn't know whether to laugh or cry. He wanted his team to win, yet the way they were doing it still affronted him immeasurably. They were doing it without him, doing it without plan or discipline. Football wasn't supposed to work like that. It was mathematics, not mysticism. It was blood, sweat, and tears, not fun and games. He looked at his top sergeant, Fred Walston, for corroboration. Walston, sitting on the bench, scrunched down into his warm-up cloak, was staring dead ahead, balefully. He understood the tragic dimensions of this palace revolt. The King is dead, long live the King.

"Coach, have something to warm you up. It's getting a bit chilly out."

Schimpf turned to find Bubbe standing with a steaming-hot plate of food in her hands. It gave off a savory, pungent smell that he had never sniffed before.

"What is it?"

"A kasha knish."

"A what?"

"It's like a dumpling, with barley. Try it."

Against his will, Schimpf bit into it. Pure deliciousness flooded down the sides of his throat.

"Not bad," he had to admit.

"Then have another. Eat, eat, darling, it's good for you."

She tried to get Walston to take a bite, tried to soften him up too. But he was implacable, unchangeable as stone. "Don't bother me with that shit," he told the old woman, turning his back on her.

Knishes, Schimpf thought. His team was eating knishes on the sideline, washed down with chicken soup. By all rights the food should've made them feel bloated and heavy—instead they seemed to thrive on it. Guys who used to pop amphetamines like aspirin and suck down laughing gas like oxygen were now scarfing *glatt kosher* instead and playing the better for it. They seemed stronger and faster each time they returned to the field, impervious to injury or fear.

The coach kept waiting for the explosion to come, the reversal to occur. But it never happened. Ziggy passed for 360 yards, the team ran for 200 more, and they finished on top of the Dolphins by thirty points. It was the most a team of his had ever won by and the well-wishers crowded round him after the game, telling him what a great job he was doing.

Schimpf smiled blandly and said thanks, but inside he was experiencing no joy at all, knowing that he didn't have a damn thing to do with the team's resurgence. He was strictly a visitor around here. It was as if General Patton had been pulled off the battlefield and given a desk job. Schimpf's depression deepened, even though everyone around him in the locker room was celebrating, hugging and kissing Ziggy and his grandmother.

Schimpf had a yearning to visit his padded cell; a little letting off of steam and pain would do him good. Yet that made him feel guilty as well; how could he justify punishing himself when his team was doing so splendidly? Was he truly crazy, the way Hogarth and others believed?

That's when his premonition came true, just in time to save him from going over the edge, so deeply that there might be no coming back. It happened about an hour later, after all the glad-handers and news crews were gone. Ziggy, finally done with the press, walked down the underground passageway that connected to the VIP parking lot where he had arranged to meet Darcy. They had just embraced and were heading to his car when Jesus Maria Gonzalez struck.

The runty Argentinian placekicker had come to the end of his rope. His groin was healed, his leg was strong, but he couldn't get into a game because of that *maricon* Ziggy. There was nothing worse for a kicker than to be relegated to the bench. You lost your timing, your rhythm, even your nerve.

Next step was the waiver list, frantic tryouts with other teams, a ticket back home.

He'd done what he could to turn the tables on Ziggy. He'd gone to see a *santera* up in Spanish Harlem. She'd gathered three different kinds of ashes and wrapped them in a pumpkin leaf, together with an old jockstrap of Ziggy's and a slip of paper with his name on it. After burying the pumpkin leaf, the *santera* had asked the god Oshun to turn Ziggy's life into ashes—or at least to see that he began missing kicks, but none of that had come to pass. Jesus had blown a couple of hundred bucks for nothing.

That had started him drinking. He began putting away a bottle of Johnny Walker a day, listening to mournful cantadas on the CD player hour after hour, and plotting some kind of revenge against Ziggy, this *judeorusso* who had taken his job away and messed up his life.

Jesus, blinded by resentment and whiskey (which he'd drunk all night long), had stumbled to a hiding place when the game ended. There he'd waited for Ziggy to appear, mumbling oaths under his breath and polishing off the whiskey. When Ziggy finally did show, Jesus was so smashed he could barely see straight.

He tried to plunge his knife into Ziggy's heart, crying, "You kick, I keel!" but ended up missing badly and nicking him on the left shoulder instead.

As Darcy screamed, Ziggy managed to slap the knife out of Jesus's hand, leaving the latter no choice but to attack him with his fists. But he was no match for someone Ziggy's size and strength. Jesus went reeling back, banging into Ziggy's car, a brand-new BMW, thereby triggering an explosive device that had been planted earlier.

The BMW was blown apart, knocking Jesus, Ziggy, and Darcy for a loop.

16

WHEN ZIGGY CAME TO, HE FOUND HIMSELF IN A HOSPITAL BED with a familiar face hovering over him. When his blurred eyes adjusted he saw that it was Dora Glick.

"Welcome back to the land of the living," she said. "Is there anything I can do for you? Would you like me to give you an enema?"

Before Ziggy could spit out his answer, a doctor entered. He too looked familiar—Irving Nobel, a member of his father's congregation. He wore medical white, a tall, robustly built man with a full gray beard and *payess* topped by a tiny white skullcap with black zigzag stitching.

After ordering Dora out, he looked down at Ziggy. "Ah," he said, smiling with relief. "Sleeping Beauty awakens. Thank God, too. If you hadn't, all of New York would've torn me limb from limb. How do you feel?"

"I've got the most unbelievable headache."

"You're lucky, Ziggy. You've come out of the whole thing with nothing but a lacerated shoulder and a mild concussion."

"Where am I?"

"At Albert Einstein Hospital in the Bronx. Your father insisted. He wanted you brought as close to home as possible."

"What about Darcy?"

"She suffered a severe concussion and some burns. Her parents belong to a flying medical service and had her shipped back to California to recuperate. She left a note for you."

"And Jesus?"

"Okay, too. He's in a New Jersey hospital, under police guard. The cops are dying to talk to you as well, plus about five thousand reporters. The hospital had to take on another dozen security guards. It's been pandemonium around here."

"Do you think I'll be able to play next Sunday?"

"Forget it. But maybe the week after, if you drink lots of Bubbe's chicken soup."

"How is she? And the Reb?"

"They're both outside—been here all night." Dr. Nobel looked at him, worriedly, through his thick glasses. "Why'd this guy attack you, Ziggy? Because you beat him out of a job—or because you're a Jew?"

"I have no idea. Maybe for both reasons."

"What is it with the goyim? Why won't they ever let us live in peace? But you don't need to hear all that from me. You'll soon get enough from the Reb, that's for sure."

That's exactly what happened when Ziggy's father was allowed into the room. Looking drawn and exhausted from his sleepless night, he sat down beside him and said, "You see? You see what happens when you violate a sacred holiday and thumb your nose at your religion?"

"I didn't thumb my nose. I simply played a game of football."

"There's nothing simple about any of this. Somebody booby-trapped your car. Somebody wanted to kill you."

"Jesus just went crazy, that's all."

"It's not Jesus, he wouldn't know a bomb from a coconut. The police are sure of that."

"How so?"

"Somebody painted a swastika on the synagogue last night."

"What?"

The Rabbi nodded grimly. "This is an organized bunch. You've brought our enemies out of the woodwork, Ezekiel. You've given them a target for their hate."

"It might be just a few demented souls doing all this. Don't overreact."

"Two different people tried to kill you. Chances are there are others behind them, so don't tell me I'm over-reacting. It's a conspiracy, an unleashing of forces from the *sitra achra.*"

Ziggy closed his eyes. His head hurt and he didn't want to argue with his father again. He wished the old man would go and read Spinoza, who had said that there was good and evil in all men, even the Jews.

The Reb was not a Reb for nothing, though. He was sensitive to what people were thinking and feeling. He put a hand on Ziggy and said with a remorseful sigh, "Ezekiel, I hate this. A father does not like to fight with his son or to be seen as a hectoring, moralizing ogre. I know you love football and are good at it. I just think you should follow your deeper and truer calling, which is to become a rabbi and lead a fine, pure Jewish life."

"Look, do we have to talk about all this now? I'm not feeling terribly well."

"Then I'll do the talking. I know you have doubts about being a rabbi. Do you think I don't? I struggle with my conscience all the time. That's the battle you should be fighting—not to become a better football player."

"I can't quit. I won't quit."

"Why are you being so stubborn? You're like the Jews of Germany who wouldn't flee the country even when they heard the sound of jackboots in the streets."

"That's unfair. This isn't Germany and we're not surrounded by Nazis."

"If we don't struggle to keep our ways and traditions the Jews will soon vanish as a people. Is that what you want?"

"No. I'm happy to be a Jew, but I don't want to be a rabbi. Why can't you get that through your head?"

"And why can't you get it through your head that your enemies don't want you to be a football player either?"

"I don't believe that. There've been other Jewish football players before. Nobody tried to stop them from playing."

"But they're trying to stop you because you're the descendant of rabbis, whether you like it or not!"

Ziggy's mouth tightened, his head throbbed painfully. He looked at his father. "So what is it you want from me?"

"That you promise to give up the game."

"And if I don't?"

"Then I'll have to renounce you," the Reb said, his voice dropping, quivering with pain and regret. "I'll sever all ties with you. You won't be welcome in my house or shul ever again!"

Depressed and hurting, Ziggy went home from the hospital to recuperate and think things over. He discovered that the Gnomes had hired two more security guards to protect him and that the NYPD had sent over one of its top detectives, Lt. Phil Friedman, to investigate the car bombing.

Friedman was in his sixties, a tall, slouched-over guy with the pouchy, constricted face of a man in a dyspepsia commercial. He wore a wrinkled, hand-me-down suit and battered shoes, but once he walked into Ziggy's penthouse, his back stiffened and his nose quivered, like a bird dog sniffing quarry.

"This joint is wired," he announced. "I can smell it, kid. It's got more bugs than a roach motel."

He commenced searching the apartment, slowly and carefully, finding evidence everywhere of his supposition. "What's your guess?" he asked. "The American Nazi Party?"

"Even worse: It's probably Dora Glick."

Freidman grunted. "Figures. Did you know that she's been a neighbor of yours ever since you moved in?"

He moved to the open French doors and pointed across the street, where Dora was sitting in her fifty-eighth floor window-seat perch observing Ziggy through binoculars. Ziggy stepped out on the patio, extended his right arm, and chopped down on it with his left. The unmistakably obscene gesture caused Dora to scramble out of view.

After thoroughly sweeping the apartment for bugs, Friedman brought Ziggy up to date on his findings, while sipping Bubbe's Chicken Soup. "We're absolutely certain that Jesus Gonzalez didn't booby-trap your car. If he had, he wouldn't have jumped you in the parking lot. On the other hand, we did learn that he went to some witch doctor on Amsterdam Avenue and paid her to put a hex on you. We found a Ziggy doll in his room, with some souvlaki spears stuck through it."

"So if Jesus didn't tamper with my car, who did?"

"Good question. That's why I'm here. Somebody out there doesn't like you. Any ideas?"

"Take your pick," Bubbe said, pushing a stack of Ziggy's hate mail at the detective.

Friedman flicked through a few of the letters and put them aside. "'Hatred for Judaism is at bottom hatred for Christianity.' Guess who said that," he challenged.

"Maimonides," said Ziggy.

"Rabbi Stephen Wise," offered Bubbe.

"Not bad. You're both smarter than you look, but not smart enough. Sigmund Freud," the detective said smugly.

"Since when do New York policemen read Freud?" Bubbe wanted to know.

"Hey, don't knock the force or the force will knock you," he warned, just before digging into a plate of her gefilte fish. "Delicious," he pronounced. "I can't believe it came out of a jar."

"It's just like the kind your grandmother used to make, right?" smiled Bubbe.

"My grandmother was a gynecologist. Wouldn't be caught dead in a kitchen." He looked at Ziggy again. "What about your girlfriends? They have any reason to want to snuff you?"

"Are you kidding? Darcy was with me and got hurt herself.

And Rachel's in Amsterdam."

"Really? How do you know? Have you talked to her lately?"

"As a matter of fact, yes. She called me early this morning, when I got home from the hospital. But where do you get off accusing her?"

"I'm not accusing, just asking. When there are two women involved, one's bound to be jealous. And jealousy and murder go hand in hand, like Jack and Jill."

"Darcy and I aren't lovers. And Rachel's become a friend, nothing more. Neither of them could have done anything like this, anyway."

"Your answer is in these letters," Bubbe said, tapping the stack.

Lieutenant Friedman finished the last of his gefilte fish and stood up. "It's been nice breaking bread with you," he said. "Much as I appreciate your comments, I'll leave you with this thought, which also comes from Doctor Freud: *'Der feind steht im eigenen lager.'*"

Bubbe worked it out from her knowledge of Yiddish. "The main enemy is at home."

"Give that lady a cigar. And think about it, Ziggy, because it's almost always the key to any attempted murder. *'Der feind steht im eigenen lager.'*"

Over the next days Ziggy had lots of time to ponder Lieutenant Friedman's parting words. While he didn't like to think that any of his own buddies disliked him enough to want to kill him, it certainly was within the realm of possibility.

Since he couldn't work out because of his injuries, he wandered around Giants Stadium during practice, checking each and every player out for signs of hostility. It sickened him to have to do this, as one of the things he liked most about football was the camaraderie and loyalty it engendered in the ranks, worthy emotions in any human setting. He'd been spoiled by his experiences in sandlot and semi-pro, he realized, where the guys all pulled hard for each other and became the better for it. But on that level of the game, the rosters were small, everyone got to play, and the monetary rewards were skimpy. The guys played for love of game, not fame and fortune.

It was different in the NFL. The competition, pressure, size of egos, and quest for riches did things to the players, affected them in strange ways. They became jealous, self-centered, mean-spirited. Profit took precedence over solidarity. You couldn't blame the players for becoming selfish. They had to cope with rapacious owners and conglomerates, live with the fear of injury, deal with contract battles and often crooked agents, face the possibility of being traded or dropped at any time.

The players were the modern-day equivalent of mercenaries. That's why coaches like Gus Schimpf were hired—taskmasters who knew how to whip a foreign legion into shape, get men to kill for gain, not God or country. In a way, the players were only a reflection of their masters, buccaneers to a man.

And yet, many of his teammates showed Ziggy how genuinely fond they were of him as the week went by. Cannon-

ball, Amen, Siffie, and Gill Kozlowski, the 400-pound nose-
guard, treated him to an expensive dinner at which
Cannonball made a little speech:

"Hey, Zig, if anybody's got it in for you because you're a
Jew, just let us know and we'll kick his ass in. You're our
leader and we're behind you one hundred and fifty percent,
Reb!"

He turned to the other behemoths with him and shouted,
"Ain't that right, guys?"

"Right!" they shouted back, cheering in unison so loudly
that the whole restaurant shook:

> Give 'em a *zetz*, give 'em a *whisk*
> Give 'em a *frosk in pisk!*
> Giants, Giants, Giants!

Good as that made him feel, Ziggy knew that not everyone
on the team had such fraternal feelings. Certainly not Schimpf.
Or two of the three other quarterbacks under contract. Only
Ferdinand Daniels was in his corner. Ferdie was a prince, a
man who genuinely enjoyed Ziggy's success and devoted
much of his time to looking out for his finances. He'd put
Ziggy on to some good blue chips and volunteered to act as
his agent as well, protect him from the sharks and hustlers
out there.

To stop the pirating in T-shirts, dolls, and bubblegum, Ziggy
gave Ferdinand the right to represent him and weed out the
schlock offers from the legit ones. As for the other deals that
continued to come his way, from the advertising agencies that

wanted him for national commercials, the corporations dying to appoint him as pitchman, Ziggy told Ferdinand to hold off until such time as he felt comfortable in those highly visible roles. He still had this nagging guilt inside that wouldn't let him forget that he was a rabbi and shouldn't exploit that status for commercial gain, even if he was a rabbi in name only.

Meanwhile, he studied the behavior of the other two Giant quarterbacks to see if they could be the culprits in Lieutenant Friedman's scenario. Robespierre he dismissed as not being bright or sober enough to hatch a murder plot. As for Walston, Ziggy supposed he was the kind of guy who could do something like that, if driven enough. He had done time with hardened criminals, was mean and cunning as a rattlesnake.

As soon as he thought these things, Ziggy was sorry. Walston had paid his debt to society, gotten himself an education, proved himself as a football player. So what if he was covered with tattoos, had a Mohawk, and rode around on a Harley? That was all image and show. Walston had been in the league for many years and had earned millions of dollars. He was a star, a success—what did he need with murder?

Still, he was the prime suspect, the man who had the most to lose if Ziggy kept his job as starting quarterback. So Ziggy tried to test him by playing detective. He went to Walston and attempted to make conversation with him, asking if there were anything he could do to help him prepare for the Steelers on Sunday.

"When I need your help, I'll come to you," Walston replied curtly.

"Just trying to be friendly," Ziggy said, studying him intently.

"Ain't that sweet."

"What's with you, Walston? Why have you got it in for me? I know you don't like sitting on the bench, nobody does. But you've had some good years and there comes a time when it's the next generation's day."

"If I want to hear a lecture, I'll watch C-Span."

Since he wasn't giving an inch, Ziggy decided that only a sneak punch would have any effect. "Let me ask you something. Did you have anything to do with the car bombing last Sunday?"

Walston showed no emotion, just said, "If I did, do you think I'd tell you?"

"No, I guess you wouldn't."

"Then get out of my face, man. We ain't got nuthin' more to say to each other. Beat it, motherfucker!"

17

THE WALSTON AND SCHIMPF SHOW HAD BEEN RETURNED TO prime time, given another shot at succeeding. The twosome didn't intend to blow it this time. Schimpf put his scaffold back up, dusted off his bullhorn, and wore khakis for all practice sessions, running them the only way he knew how, like boot camp. Standing spread-eagled atop his tinkertoy mountain, the sunlight glinting off his wraparound combat sunglasses, stopwatch in one hand, bullhorn in the other, Col. Schimpf tore into his players, insulting and haranguing them, ordering this one to do extra laps for an infraction of the rules, that one to do another twenty push-ups for running a wrong pass route.

When the workout didn't proceed with the military precision and obedience he favored, Schimpf ordered the players to put on pads and start hitting again. It was unheard of, a contact drill this late in the season when everyone was nicked up with injuries and needed the time between games to recuperate. But Schimpf believed the troops needed toughening up. "Hit!" he screamed at them, "hit, hit, hit! Get mean again, dammit. Kill the enemy before he kills you!"

The players grumbled and cursed him out under their breath as they hurled themselves at each other, under near-game conditions. When Siffie had to be helped off the field with a severely bruised thigh, Homer tried to get Schimpf to curtail the drill, only to be rebuffed for being disloyal. "Which side are you on, goddammit?" Schimpf demanded. "Do you work for me or not?"

"Of course I do, but—"

"But nothing. This is my team again and I'm going to run it as I see fit."

"We're losin' players we can't afford to lose."

"Tell 'em to see the trainer, or take a whiff of laughing gas. Nobody shirks in this man's army, nobody! Even the walking wounded are expected to fight."

Walston was just as driven where the Steeler game was concerned. With only one shot at winning back his starting role, he worked feverishly all week. The pressure on him was enormous, thanks to the screwup when Ziggy ended up in the hospital instead of the graveyard. That's what happened when you didn't do things yourself, the damn help always let you down.

Angry at having blown money on that fiasco, even angrier that Ziggy was still in competition with him, Walston worked overtime to sharpen his mechanical skills, staying out until dark throwing passes and running plays. With Schimpf's permission, he also made a speech during a team meeting: "There ain't gonna be no Jewish shit this week, got it? We're gonna play the game the way it was meant to be played, straight and hard, with no tricks."

Bubbe and her catering crew were banned from the sidelines and the cheerleaders were instructed to go back to Anglo-Saxon chants. When Cannonball protested, pointing out that the team hadn't lost since Bubbe became their mascot, Walston shouted him down, reminding him that "this ain't Israel, man, it's the U. S. of A. and we are goin' back to playin' the game the American way!"

Hogarth screamed bloody hell when he learned of these developments, threatening both Schimpf and Walston with suspension. But when Sam Robespierre overdosed Thursday night on some bad acid and had to be carted off to a rehabilitation clinic, it left the team with only one healthy backup, Ferdinand Daniels.

Ferdinand, still on a roll in a bull market, was too busy making millions for himself to practice much. And since he was much in demand for dinners and parties these halcyon days, his predilection for French food and wine had caused him to put on another ten pounds and resemble a pregnant woman. He'd be no help at all if Walston went down against the Steelers.

Hogarth, with the Gnomes backing him, fumed and threatened, but was powerless to back his threats up with action. It was Schimpf's and Walston's call and there wasn't a thing he could do about it, not even when Walston insisted that The Hook be benched for the game. "You better get him outta there," he warned Schimpf, "because he ain't even gonna see a ball from me!"

Thus when Sunday came, The Hook spent all of his time at

the far end of the field, sulking. It did give him time, though, to hit on the next Giants' cheerleader on his list, Nancy DeGallo, a vivacious, big-chested twenty-three-year-old with black eyes and medium-thick ankles. If he scored with her, as he knew he would, it would be seven down and six to go, with a like number of weeks to do it in. As for Ziggy, he prowled the sidelines restlessly, his left arm in a sling, watching the team trying to act gung-ho and please their commanding officer and topkick. They did the best they could, but it was never quite good enough for Schimpf, who was his old demented self again, screaming at them on every down, arguing with the refs, cursing out the opposing team, working himself up to nervous-breakdown level with his voice beginning to crack and the sweat steaming off him like a racehorse after the Derby.

On the field, Walston mirrored his coach's behavior, driving the team with equal fury. He was a superb QB today—quick, forceful, relentless. When his passes were on, he could zap the ball in there with laserlike accuracy and speed. His play execution had always been outstanding and he was fearlessly, even recklessly, brave in the pocket, able to stand up to the most ferocious rush without blinking or weakening.

Ziggy respected him as a player. Walston was a formidable competitor, a gifted athlete, but he couldn't warm to him as a man. All the joy and humanity had been squeezed out of him, all the *naches*. Walston tried to make up for it with an excess of determination and will, whipping the team on, tongue-lashing it.

If a receiver deviated from his route by so much as two feet,

Walston was all over him in the huddle. Pity the guy who missed a block or fumbled a pitchout: his punishment and humiliation would be unbearable.

Watching him, Ziggy understood why Walston had never made it into the ranks of the top quarterbacks. He was a prisoner of his own shortcomings, handicapped not by a lack of skills but by an absence of soul.

And soul was what football was all about, Ziggy understood anew. The game required spirit and humanity as well as muscle and flesh, even on the play-for-pay level. The contestants were the same size and equally talented, generally speaking, but what separated the winners from the losers was heart. And that's what Walston didn't have—not courage (he had plenty of that) but heart. That's why robots made lousy lovers. And why quarterbacks sometimes couldn't win, no matter how good they were or how hard they played. A quarterback had to feel as well as think. He had to not only understand his players but care for them, love them, inspire them.

The game against the Steelers bore all that out. Walston got the team off to a decent start, but as nothing they did ever seemed to please him (or Schimpf), the team began to falter, ever so subtly. Little things began to go wrong. Ziggy would have laughed them off and teased the guys; that way you kept morale up and stopped the goofs from snowballing. Walston never smiled once, though. He never let up, never called a trick play or asked a lineman for advice. And so things got worse. The Giants began pressing, trying too hard. Suddenly they weren't playing against the Steelers but against their own leaders. It was class war, civil war, only Walston and Schimpf couldn't see it; neither could the rest of the team. Consequently, the Giants lost impetus, gave up points, and fell behind.

If it weren't for Jesus and his field goals, the Giants would have walked off the field at halftime big losers. But the little Argentinian, still suffering hearing loss and second-degree burns from the car-bomb explosion, tottered out and managed to kick three three-pointers and kept the Giants within shooting distance of their opponents.

"Nice going, Jesus," Ziggy told him between halves. "You're showing the league you can still kick. You don't have to worry about a job, *amigo.*"

Jesus, grateful that Ziggy hadn't pressed charges against him, gave him a smile.

"I guess you're right, Zeeggy. I made myself crazy for no good reason. I should've knifed that *santera,* instead of you."

Somebody slipped Walston some good blow during the break; it was primo, uncut stuff, the kind you could fly to the moon on, but the quarterback's internal machinery ground it to dust and he went from bad to worse in the second half, overthrowing receivers, bobbling snaps, making a fool of himself.

Ziggy hated to see it happening, tried to talk to Walston and calm him down. "Relax, stop trying to do it all on every play. Have a little fun out there," he suggested.

Walston said nothing, just glared at Ziggy as he sat on the bench, a towel wrapped around his sweating, bruised face, but into his eyes crept such a look of hatred that Ziggy could only back off. This was hatred that went back to Walston's youth, the years he had spent in juvenile detention and prison, stewing away in some dingy hole. Walston was still a prisoner in a way, still an outcast, a man with a huge chip on his shoulder that he could not do anything about.

Ziggy understood everything now. He understood not only Walston's tragic nature but that he had indeed tried to kill him last week.

Devastated, sick at heart, Ziggy found a seat on the bench and watched the rest of the game from there, taking no pleasure at all in Schimpf's decision to pull Walston late in the third quarter. The QB didn't come out willingly. He kicked over the Gatorade tub when he reached the bench, gave the finger to those watching on TV (costing him a fifteen-thousand-dollar league fine), and got into a shouting match with Schimpf. It was all to no avail: Walston's comeback had gone down the tubes.

Ferdinand Daniels had to lumber onto the field and try to save the day. The potbellied stockbroker was an embarrassment. He couldn't connect on a single pass and had to be yanked in turn by the now totally berserk Schimpf.

Walston came back in. Pressing too hard, he threw an interception each time the Giants got the ball.

The final score was Steelers 47, Giants 16.

It meant that the Giants were now three games behind the league-leading Eagles and in serious danger of not making the playoffs even as a wild-card entry, unless they won just about every one of their eight remaining games.

Later, after the press postmortem, a wrung-out and deeply depressed Gus Schimpf made his way to where Ziggy was sitting.

"You'll start next week, if you're ready," the coach said morosely. "And Bubbe and The Hook can come back, too. It's obvious we can no longer win as a gentile football team."

When Walston left the stadium, he rode his Harley home, put a frozen dinner in the microwave, and killed half a bottle of tequila before opening the wall safe in his bedroom and drawing out the small package that had been stored there for a few weeks. He stared at it as he finished eating and drinking. Then he got back on his bike and drove down the East River Drive and parked near the Fourteenth Street dock. Jake was waiting for him when he walked up, a small man with sallow skin and cold eyes. He had his collar pulled up for warmth on this damp, chilly night.

A tugboat glided by pulling a couple of garbage scows. "You got the rest of my money, Fred?"

"Yeah, though you don't deserve it. You fucked up the job, Jake."

"What do you mean? The bomb went off prematurely, that's all. How'd I know the spic was gonna get in on the act?"

"You didn't use enough explosives. You economized, asshole. Those people should have been blown to bits, not just bounced around."

"If Ziggy had climbed in the car he'd have had it."

"But he didn't and now he's come back to haunt me again."

"Fuck that, I did what I was supposed to. Give me my money."

"Yeah, I'll give it to you all right."

Walston brought out the package and opened it. Inside was a U.S. Army .45 with the serial number obliterated.

Jake let out a curse when he saw it. "You son of a bitch. I thought we were friends."

"That's right. We were."

Walston shot him in the head, three times, and kicked his fallen body into the swift-flowing river. Tossing the gun in as well, he turned and went back to his bike and drove home, arriving just in time to catch the 11 PM sports show on ESPN.

18

JEW JEW JEW JEW.

Rabbi Rabbi Rabbi Rabbi.

They wouldn't let him forget it, no matter what he did.

The mail continued to pile up. Most of it was favorable, especially the letters from ecstatic Giants' fans and from out-of-towners who reported being inspired by Ziggy's story, either refinding or converting to Judaism. They told Ziggy how much they liked and admired him and wanted to emulate him in the way he played football and represented his people. Ziggy was astounded by this outpouring of affection and goodwill, and was touched to the quick. Like it or not, he had become a role model.

Not everyone approved, however. There also arrived dozens of letters crawling with maggoty anti-Semitic slurs and death threats. These he turned over to Lieutenant Friedman.

At times Ziggy found himself wishing that he'd been born a Mormon or a Rosicrucian, because not even his teammates would let him forget his religion.

On the Monday after the Steeler game, a bunch of the guys

had approached him—Schimpf and Homer included—and asked him to conduct daily lessons in Judaism so that they could, as Schimpf put it, "get a better handle on this Jewish thing."

Homer was even more serious about these studies. "I'm thinking of converting," he explained. "For Bubbe's sake."

Ziggy was overjoyed to hear the news. But fond of Homer as he was, he told him that it would be best if he studied with a working rabbi, someone with experience in helping non-Jews find their way to Judaism. He referred Homer to an old Yeshiveh classmate who was now an assistant at Emanu-El Temple.

When he called Bubbe to congratulate her on her engagement, she sounded as happy as he'd ever heard her. Not only was she in love and dying for the day when she could stand under the *chuppah* with Homer, but everything was going swimmingly with her professional life. Her line of kosher food products was catching on and her TV commercials were among the most popular in the country.

Darcy took to study, too. She called from California to ask for a list of books on Judaism so that she could bone up while recuperating. Ziggy was pleased to hear that she was feeling better and looking forward to seeing him when the Giants came out to L.A. to play the Disney Quacks in a few weeks.

"You've been getting a lot of press out here," she reported, adding that one of the local papers had just run a story on him headed, ZIGGY CANTOR—THE HEAVIN' HEBREW.

That did it.

If no matter what he did, people wouldn't let him forget

that he was a Jew Jew Jew Jew, Rabbi Rabbi Rabbi Rabbi, then he was going to give them more Jewishness than they had ever bargained for, friend and foe alike.

The next day, when he reported to practice, he was wearing a large white yarmelkeh. He was also carrying a tallis, the one his father had given him when he was bar mitzvahed, and a tefillin, both of which he donned in the dressing room to say a morning prayer in Hebrew.

Most of the team gathered round and watched thunderstruck as Ziggy draped the prayer shawl over his shoulders and went through the elaborate process of putting on the tefillin. One of the small leather phylactery boxes was placed on the inner side of his left arm, above the elbow, and its leather strap coiled round his forearm seven times; the other was put in the middle of his forehead and tied around his head, with the two ends of the strap joined over his shoulder and brought forward. Then the armband strap was wound around his wrist and upper knuckle.

He taught the prayer to all those who were interested: "Hear O Israel, the Lord our God, the Lord is One!" He also taught them how to daven while saying it, standing upright and rocking back and forth from the waist. "And thou shalt love the Lord thy God with all thy heart, and with all thy soul, and with all thy might."

Those praying with him wore towels and caps (or even football helmets) in lieu of yarmelkehs and tallises. Naturally, they wanted to know why the headwear. "The hat is worn as a sign of respect before God," Ziggy explained. "Donning of tefillin is derived from the injunction in Exodus, 'And it shall be for a sign unto thee upon thine hand, and for a memorial between thine eyes, that the Lord's law may be in thy mouth' . . . the tallis is worn by a man to remind him of his bond and duty to God. The black bands across the shawl symbolize the destruction of the Temple and mourn it forever. Traditional Jews are buried in a shroud and tallis just like these."

"Where can I buy one?" Amen Armstrong asked. "My wife just loves evening shawls."

"What the hell's the matter with you?" demanded Cannonball Murphy, who took his religion seriously. "Show a little respect. That thing ain't for parties."

"Hold on now," Ziggy said. "The tallis was actually worn as a cloak or gown in olden times, but because it marked a Jew and singled him out for discrimination, the rabbis decreed it be used in the synagogue or during private prayer services only."

"I'd like to get me one of them trellises," Homer said.

"Tallis, not trellis."

"Me too," Cannonball said. "I'd also like to pray with you every day—if you'll say a Catholic prayer with me afterward."

"That would be wonderful," Ziggy said. "Why don't we say Protestant and Muslim ones as well. We'll have our own Ecumenical Council going."

"The emphasis has gotta be on Judaism," Coach Schimpf insisted. "That's what's bringing us luck this year and we gotta go with it."

"Amen," said Amen. "We must make like Jews if we're going to make it to the Super Bowl."

Cannonball took the issue even farther. "I think we should

pick up some official prayer gear and really get into the religion so that Old Man Moses will stay firmly in our corner."

The team captain had spoken. That evening ten players, accompanied by coaches Homer Bloetcher and Gus Schimpf, and by the front-office executive Russell Hogarth, made a semitic safari down to Delancey Street on the Lower East Side. Ziggy took them to The Hatikvah, a shop for religious articles owned by yet another member of his father's congregation, Morris Farber.

Rejecting the short prayer shawls worn by Reform Jews, the players bought the kind of voluminous, robelike shawl that Ziggy had—the better, as Cannonball said, "to take refuge in the shadow of God's wings."

When it came time to outfit the Giants with yarmelkehs, Farber was hard-pressed to find enough extra-larges to fit the prodigious skulls of these oversized athletes. There were other problems as well. Ferdinand Daniels wanted to know, for example, whether his yarmelkeh would go with his navy blue Brooks Brothers blazer.

Amen Armstrong was distressed to discover that The Hatikvah did not sell color-coordinated accessories to go with the prayer sets. "I need socks, handkerchiefs, and a tie to go with this beanie," he said. Farber recommended a haberdashery on Grand Street.

Later, Ziggy took them all to Katz's Delicatessen on Houston Street. The sight of all those salamis and sausages hanging from hooks, the food cases bulging with goulashes, stews, and briskets, the barrels overflowing with sauerkraut and pickles, the pots of potato and pea soup and gravy bubbling away, made them cry out with joy. They couldn't get over the size of the place, the amount of food available cafeteria style, the warmth and clamor that made it so inviting, especially the bar where tap beer flowed like a river of foam.

They wanted to know from Ziggy what each and every unfamiliar food being served was—the *kasha varnishkes,* the brown *farfel,* the carrot *tzimmes,* the *plov,* the vegetable *kishkas.* They also eyed all the different kinds of breads, not just the ryes, whole wheats, and pumpernickels but the kaiser rolls, bagels, and bialys, not to speak of the cookies and cakes, the rugelahs, strudels and *hamantaschen.*

The huge, hungry men went up and down the food lines, piling up their trays, breathing in the pungent smells of the spices, mustards, and sauces, grinning ecstatically as they made their way back to their tables.

But before they sat down to eat, Ziggy suggested that this might be an appropriate time to break in their new prayer sets. The guys agreed, donning yarmelkehs and tallises and following Ziggy as he led them in prayer, the whole bunch of them standing at table and bobbing up and down like go-go dancers as they davened and parroted the Hebrew words that blessed and thanked God for providing them with this bounteous feast. Then they attacked their hillocks of food with a ferocious kind of gusto.

Max, the night manager at Katz's, told Ziggy later that the amount of food consumed by the Giants had set some kind of record for the restaurant. "We've served some great *chozzers* in our time," he said, "but these guys make them all seem like pikers. I've never seen so much food disappear so fast."

Leading the attack of the killer trenchermen was the rotund Buford Sifton, who used up three tickets to keep track of his food orders, polishing off a whole roast chicken and two *kugels* all by himself, in addition to a dozen other side dishes and four extra-large glasses of beer.

"Why didn't you tell us about this place before?" Siffie demanded as he speared another piece of carrot cake and gobbled it down. "It's got the best food in town."

"It's good, but you can't compare it to Bubbe's home-cookin'," Homer said loyally. "Don't you agree, Ziggy?"

"Nobody can touch our Bubbe," he replied.

"Tell me somethin'," Homer continued, sipping from his glass of tea, "how am I doin' with her? Do you think she really loves me and wants to marry me?"

"Yes on all counts, Homer. She's got the old-fashioned hots for you."

Homer smiled luxuriantly. "My whole life turned around when I met you, son. I never thought I'd be happy again. You've made me fall in love with football again and you've led me to the most wonderful woman in the world. I only hope that I can be a good husband—a Jewish husband."

"I'm sure you will, Coach. How are you doing with your classes?"

Homer wagged a finger at Ziggy. "Those of us in the class over at the Temple were told not to call it a class but an 'introduction to Judaism.' Anyway, it's hard learnin' all this new stuff at my age, but I'm managin'. As the Talmud says, 'Where people truly wish to go, there their feet will manage to take them.'"

"Outstanding. You're going to end up a better Jew than I am," Ziggy said.

"What I like about the religion is how oriented toward this life it is, this world. Christianity's pretty cool too, but it always points you toward heaven. I like it that Judaism is more down to earth, emphasizin' livin' with your fellow man in *this* sphere."

"How about the Hebrew lessons?"

"Goin' well, too. I've got most of my tongue around the Shehecheyanu. We also learned a song the other day. Like to hear it?"

Homer closed his eyes and sang as melodiously as he could:

> *Ha-nu-ka o ha-nu-ka*
> *ha-nu-ka o ha-nu-ka*
> *hag ya-fe kol kah . . .*

"That's beautiful," Ziggy said.

"Wait a minute, I ain't finished."

Homer plunged on valiantly:

> *Or ha-viv mi—sa-viv*
> *gil l'ye-led rah—*

"*Ha-nu-kah s-vi-non sov sov sov*," Ziggy joined in, spontaneously.

Both of them were harmonizing now, heads together, arms over each other's shoulder:

Sov sov sov ma na-im va-tov!

The catchy melody, just right for children, was soon picked up by the others at the table, who turned it into a round that everyone in the restaurant could join in on:

Ha-nu-ka o ha-nu-ka
ha-nu-ka o ha-nu-kah . . .

Ziggy was so taken by the spirit of the moment (and by the two beers he'd knocked back) that he jumped up and made like a conductor, waving his arms around exaggeratedly.

That's the pose he was caught in by Dora Glick, who stepped out of the ladies' room with camera in hand, firing flashbulbs at him in machine-gun fashion.

"Don't you ever give up?" Hogarth shouted at her.

"I don't know the meaning of the words," she shot back, aiming her camera at the players in their brand-new yarmelkehs.

When the singing came to an end, Dora plopped down at a nearby table and opened a bottle of seltzer.

"You might as well join us, there's plenty of food to go around," Schimpf said.

"No thanks," Dora said. "I'm on a diet."

"Dora Glick on a diet? I don't believe it; it's a contradiction in terms," Schimpf jeered.

"Oh, fuck you, Gus," she shot back. "Just go and stick it up your rusty-dusty!"

"What a charmer you are," Schimpf said. "A prime specimen of American womanhood."

"Ain't nothing wrong with Dora that a little sex wouldn't cure," The Hook ventured.

"A whole lot would be more like it," Hogarth said. "Why don't you try and get on The Hook's list?"

"Not even The Hook could cure what ails her," said Schimpf. "There is no known cure for terminal hostility."

"You should know, since you're perishing from it yourself."

"Whooee! Got you there that time, Coach," said Cannonball.

Schimpf was too full of good food and drink to be upset. He just smiled a crocodile smile at Dora and said, "If it's war you want, it's war you'll get."

19

DARCY AND CALIFORNIA WENT TOGETHER LIKE MUSIC AND dancing, France and adultery. With her blazing red hair and flashing green eyes, she seemed part of the chromatic landscape of Los Angeles, the tall, tinted palm trees and stucco houses draped with oleander and bougainvillea framing her as she tooled around at the wheel of her Porsche, handling it with ease and skill, sound system exploding with hip-hop and rap.

Ziggy found her changed. She was still beautiful, of course, still able to flash that captivating smile of hers, but it only came and went now, replaced by a mixed look of pensiveness and anxiety. Her bright, cheerful existence had been shattered in more ways than one by that car bomb. The physical scars— pink patches of burn on the left side of her face—had almost healed, but the psychological scars were another matter. It was the first time she'd been touched by violence and evil.

She wasn't bitter about it, though, at least not toward him. "It's not your fault some people are bastards," she said when they were together.

"Still, nothing would've happened if you hadn't hung out

with me," he pointed out guiltily.

"Ziggy, please don't feel bad. I'm okay, I really am. I want to be with you more than ever," she said, flicking back the hair from her face.

"Even though something like that could happen again?" Ziggy asked, hiking a thumb over his shoulder.

She looked in the rear viewmirror and saw the car following them. "Jesus Christ—!" she blurted in fear. Ziggy tried to calm her.

"It's not a terrorist," he said, "just an L.A. detective keeping an eye on me. Lieutenant Friedman back in New York told me he was arranging it. Point is, though, you are taking a chance being with me."

"That's just what my parents said, but here I am."

"I guess you just like living dangerously."

"So do you, obviously. A lot of other guys in your shoes would've dropped out by now."

"I can't quit," he said. "I'm too proud and stubborn for that. But you could walk away from all this and nobody, including me, would ever say a word."

"I'm not walking," she said, "not unless you want me to." She looked at him. "Do you?"

He leaned over and kissed her.

"Hey," she said, "you haven't shaved."

"I'm growing a beard," he admitted. "And *payess*."

"What?"

"Side curls. All Orthodox Jews have them."

"You're going Orthodox again?"

"Not really. Just want to give the Jew-haters the finger."

"You're a funny guy, Ziggy Cantor."

"Funny ha-ha or funny weird?"

"Both," she laughed. And kissed him back.

It was such a nice kiss that she decided she wanted more and pulled the car onto the shoulder of the freeway, cutting the engine. They started necking furiously and Darcy made it clear that she was perfectly willing to get it on right there and then. But Ziggy had to nix the idea because Schimpf had scheduled an early practice session at Anaheim Stadium. He also didn't think he could perform with the eyes of passing truck drivers on him.

"I know, you'd rather be with the boys than make love to me," she said teasingly. "I read that article."

She drove him to Anaheim, watching the whole boring workout from the stands, wearing a duck-billed cap to keep the sun off her face. It made her look younger and perkier; Ziggy couldn't take his eyes off her.

After practice, she took him on a mini tour of Los Angeles, showing him the Hollywood Hills, Melrose Avenue, Rodeo Drive, and finishing up in the rooftop lounge of a Santa Monica hotel where they drank margaritas and ate nachos and watched a fat, blurry-red sun slip down into the dark green, long-rolling Pacific Ocean. Then it was time to drive out to her house for dinner.

"Will your parents be there?" he asked.

"I asked them to clear out for the weekend, which they did, so we've got the place to ourselves."

Ziggy couldn't get over it.

"Did they really leave town so that we could shack up? Next thing you'll be telling me is that your mother made up the bed for us."

"As a matter of fact, she did," Darcy grinned. "She also picked up my birth-control pills from the pharmacy for me. I told you that I have very sophisticated parents."

"It couldn't happen where I come from. Relations between the sexes are a lot more Neanderthalish."

"So I gather, from reading those books you recommended to me. Those old boys with the white beards were not exactly crazy about women."

"They just never met a girl like you, I guess."

"I got a whole other insight into you," she reported. "I was able to understand why you acted so cold toward me."

"Cold? I acted cold?"

"Cold and cruel," she corrected.

"You're beginning to sound like The Hook. He's convinced I've got all kinds of complexes and phobias about sex."

"Is it true, Ziggy? Am I too unkosher or something like that for you to really care about me?"

"It was only my attachment to Rachel that kept us apart."

"Where do you stand with her these days?" she asked.

"It's over with her," was his answer. "She wrote and told me she has a new boyfriend, a Dutch jazz musician."

A look of relief blossomed on Darcy's face.

Let's go," she said urgently, "let's go and stain my mother's sheets."

On the way to Pasadena, with the LAPD detective still following (and Dora right behind him, sucking on a can of Optifast), Ziggy remembered something: Schimpf had put a curfew on the team while it was on the road. Everyone was supposed to be back at the hotel by 11 PM for bed check.

"Oh, shit," Darcy cried. "We'll just be getting warmed up by then. Can't The Hook cover for you?"

"The Hook, are you kidding? He disappeared right after practice with a stewardess he met on the plane. She took him off to the Playboy mansion and is probably humping him to death right now."

"How does he do it? How does he get all these girls when they know he's just a Casanova?"

"There's a reason, a big reason."

"Is it just size that does it for him? Is life really that simple and primitive?"

"Give The Hook credit. When he wants a woman, he gives himself completely to her. He wines and dines her, sends her flowers, asks her for the story of her life. He dotes on her, gives massages and hot rubs, makes her feel like a goddess. And when he finally gets her in the sack, he gives her pleasure, such incredible pleasure, that she never forgets him. Just about every cheerleader he's made it with this season, for example, keeps calling him and begging him for another date."

"What about Devrah?"

"She keeps chasing him, too. You can't imagine how many other women do the same. Wherever he goes, girls follow him, trying to slip him their phone numbers, touch him between the legs."

"That's not true."

"What do you mean? That huge, curved thing of his has become famous. It's a kind of New York landmark, like the Statue of Liberty."

It was dark by the time they reached her house, which sat off Arroyo Parkway. It was a landmark house, built by Greene and Greene back in the early part of the century. Everything about the house was handmade, not just the exterior but the interior as well, which was all warm hues of burnished pine, teak, and mahogany. The Greenes had even designed the desks, closets, and tiles, making sure that every detail was touched with love and care.

The house sat on a bluff and overlooked magnolia trees, flower beds, and a gazebo that served as Darcy's dollhouse when she was small. Darcy had obviously always been the center of attention around here; there were photos and portraits of her everywhere—Darcy riding a pony, Darcy playing Cinderella, Darcy graduating high school. Darcy Darcy Darcy and why not, because she'd always been beautiful and animated and appealing, a fresh-faced, athletic, well-adjusted American girl, the kind of girl who'd always got what she wanted—and enjoyed it when she did.

Now she wanted him. She'd cleared her parents out, cooked dinner to be eaten over candlelight, with wine from her father's cellar. And before they tucked into the spread, she held up a hand and rattled off a *broche* that she'd learned from one of the books he'd recommended. Ziggy laughed and hugged her, congratulating her on her pronunciation, thinking yet again what a fantastic girl she was.

Yet once the meal was done, the wine drunk, the dishes

washed, he still couldn't bring himself to get up, take her hand, and lead her down the hall to the bedroom. The Hook would've put it to her twice by now. Ziggy knew that, knew she was waiting impatiently for him to make his move, but he just couldn't get going. His old shyness with women, his lack of experience, had asserted itself. Finally, after they had talked and talked and run out of words, Darcy looked at him and asked, "Ziggy, what's the problem? Is it that you really don't want me after all?"

"No, that's not it."

"What then? Is it the Jewish thing?" He was about to scoff at that, until he realized something. She was indeed the first non-Jewish girl he'd ever tried to become intimate with.

When he told her that, she showed surprise. "Am I really your first shiksa?"

"Cross my heart, if you'll forgive the expression."

She giggled and said, "Well, we're even. You're my first Yiddisher boychik."

"Love the way you speak Yiddish."

"Ziggy, I'm as nervous as you are. I keep thinking that maybe you won't like me as much as you did Rachel."

"It's hard to believe anybody as beautiful as you could be unsure of herself."

"If only beauty were the answer to my problems," she said. "I'd have nothing to worry about."

"I've got problems," Ziggy said teasingly. "You've got minor irritations."

"Oh, I see. Is that because you're Jewish?"

"It goes deeper than that. I've got all these rabbis looking down at me now. You can't see them, but they're here with us. My ancestors are watching and waiting to see if I would dare make love to a gentile girl."

"Try, Ziggy," she urged. "Please try. I don't have horns. Or three breasts. Or a tattoo of Jesus Christ on my behind."

They stared at each other again.

Then she sighed and said, "Oh, what the hell." She got up, came over, took his hand, and dragged him off to the bedroom. There she quickly took off her clothes. In the half light, her nude, smooth, hard-nippled body looked lustrous and lovely. She embraced him and began unbuttoning his shirt.

It was the reverse of what was supposed to happen. It was she who was running the show, doing the seducing. But he found himself responding nonetheless. He kissed her, shivering all over when her warm tongue flicked at his, stirring the desire in him, bringing it up from the bottom of his feet and into his chest, his throat, a powerful loving urge that soon took hold of him.

He caressed her, passionately. All he knew was how young and lovely her body was, how sweet she smelled, how soft her mouth was, how exciting her hips and breasts and loins. He was past needing her to guide and lead him; his desire and manhood had taken over and things suddenly became as easy and natural as they had been with Rachel and he was able to lose himself in the act of love, give himself over completely to the power and wonder of it.

He and Darcy threw a Saturday afternoon barbecue in her backyard at which he cooked kosher steaks and hamburgers

for his teammates and their dates, most of whom were girls
The Hook had rounded up at the Playboy mansion. A lot of
wine and tequila flowed and it got pretty wild by nightfall
with people dancing in the nude and slipping off frequently to
the bedrooms and even swapping partners once in a while.
They partied on and on into the night, long after the eleven-
thirty curfew Schimpf had established. Back at the hotel, the
coach blew up when he discovered his rules had been ignored.
He ended up trying to turn his room into a substitute padded
cell, running amok and smashing to bits a thousand dollars'
worth of furniture and wall fixtures before finally knocking
himself out so severely that he did not recover consciousness
until game time.

By then it was too late for him to punish anyone. Gashed
head wrapped in bandages, he watched in a fury as the hung-
over, fucked-out Giants took the field against the Quacks—
and proceeded to whale the shit out of them.

The Quacks, owned by the Disney media empire, were
coming off ten days' rest and an early night, but it did them
no good against the Giants, who couldn't seem to do wrong,
no matter how foul their breath or how shriveled their peck-
ers. They scored on the first play of the game, on a long bomb
from Ziggy to The Hook, who was much lighter and faster on
his feet thanks to the seven orgasms he had enjoyed last
night, and kept pouring it on the Quacks from there on.

It helped that Bubbe was around, dishing out various goodies on the sideline. Yesterday she had found some nice fresh
fish for sale on Fairfax Avenue and had cooked up a big batch
of patties, going heavy on the matzoh meal and garlic powder

to give her *chukkelehs* extra strength. They just loved the dish and kept coming back for more; several asked for the recipe to send back to their wives and mothers.

Schimpf couldn't believe that a night of dissipation could have results like this, that a bunch of drunks and whoremasters could beat a team of straight-arrows. But all his notions of right and wrong, cause and effect, had been knocked for a loop. The Giants kept wasting the Quacks as the game went on. They did it in their inimitable fashion, with Ziggy calling signals in Yiddish and conversing with The Hook and others in the same pidgin tongue, while the Giants' cheerleaders cavorted during timeouts, exhorting the crowd to:

Give 'em a *zetz,* give 'em a *whisk*
Give 'em a *frosk in pisk!*

The game ended with the Giants romping to a 34-10 victory, putting them in first place in the Eastern Division, one game over the Eagles. On the flight back to New York, Ziggy and Darcy kissed and petted and joined in the group sing Bubbe had organized. Tonight she taught the team a new song, "Tzena, Tzena," which they sang over and over again as the plane headed east. Equally popular were the songs Bubbe and Homer performed as a duo, "My Yiddische Mama" and "By Meir Bistushein." Schimpf stared openmouthed at Homer, a singular figure in his yarmelkeh and tallis, with his stringy new earlocks hanging down like the tassels on a lampshade.

"You are really and truly becoming a Jew," the disbelieving, still-bandaged coach said to his assistant later, as the cabin attendants began to serve the late snack that the team had requested in advance: *kreplach, mandelbroit* and egg creams.

"I wonder if I'll qualify in the end," Homer confided to his old buddy as he sneaked a little chew of tobacco.

"Why's that? You having trouble learning the Torah?"

"It's not the spiritual part of my conversion, it's the physical."

"Physical? What gives—they going to test you for a bad heart?"

"Worse. They're going to do some snippin' and sewin'."

"Say what?"

Homer pointed to his groin.

Schimpf's head jerked back, like a fighter who'd just taken a shot to the jaw.

"You mean—?"

"Yeah, I'll have to go through with it if I'm going to marry Bubbe. Even the Reform Jews require it." Homer spat a brown stream into a paper cup.

"But—but that's crazy," Schimpf spluttered. "They're supposed to do that on infants, not grown men."

"Yeah, I know. I blame that damn 'intact child' movement. But rules are rules. Your ding-a-ling's gotta be trimmed before you can join the tribe."

Schimpf sat for a long time after Homer left him, so devastated by the thought that he was unable to move or speak.

"What's the matter with you? You look like shit."

That could only be Dora Glick, though Schimpf hardly recognized her, so much weight had she lost lately. She'd also changed her hairstyle and shed her usual potato sack for a frilly dress that showed off the makings of a passable body.

"I wish I could say the same to you," Schimpf admitted. "What have you done to yourself, Dora? You look almost human."

"Been on a special weight-loss program," she said. "Seven hundred and fifty calories a day and one hour with a personal trainer pummeling me with boxing gloves. Works like gangbusters. I went from a fifty-four triple E to a thirty-four A," she said, hefting her breasts. "Feel for yourself."

"Not just now."

"You haven't answered my question," she pointed out. "How come you're so down in the dumps when your team's in first place?"

"It's not my team, everybody knows that."

"Well so what? You should be laughing all the way to the bank."

"There's a principle at stake. Dangerous things are happening here, even if we are winning."

"What things?"

"Anarchy, for one. It has the upper hand. The established order is crumbling, people are making fools of authority. What happens if those ideas begin to spread and infect the populace at large? It could mean revolution, the end of the free enterprise system and corporate capitalism."

"Oh come on, Gus. This is only football, it's not life."

"Today football, tomorrow the world."

"Nah. It can't happen here."

"I say it can. Strange things are occurring all the time. Look at Homer in his beanie and shawl—I do believe he is going crazy."

"Hey, you're the nutcase. I heard about the way you destroyed that hotel room in L.A."

"I need to blow off a little steam every once in a while," he admitted.

"You know what your real trouble is," Dora said. "You are sexually frustrated. You need a woman, Gus."

"Look who's talking about sexual frustration. I'll bet it's been years since you were laid."

"It's true," Dora admitted. "The last time I had an orgasm, gas was thirty-five cents a gallon. But I'm doing something about it now. You should follow suit."

"I've gone out with a few women since my wife died, but can't seem to get them to warm up to me. Guess I'm too much of a taskmaster," he said.

"Nonsense," Dora sniffed. "If I can change, so can you."

"I don't need somebody pummeling me, I can do that to myself."

"I'm not talking physical here, I'm talking spiritual. You've got to open yourself to love."

"Holy shit. This I don't believe.: Dora Glick sounding like a radio psychologist."

"Fuck that. I'm just being real. You need some good pussy, Gus. Mine."

Schimpf's jaw dropped again.

"Don't act so surprised. We're kindred souls, buster. We're hard-assed overachievers but we still need love. I thought I could find it with Ziggy, but he's hitched up with that California cooz and won't even give me a tumble. He's all wrong for me, anyway—too goddamn sensitive. You're more my type."

"Dora. . . . "

"No, don't say anything. Just think about what I said."

She leaned over and kissed him, her mouth surprisingly soft and yielding.

"See? You like? There's lots more where that came from. I was once voted the best french kisser in junior high school. I do stuff in bed you never dreamed of. You'll learn, Gus. You'll learn what a great little piece of ass Dora Glick is."

T HE GIANTS RETURNED TO THE WEST COAST THAT NEXT WEEK, this time to Seattle for a game in the Kingdome. As well as things had gone in Los Angeles, they went poorly in Seattle, starting with the flight itself, which had to be grounded in Denver for two hours while a faulty engine was repaired. It made everyone tired and grumpy, especially Gus Schimpf, who was feeling especially out of sorts these days. He resented the way his orders were continually ignored, not just by the rogue elephants Ziggy and The Hook, but by the rest of the team, even the bit players and guys on injured reserve. As a show of force, he decided to impose martial law on the Giants when they arrived in Seattle. Nobody would be allowed out of his room after supper. Coaches and trainers were assigned posts in the hotel's hallways to see that the restriction was obeyed.

The guys bitched out loud, especially The Hook, who had a hot date with Lynne Favola, one of the Giants' cheerleaders who had accompanied the team to Seattle. She was number ten on his hit list, a black-haired beauty with a mischievous and independent spirit. She had resisted his blandishments all season long, laughing in his face when he dropped his usual lines on her, telling her how irresistible and desirable she was. She told him she normally only dated professional men, as befitting her status as a third-year student of veterinary medicine.

The Hook had his work cut out. Relishing the challenge, he threw himself into the seduction process with renewed vigor and spirit. He sent her a thousand dollars' worth of flowers over a three-day period, invited her to the opening of a new Broadway musical, took her to a rock concert at the Garden, acting the perfect gentleman all the while.

He let her do most of the talking, encouraging her to specify all the reasons why she couldn't and wouldn't sleep with him. He offered no arguments, made no passes, told no lewd jokes, showed her only his sympathetic, new-male side. She knew he was playing a game, but he played it so well that she couldn't help but be amused and a little flattered.

By the end of the week, she had begun to soften toward him. His dark, smoldering good looks had gotten to her, not to speak of his sensuality, which just oozed out of him, influencing everything he said and did like an actor's subtext.

The Hook made it clear that while it was a game he was playing, he played it with everything in him, offering as much of himself as he wanted from her. My surrender will be as complete as yours, his attitude implied. Our night of love will be so close to the real thing that you won't be able to tell the difference.

Lynne became uncomfortable with how tempted she was, and turned aggressive, attacking The Hook for his macho ways. She insisted she was not attracted to guys who fancied themselves great lovers, and began to drop insulting remarks about the size of his dingus, about which she'd heard from her sister cheerleaders, and had seen dangling in the latest issue of *Cosmo*.

That's when The Hook knew he had her, when she kept talking about "that silly old peenywhacker of yours" and how she placed no importance on a man's size, only his character and accomplishments. Those that protested too much, always ended up wanting it the most. Still, he bided his time with her, letting nature take its course. Which it finally did, in quite innocent fashion, right after the plane had left Denver for Seattle. When Lynne couldn't quite reach the pillow in the overhead rack, The Hook got up and tried to help, leaning inadvertently against her. What she felt of him when he pressed against her rump gave her the shock of her life.

"Ohmygod," she heard herself exclaiming. She had to sit down, so weak were her knees and short her breath. The Hook took his seat too, spreading a blanket over their laps with a little smile of understanding and humility. He never gloated at a time like this because he knew what a miracle that schlong of his was and what it could do to people, himself included. Only those who have power know it can bring as much pain as pleasure.

He let her check him out carefully and scientifically, to make sure no trickery was involved. Once she was satisfied that he was indeed for real, that he hadn't concealed a length of steel rope in his pants, it only remained for them to work out how they would spend the night together. The Hook instructed Lynne to rent a motel room, hire a car, and come collect him at the Giants' hotel.

"But how will you get away?" she asked. "You heard what Coach Schimpf said."

"That's my problem," The Hook replied. "You just find some wheels and a water bed. I'll do the rest."

Easier said than done. Schimpf himself camped right outside Ziggy and The Hook's hotel door, stretching out for the night on a foldout cot. The Hook stepped to the window and looked down three flights as Lynne rolled up at the curb in a rented '57 Chevy classic convertible. She was dressed in a white mini-skirt that showed off her long, curvy legs. Cutting the engine, she leaned back against the seat and sat with thighs spread apart: ready and waiting.

"Look at her," The Hook exclaimed. "Have you ever seen a more beautiful sight in your life?"

He turned and yanked the covers and sheets off the beds, knotting them together into a single strand, like the hero of an old-time prison movie.

"Not a good idea," Ziggy said. "It's a long way down."

"You think I'm going to let Schimpf beat me?"

"It's too risky, Hook. You could fall and die."

"I'll die if I don't sleep with her tonight," The Hook said.

"Come on, you'll make it with her tomorrow night, when we're back in New York."

The Hook started yanking on the rough knots, testing them.

"Tonight," he said. "It's got to be tonight."

He glanced over at Ziggy as he tied one end of the escape

rope to a bedpost. "If something happens to me, you can have my Bruce Springsteen records."

"Come on, Hook, cut it out."

"I'd like this inscribed on my tombstone: HE GAVE HIS ALL FOR LOVE.

The Hook turned away and opened the window, tossing the rope out. Then he took a deep breath, crawled out on the sill and started lowering himself deliberately, hand under hand. He made it look easy until he reached the first floor and discovered that the rope was too short. He hung there, dangling precariously in midair.

Minutes went by. Lynne glanced at her watch with obvious impatience.

The Hook, making like Tarzan, gave a kick and tried to swing to the nearest window, but the strain caused one of the knots to unravel, sending him plummeting downward. He hit the awning over the hotel's entrance and bounced up and down several times, like a trampoline artist, before landing on the curb, hard.

Lynne gave a scream and rushed out of the car. But The Hook picked himself up, dusted himself off, and staggered toward the car, one hand already reaching for her butt.

The Hook was able to perform in bed that night, but not on the football field the next day. He had sprained an ankle.

Schimpf suspended him, Ziggy too for his complicity in the caper, but when both Hogarth and BBU screamed bloody murder, the coach had to back down. Ziggy was allowed to start, but as things went, he would have better off on the bench, because no matter what he did nothing went right. It was his first bad game; Homer blamed it on the loss of his favorite receiver and on the decibel count in the Kingdome, where the screaming hometown crowd was always an unnerving factor.

Ziggy knew differently. He knew that it was his inexperience, particularly his unfamiliarity with indoor arenas, that was affecting his performance. He had never played in a completely artificial environment before. Even the astroturf here felt strange. He kept slipping and sliding, going out of sync.

He also hated the way the stadium looked and smelled, the glare of the lights, the heat and closeness of the air. It was his first taste of the modern, synthetic version of the game and he found it profoundly unpleasant. It was like playing football in an Iranian pinkie ring. On top of that, he suffered a terrible carpet burn when he was sacked hard on the third play of the game. Then he stumbled on a seam and gave his right knee a wrench.

Ziggy began to improve in the second quarter, but by then the score was 21-7 against the Giants and Schimpf decided to take him out. Body bruised and hurting, Ziggy sat and watched as Walston came in and proceeded to rally the team with a couple of long, sustained drives.

Once again, Ziggy had to admire Walston's skills. The man played a hell of a game against the Seahawks, throwing the ball well and not letting the crowd ruffle him.

Behind him, the Giants almost caught up to the Seahawks in the waning moments of the game. With a chance to tie, Ziggy limped in and tried for a field goal. But Robespierre, filling in for the banished Hook, gave him his usual lousy spot and Ziggy slipped on the turf as well, causing him to hit the ball poorly and miss a twenty-six-yarder.

When the Giants finally returned to New York early Monday morning, they had dropped to third place in their division, with a record of 9-5. They still had a chance, though, to qualify for the playoffs as a wild-card entry if they could win their remaining four games, all of which were scheduled against top-notch opposition.

It was going to be tough for Ziggy from here on in, Homer told Bubbe that night as they held hands over dinner at Moscowitz & Lupowitz. "What happened in Seattle showed the league that he's human after all and could be beat."

"Everybody's entitled to a bad game," Bubbe said.

"Of course. But I know how things work in pro ball. Teams are going to go after Ziggy in a big way again. It's not going to be pretty, Bubbe. I think we'd better say a *broche* for him and call on the Ribbono Shel Olom for help."

ON TUESDAY MORNING, FRED WALSTON MARCHED INTO THE meeting he had called with Schimpf and Hogarth and gave them an ultimatum: "Either start me or trade me. I'm not sitting on the bench anymore, not after what I did in Seattle on Sunday."

The response he got wasn't the one he expected.

Hogarth, crouched behind a desk framed by a Star of David and a menorah, got up and screamed, "You fucking criminal, don't come in here and make any threats."

Hogarth punched a button on his desk.

Enter Lieutenant Phil Friedman, pride of the NYPD, clad in a garage-sale suit and green and yellow running shoes.

"You and Jake Warburton tried to have Ziggy offed," the detective said to Walston. "It's taken me a little while but I've put it all together now. How'd you ever figure you could get away with it, Walston? Think we're a bunch of schmucks or something?"

"You sure dress like one."

"Yeah? Well, if I wanted to, this schmuck could run you in

right now."

"Why'd you do it?" Hogarth asked.

"I didn't do anything," Walston said, crossing his arms defiantly over his chest.

"Stop the bullshit, we've got you dead to rights," Lieutenant Friedman said. "We know everything about you, Walston—how you lost four million bucks on a drug deal, for example."

Walston, remembering what he'd learned back in the slammer, sat back and clammed up.

"You're just lucky that no one was killed and that the Giants have used all their influence to keep your involvement out of the papers," Hogarth continued.

"I'm really disappointed in you," Schimpf said sadly. He looked shattered, betrayed. "You've done such a terrible thing . . . in the middle of a championship race, no less."

Walston kept stonewalling it. All they could do was stare at him.

"Here's the deal," Hogarth said finally. "If you'll be a good boy until the season ends and give us your personal best when called on, we'll continue to keep the lid on this thing."

All eyes stayed on him, awaiting his reaction.

"Aren't you going to say anything?"

"The only thing I got to say is what I said before—I'm not going to keep playin' second fiddle."

"Well you'd better keep playing it!" Hogarth shouted, "because if you don't, we'll see that you're charged with murder! Even if you get lucky and beat the rap, you'll still be washed up as a player."

Walston's smarts were working at full speed. He was certain they didn't really have proof that he was involved. If they did, they wouldn't be making these threats, but would have booked him by now. Obviously, they had their suspicions, had maybe even amassed some circumstancial evidence, but that wasn't worth shit. No corpus delecti, no case.

They weren't about to tip the press to the story. Not only would it make a bad stink and ruin morale, the team would have to go into the playoffs with just one good quarterback on the roster. Its chances of making the Super Bowl would be greatly reduced.

And that's all the Giants really cared about; not seeing that justice was done, but making all those postseason bucks. A whole lot of zeroes were at stake.

This meeting was just for show. They might think they had a case, but the only man who could prove it was floating toward Portugal right now. Friedman had dropped Jake's name, giving him a little scare, but he had a hunch the cop didn't really know what had happened. Walston sat back, sure of it. Friedman was bluffing, pretending to hold aces when all he really had was a couple of treys.

Walston's mind raced ahead. He knew they'd been watching him closely ever since the car-bomb fizzle. Now they'd be on his ass even more, to make sure he didn't do another number on Ziggy.

That's exactly what he meant to do, though. If the Giants got to the Super Bowl, there was no way he was going to let that rabbi cop all the glory and gold.

It would be the finish of his career if that happened; they'd release him after the season ended and, out of spite, would make sure nobody else signed him, either.

But if he could dust Ziggy off and excel in the Super Bowl, the Giants would be backed into a corner. They couldn't very well announce they'd let a murderer quarterback the team; it would be admitting they loved money more than morality. If nothing else, they'd trade him to another team, enabling him to sign a three-year contract for big money.

It would have to be done right, though. That much was obvious. There was no room for errors of any kind. Nor could he depend on anyone else to help him. It was do-it-yourself time. Don't-get-caught time.

That's what it all came down to. Walston wasn't sure how he was going to take Ziggy out, just that the deed must be done, and done well.

BRING ME THE HEAD OF ZIGGY CANTOR.

The cry went up around the league, just as Homer Bloetcher had predicted it would.

With the season drawing to a close (just four games left for each team) and all the front-runners fighting either to make the playoffs or win home-field advantage, the competition became more ferocious than before, with the contending teams zeroing in on the Giants and their rookie quarterback as being the weakest boys on the block.

San Diego, next up for the Giants, employed psychological warfare tactics, accusing its opponent of using illegal drugs to boost performance, Ziggy especially. The Chargers demanded that the league test him for traces of controlled substances in his bloodstream.

"The only controlled substance you'll find in my bloodstream is Bubbe's Chicken Soup," was Ziggy's response.

The quip made headlines all across the country and was also the inspiration for a skit on *Saturday Night Live* in which the comic playing Ziggy was found to have an excess of

"Jewish penicillin" in his veins and was sent to a chicken-soup rehabilitation clinic to recuperate. Bubbe and The Hook made surprise appearances in the skit as doctor and patient, respectively. They brought the house down when Bubbe peeked down The Hook's drawers and recoiled, shouting, "That's what I call *shmaltz!*"

Anti-Semitic nerves were further twanged when Russell Hogarth called a major press conference to announce that the team had entered into a licensing deal with the Gucci Company to produce the Official New York Giants/Gucci Yarmelkeh—a white and blue polyester skullcap imprinted with the Giants' logo. Priced at $12.95, it would go on sale immediately at the ballpark and at all Gucci boutiques throughout the city.

It was bad enough that most of the Giants' players and coaches were walking around in yarmelkehs these days; now everyone in the stands would be wearing them, too. It made quite a sight on Sunday when the Chargers came to town and at least half of the seventy thousand onlookers got up in their designer caps, faced east, and began davening in loud, singsong fashion.

The power of prayer seemed to help. Ziggy regained his touch that day. The tall, now heavily stubbled young quarterback had a fine game, throwing and kicking the ball as of old. His teammates, many of whom wore skullcaps under their helmets and were growing House of David beards, also played with zest and flair. Amen Armstrong ran for over 200 yards, Siffie picked up a fumble and rumbled for a touchdown, and The Hook, dicey ankle and all, caught twenty passes and scored three times himself. The final score was 44-14, Giants.

These numbers made the Indianapolis Colts, next on the Giants' schedule, even more determined to intimidate Ziggy in tried-and-true football fashion, by punishing him physically.

Bring me the head of Ziggy Cantor.

Most football players liked to play rough, not dirty, but the Colts didn't need too much prompting to cross the line, as a Giant victory would eliminate them from wild-card consideration. The owners of the Colts, two South African diamond moguls, offered a secret bounty of a hundred thousand dollars to the player who knocked Ziggy out of the game. "Don't hurt him for life," they emphasized, "just for today. Break that bloody kaffir's leg!"

The Giants did their best to try to protect Ziggy from being injured, blocking for him with all their skill and might. Usually there was only one certifiable psychopath per team, such as the Bears' Mad Dog Marlboro, but today all eleven Colts seemed bent on beheading Ziggy. That made defending him difficult, if not downright impossible.

The Colts kept coming on all-out blitzes, rushing everyone but the ball boy, and it was all Ziggy could to do to save his skin. Ducking and dodging, bobbing and weaving, he was like a beleaguered boxer back there, eluding most of the wild blows aimed at him, taking the count when it was prudent.

Somehow he managed to move the ball. Throwing quick, instinctive slants to The Hook, sending Amen up the middle on sudden hits, drawing the Colts offside by switching from Yiddish to Hebrew signals, running with the ball himself when he was trapped, Ziggy pushed the Giants downfield in trench-warfare fashion, hacking out a few yards at a time. They couldn't reach the Colts' end zone but they could get close enough for him to kick a field goal, which he did, six times on the day, giving the Giants an 18-14 victory.

A week later, Dallas tried to outmuscle the Giants, but when the Cowboys lost four key men to injuries in the first half, the Giants blew things open and built an insurmountable lead. Things didn't go so easily, though, in the season's finale against the Oakland Raiders. The game was played at home a few days after Christmas. The Raiders, eliminated from the playoffs, were full of spite and fury and kept coming at Ziggy, cursing and spitting at him, trying to rip his head off. Harried as he was, Ziggy knew the Raiders couldn't win this game unless they managed to land a lucky cheap shot. Teams that played with hatred in their hearts did not win football games. Football was meant to be played with love, or at least enjoyment. The more you liked what you were doing, the easier it became.

That's why he cautioned his team against taking reprisals against the Raiders when somebody held or tripped them. Turn the other cheek, he counseled. Play the game by the New Testament, not the Old. He even quoted one of his father's homilies: *"Az men ken nit iberharn dos shlekte, ken men dos gute nit derlebn."* (He that can't endure the bad, will not live to see the good.)

"The *shlekte,* you gotta live with the *shlekte!"* the guys kept telling each other on the line of scrimmage, to the mystification and annoyance of the Raiders.

Not that the Giants didn't do some hitting of their own.

Buoyed up by Ziggy's advice, they came off the ball with explosive force and strength. Three-hundred-pounder hit three-hundred-pounder with thunderous results, making the field shake under Ziggy's feet and threatening to rouse the Mafia dead. But there was love and pleasure behind those blows, not spite and spleen, and it served to keep the Giants from committing stupid fouls and giving up unnecessary yardage.

This time it wasn't even close. The Giants came out on top, 27-10, qualifying them for the playoffs. The deliriously happy sellout crowd refused to leave the park after the game. Linking arms, the yarmelkeh-topped mob of 73,500 swayed this way and that as they sang along with the new song Bubbe had taught them:

> *Zum galee, galee, galee*
> *zum galee, galee . . . "*

Many of the Giants remained on the field after the game as well, dancing together and showing off some of the tricky steps they'd learned in recent weeks.

> *. . . zum galee, galee . . .*

It was only when Russell Hogarth, on orders from the Gnomes of Zurich (who did not like to waste electricity), had the stadium lights turned off that the celebration finally came to an end, but it went on until the wee hours of the morning around the rest of New Jersey and New York, where Giants' fans partied hearty in their Gucci skullcaps, drinking Motherhens on the rocks (Bubbe's Chicken Soup spiked with vodka) and singing songs dredged up from Hebrew school days and taught to fans of all faiths.

W HEN SCHIMPF GAVE THEM MONDAY OFF TO RECOVER FROM the primordial battle against the Raiders, Ziggy took advantage of the free time to try to see his father, who had not returned any of his phone calls in weeks. But when he drove up to the Bronx and knocked on the door of the Reb's shul, Mrs. Karp told him that his father did not wish to see him.

Ziggy, distressed, returned to Manhattan and locked himself up in his penthouse, refusing to leave the premises except to attend practice.

This made Ferdinand Daniels frantic. "I could make you a fast quarter of a million dollars in endorsements," he told Ziggy. "Everybody wants you, but you're making like Greta Garbo all of a sudden."

"Sorry, I'm just not up for it right now."

"You're being foolish. You might never have a chance like this again. Suppose you get hurt next Sunday, break your leg or something? Goodbye career. That's why I think you should take what they offer you, as long as the products are known and respected."

"Ferd, give these companies my regrets and tell 'em to try me another time."

"Ziggy, I feel bad about this. I'm helping everyone to cash in on Ziggymania except the very man who's responsible for it."

Ferdinand enumerated the deals he'd closed for the "mishpocheh" (his word) in the last few days: a five-day tryout as sports commentator on the *Today Show* for Dora Glick; a daily chat, cooking, and beauty-tip show on BBU for Bubbe; a McDonald's commercial for Cannonball Murphy (a hundred thousand bucks to scarf down a whole chicken in thirty seconds); a Trojan commercial for The Hook; and, biggest and best of all, a million-dollar modeling contract with Revlon for Darcy Dalton, who was to become the cover girl for a new perfume called "Jailbait" aimed at the lucrative teen market.

Darcy wanted to celebrate, of course, and asked Ziggy to help her do it. He tried for her sake to lighten up and be good company, but just couldn't shake his depression, the feeling that he'd gained the world playing football but lost his soul. Also, it had become near impossible for him to go anywhere in public these days. The groupies and fanatical Giants' fans would descend on him, clamoring for his attention, trying to press his flesh.

So he stayed at home every night, joined by Darcy when she got finished modeling. Together they ate the wonderful meals that Bubbe (and Homer) prepared for them, drank French champagne, listened to the Grateful Dead, read, watched TV, and made love.

No problems in that department now. He didn't love her as much as he'd loved Rachel, simply because she wasn't as deep a person as Rachel was, but what he felt for her was indeed love and that made it easy for him to want her, as the two things went together for him. What also helped was the way she behaved in bed—no inhibitions or hang-ups, just a completely open, free-spirited, passionate woman who got all wriggly and horny and locked her legs around him saying these incredibly erotic things that made him outdo himself as a lover.

Her beauty also never ceased to astound him—not just the way she looked, but the way she felt and smelled, the creamy consistency of her skin, the softness of her mouth, the emerald glitter of her eyes, the lithe fullness of her thighs. She was a miraculous and magnetic creature and when he was making love to her, he felt certain that it was a holy act, even if they weren't trying to perpetuate the species. Maimonides and his followers were wrong about that whole business. They had tried to separate the spiritual from the physical, insisting that the sense of touch was the lowliest of the five senses. But Ziggy could find nothing repulsive in sexual intercourse. On the contrary, it was a worthy and exalted act, beneficial even to the soul, and when he lay in Darcy's arms after they had climaxed he sometimes felt it was God's arms that were wrapped around him.

Happy as that made him, he would have been happier had his father not rejected him. The Reb was such a stubborn and dogmatic old fool at times. He was hurting not only Ziggy but himself with his unreasonable stand on football. He could have raised all kinds of money for his causes, gotten the mayor and other bigshots behind him, if he'd played his public relations cards right and accepted Hogarth's offer to become the Giants' team chaplain. He would have become a famous rabbi, an articulate and persuasive spokesman for Orthodox Jewry, someone who commanded respect and attention as an inspirational force in the world. His influence would have become permanent and indelible, thanks to his intellect and scholarship, his charm and vigor. He also could have been a big help to the team, being a friend and counselor to the players, helping with their problems, teaching them what Judaism was really all about.

Right now, the Giants were practicing a motley kind of Judaism, half serious, half tongue in cheek. Practice began with about two-thirds of the squad gathering in a side room to recite the Shema with Ziggy, who was obliged to wear his full prayer gear because the guys liked to see him in it. "It's only right," Cannonball Murphy pointed out. "After all, what's a priest without a turned-around collar?"

Ziggy would have felt a lot better if it were his father up here, doing things properly. He felt something of an imposter but had to go through with the charade, reciting the morning prayer with a couple of dozen mammoth football players standing in full pads and yarmelkehs and talassim as they made davening noises. After that, Ziggy led a brief discussion on various questions relating to Judaism: what was the meaning of the Star of David, did the Jews believe in life after death, were Jewish dietary laws ordained for health reasons, did the Jews really kill Christ, and so on.

Ziggy did his best to answer these and other questions, separate myth from reality, but he knew his father would have done a lot better job, being the kind of man he was. He would have led these men to the true heart and soul of Judaism, not just semi-enlightened, semi-entertained them in a superficial way.

Not that the Reb had ever looked to make converts. "Proselytes are as difficult for Judaism as a sore," he had once said to Ziggy, even though he knew that the Talmud had contradicted him: "When a prospective proselyte shows an interest in Judaism, extend to him a hand of welcome."

That was another reason Ziggy wished he had his father by his side: to help Homer in his slow, difficult struggle to become a Jew. The Reb would have made Judaism not only comprehensible but compelling to a man who four months ago didn't know a yarmelkeh from a *yentzer*.

Ziggy also believed that if he had only been able to persuade his father to attend just one practice session, he would have seen there was nothing satanic about football players or the game itself. But the Reb kept refusing to return his phone calls or to have anything to do with him.

Ziggy's heart was heavy as he threw himself into practicing for the wild-card game against the Bills in upstate New York. He tried his best to shake his depression, running plays with the backs, taking part in seven-on-seven passing drills, reviewing one game film after another.

Normally, he was the most ebullient player on the field, cracking jokes and hurling insults, but now it was the other way around; the guys did all the ribbing while he was the dead-serious one. For the first time ever, football felt like a chore to him. The Hook had to drag him out of bed in the morning and force him to go to practice.

"We've come this far, so don't blow the deal, Ziggy. Forget your father and concentrate on winning us a few more games. Then the season'll be over and you two can kiss and make up," The Hook noted.

Easier said than done. Ziggy knew his father, knew how stern and unforgiving he could be, especially when his authority was challenged. He'd been a patriarch for too long to accept being criticized or contradicted, not by Ziggy anyway. Sons were expected to obey their fathers, not defy them: it went all the way back to the Prophets. Chances were, by the time the playoffs ended the Reb would have made good on his threat to repudiate him. He could just see the old man sitting shivah for him, as if he had died or become an apostate.

Saddened and upset, Ziggy moved through the week as if by rote. So cheerful was everyone else, though, that hardly anybody but The Hook and Darcy noticed. You couldn't blame the guys for feeling good; not only were they in the playoffs but they were earning extra money through paid personal appearances at mall openings and sporting goods stores. Schimpf did a recruiting commercial for the U.S. Army and Homer picked up a quick fifty thousand bucks endorsing his favorite chewing tobacco.

Fattest cat of all was Russell Hogarth, who sat in the counting house rubbing his hands with glee, having been rewarded handsomely by the Gnomes. They'd given him two more years on his contract as general manager and deposited two hundred thousand dollars in a numbered account in Geneva. The Gnomes were particularly appreciative of the way he'd marketed the Giants' skullcaps, which had now become a national fad on a par with the hula hoop.

Thanks to him, people all over the country were walking around in designer yarmelkehs. Men and women alike wore them to work, to tennis matches, even when decked out in formal evening wear. It was an accessory that went with everything, one that also suggested success and sophistication, with a hint of spirituality. Hogarth had factories in Haiti, Bangladesh, and China working around the clock to keep up with demand. He'd also made a special deal with the CIA to ship his goods on a space-available basis on the planes they normally used to fetch back heroin and cocaine for the American market.

Hogarth had never been so happy. The Gnomes kept approving every marketing idea he suggested, such as serving only kosher food at Giants Stadium and having the Hebrew words to the Shema flashed on the electronic scoreboard so that the home crowd could pray along with the players before the game, with a follow-the-bouncing-ball feature to give the rhythm, just like in the movie houses of old.

Jewish was hot, Jewish was in, and Hogarth exploited the phenomenon fully, wracking his brains for new ways to sell an old, much-despised minority religion to the masses, in a secular way, of course. He came up with New York Giants Mezuzahs, a dreidel with Ziggy's picture on it, the official *New York Giants Yiddish Phrasebook . . . Joke Book . . . Cookbook . . .* the prospects were endless, the competition nil, the profits unlimited. Hogarth laughed himself to sleep every night.

So did the Gnomes. He had never met any of them in person, but he could see them in his mind's eye—five misshapen trolls with pointy heads gamboling on a Swiss mountaintop. Nah, that was silly. The Gnomes of Zurich were not trolls. They were big, powerful, overweight men in dark suits and vests with stubby cigars drooping from their lips. They were serious men, sober men, ex-bankers, lawyers, and stock-traders who met every morning in their Situation Room deep in a subterranean bombproof chamber stocked with enough food, water, and toilet paper to last thirty years. Here, surrounded by state-of-the-art computers, faxes, telexes and satellite dishes, they ran the vast, complicated multinational called HEN, sifting through worldwide stock market results, interpreting historical trends, anticipating global shifts in balances of power.

The Gnomes bought a new business every twenty minutes, sold an old one every half hour, laying off five hundred workers here, hiring a thousand there. The Gnomes never made a mistake, they were infallible, all-seeing and all-powerful, like the Greek gods. They had made billions in junk bonds when that market was hot, using them to finance raids on undervalued corporations that they later dumped after stripping their assets. Masters of the leveraged buyout, the hostile take-over, the Gnomes had taught the world that debt is worthy, greed holy.

Now the Gnomes were out of junk bonds and LBOs and into the buying and selling of third-world and Eastern European countries, always buying cheap and selling dear. They caught markets on the upswing, unloaded before the downswing. They understood credit as no one else did, always keeping the big picture in mind, yet showing a firm grasp of details as well. They never allowed anyone to get in their way, would crush you if you were smaller, join forces if you were larger. They'd written the book on greenmail and blackmail, these cool, calm, rational men who never laughed or wept or raised their voices. They never gave in to sentiment or nostalgia, had no politics or allegiances. They never read fiction or listened to poetry, and had done everything humanly possible to keep from ever taking sides in a war.

The Gnomes believed in two things only: power and black ink.

Feed them black ink and they fed you back with it. Hogarth's two-hundred-thousand-dollar bonus was just an appetizer, a tidbit. The Gnomes had made it clear there would be more to come, lots more, if the Giants got into the Super Bowl and won it, because the worldwide pay-TV take on the event should be a cool billion dollars. Yes, one billion, which was a lot of gelt even to the Gnomes, instant cash flow which they could use to buy another bankrupt communist or African nation, depending on whether they needed cheap labor or raw materials. They wouldn't forget him if it happened, no way, not the Gnomes, who always lived up to their word and were never late with a salary check or an expense-account refund. They had promised him two million tax-free dollars if the Giants became king of the football mountain.

For that kind of money Hogarth was willing to do anything, even become a Jew. In light of what Ziggy meant to the team, what thinking and acting Yiddish had done for all of them, it seemed the prudent thing to do. The Giants were winning as a Jewish football team in a Jewish city and that was good enough for Hogarth. He had already had a hair and *payess* implant to make himself look more Jewish and was now thinking about joining Homer in his conversion classes. The Gnomes approved of the idea, had even suggested that the Giants donate a million dollars to the UJA if they made the Super Bowl, just to show good faith.

Hogarth decided to go them one better. He'd build a shul right in Giants Stadium—yes, a house of worship where Ziggy and his teammates, joined by selected VIP ticket holders, could gather before each game and daven together. It might be too late to get it done for this year, but the plans could be announced at a big press conference on the eve of the Super Bowl. The Synagogue of the Stars. Might make sense to install an autotronic rabbi, one that davened around the clock, like Lincoln giving the Gettysburg Address at Disneyland. What an attraction: They'd be able to rent the shul for weddings and bar mitvahs when the Giants were on the road. It was a just what the Gnomes loved, a surefire moneymaker.

But first the Giants had to get by the Bills on Sunday. The outcome of this match was by no means guaranteed, particularly in light of the advance weather report Hogarth had received from HEN's orbiting space platform, which was predicting heavy snow in Buffalo this mid-January weekend. The Bills, owned by former Colombian drug lords who had branched out into the entertainment field, were an erratic team, one week looking like champs, the next like chumps. But they were mudders: The worse the conditions, the better they performed.

Hogarth wondered if the Jews had a prayer for good weather.

If so, he would ask Ziggy to recite it in public and call on the team's many supporters to do the same at home. He could see the headlines on Sunday night: POWER OF PRAYER WINS GAME FOR GIANTS. He prepared his own quote for Dora Glick's column: "God shone His ever-loving light on His devoted and devout disciples."

Too soon for all that, though. First you win, then you wax philosophical. No win, no words.

Even more important, no win, no tax-free bonus.

Hogarth knew a moment of panic as the dread, forbidden American word *failure* popped into mind. His heart began to palpitate, his breath to come short. Could they really lose on Sunday, after coming this far? It would be no disgrace to lose in the Super Bowl, but in a preliminary title match in a Buffalo suburb, with sleet and snot hanging from your nose? How ignominious. How anticlimactic.

Draping his New York Giants Prayershawl around his shoulders, adjusting his Giants/Gucci Yarmelkeh, Hogarth opened his *New York Giants Prayerbook* and tried, for the first time, to get his tongue around the words of the phonetically spelled out Hebrew prayer on the last—but first—page (leave it to the Jews to do it ass-backward), thinking that if he called on God in Hebrew it would make a much better impression on him: "*Shemah Yis-raw-el. . . .*"

As he davened, he flashed on his father, the old gaunt wild-eyed fanatic on the subject of Jews and blacks, the KKK honcho who lit crosses on front lawns with the ease of a man igniting barbecue logs. What would he do if he walked in right now and found his only son in payess and yarmelkeh, gibbering away in Hebrew?

Hogarth shook his head, as if to dislodge the image, and concentrated on the prayer, his petition to the Ribbono Shel Olom to help them begin the ascension to the Super Bowl.

When Sunday came, it looked as if God had turned an indifferent ear to any and all Giants' prayers, whether in Hebrew or not. Just as predicted, the weather was bad, with snow falling steadily and a twenty-five-below windchill factor powered by a twenty-knot breeze that squeezed tears from Ziggy's eyes and froze them to his cheeks. The Bills' stadium also had lousy artifical turf that got hard and slick on days like this. The weather was particularly rough on quarterbacks, as it made the football inelastic and slippery when the leather began to shrink.

Ziggy had a rotten time of it in the first half, trying to get a handle on the ball, fighting to keep his feet. The Bills, on the other hand, were romping around in the snow like kids let out of school. They were used to these conditions and had no trouble moving the ball against the Giants, scoring three touchdowns and a field goal. Also, they had brought a teacher in to instruct the team in basic Yiddish, forcing the Giants to abandon their no-huddle offense.

The best Ziggy could do all half was kick a field goal from a puddle of water on the forty-yard line, which soaked his shoes and froze them like blocks of ice around his feet. He hobbled off the field and had to go straight to the locker room to thaw the frostbite out.

As he sat in front of his locker, feet wrapped in hot towels, a cup of Bubbe's soup by his side, The Hook came over.

"This is terrible," he said, his face rubbed raw and red by the abrasive wind. "Do you know what'll happen if we lose this game?"

"Yeah, it'll cost us and the club a bundle," Ziggy replied.

"Fuck that. I'm talking about Michelle."

"Michelle?"

Then Ziggy understood. Michelle Bradford was the last cheerleader on The Hook's hit list. Eleven others, including Lynne, had succumbed to his charms, but not Michelle. Ironically, she was probably the most beautiful and desirable girl on the squad, a six-foot-tall blond-haired blue-eyed Amazonian queen. No doubt The Hook had been saving the best for last, but suddenly time was running out on him.

"If our season ends today, she disappears. They want her out on the coast for some commercials and movie tests. I know I'll never see her again once she splits."

"Well, so what? So you only sleep with eleven out of twelve, who cares?"

"I care, goddammit! I've put my whole heart and soul into this challenge, even risked my life for it. You think I'm about to accept defeat now?"

"Hook, please don't bother me with your sex problems. I'm trying to figure out how to get us rolling in the second half. But the weather is against us; they oughta call this game the Hypothermia Bowl."

"Fuck that, you grew up in this stuff. Remember how we used to get our sleds and stay out all day when it snowed, bellywhopping in Bronx Park? So what's the big deal now, for a few hours? You got ski underwear on, don't you?"

"It's not me, it's the ball—"

"Fuck the ball!" The Hook said crossly. "There's nothing wrong with it, dammit. Just give it to me and I'll prove it to you."

"I've been trying to get it to you, but—"

"But shit. Let me get my hands on it myself. Tell Schimpf to let me handle the second-half kickoff—and then go in as a running back."

"What—?"

Ziggy broke off arguing when he looked into his friend's eyes and saw that look. That look of quiet, determined madness that he knew so well. He'd seen it in The Hook's eyes that night in Seattle, when he went out the window after Lynne.

No stopping him now, either. When Schimpf began to give the team a pep talk, The Hook pushed him aside and took the floor from him. He stood there for the longest time before he spoke, not saying a word, just fixing his teammates with that unworldly look of his. Then he turned and withdrew from his locker a current issue of *Hustler,* opening it to the centerfold page and revealing Michelle posing naked.

The Hook waited as all eyes feasted on that sight before uttering a single word: "Rosebud."

That did it, that broke them up and sent them charging on to the field impervious to the cold and ice, indifferent to the losing score. They were still grinning when The Hook took the kickoff and set off downfield, eyes fixed on the distant goal line. Dancing, dodging, reversing his field not once but twice, The Hook broke through the pack by sheer willpower and obsessive sexual desire, streaking ninety-seven yards for a touchdown.

His run set the stage for a memorable Giants comeback. Although Ziggy refused to let The Hook play halfback, he did keep dropping off short passes to him. Aided by the bone-crunching blocking of Cannonball Murphy and Buford Sifton, The Hook converted most of those nothing plays into big gainers, bucking, clawing, and sliding his way to one first down after another, propelled by sheer lust.

Momentum stayed with the Giants all through the rest of the game. With the wind and snow swirling all around them, the Giants blew the stunned Bills off the field, scoring four touchdowns in the third quarter alone and going on from there to finish on top, 52-28.

All together, Ziggy threw for seven touchdowns, a new playoff record. The Hook scored three of them, also a record mark for a rookie.

They were both celebrating raucously in the locker room when Bubbe came over, looking drawn and tearful. *"Chuk-keleh,"* she said, "you'd better hurry back to New York. I'm afraid your father's had another heart attack. It looks bad."

It was too late. By the time he got back to New York, his
father, Rabbi David Saul Cantor, was dead.

"You killed him!" someone shrieked in the hospital waiting
room. "You and your football *mishegass,* you killed your own
father!"

The room was jammed with dark-clad, heavily bearded men:
members of his father's congregation, but the one doing the
shrieking was Mrs. Karp, the large, excitable woman who had
kept house for the Reb after Ziggy's mother died. Beside herself with grief—and making sure everyone knew it—she ripped
into Ziggy the way she used to when he left toys on the floor
or played the TV too loudly.

Ziggy's dream came back, with its damning refrain that the
old woman had echoed eerily, as if privy to his innermost
thoughts: "You killed him, you killed him!"

Choked with sorrow, Ziggy passed through the rest of the
evening as if in a trance. If Bubbe hadn't stayed by his side, he
would never have been able to deal with all the funeral and
other family arrangements that had to be made.

On top of that, shortly after arriving at the Reb's house, Ziggy received a visit from Rabbi Gershon Kohut, the chief rabbi of New York's Orthodox movement.

After expressing his heartfelt condolences, the Rebbe, a small, caftan-clad man with a deep voice and discerning brown eyes, took Ziggy's hand and looked at him.

"Ezekiel, I was present at your *bris* and I watched you grow up," he said in deliberate but consoling way. "You were always a special kind of boy, a different one to be sure. But I always felt you would do something remarkable, which you have with your football playing.

"It's not a game I know much about, of course. My life has been lived for the Torah and its commandments. Nothing in my studies or life experience prepared me—or your blessed father, *avah sholem*—for such a thing as football. But we, no doubt, are more traditional Jewish males, descended from the sons of Jacob, who sat close to their father's tent, while you seem to have genes that connect to the tribe of Esau—the hunters and fighters of biblical times.

"I know your father condemned you for playing the game," the Rebbe continued, still holding Ziggy's hand. "I felt he was being too harsh with you but could not interfere because it was mostly a father-son quarrel—and what transpires between a father and son is always difficult and complicated."

Now the Rebbe paused and took a sip of Bubbe's lemon tea, savoring its bracing qualities.

"I don't wish to resume your father's quarrel with you," he explained. "It's not my argument and you're not my son. And I believe you have been a force for good among the Jews, made our people take pride and strength in your exploits on the field."

"I'm relieved to hear you say that," Ziggy said, "because I've come in for a lot of criticism from some Jews who felt I was making a mockery of the religion. I know some odd and crazy things have happened, but I never intended it that way. All I wanted was to have some fun and help my team win a few games."

"The Jewish religion has survived the pharaohs, the Spanish Inquisition, and Adolph Hitler, so I don't think it will be harmed by a little laughter," the Rebbe said, smiling fondly at Ziggy. "I myself was delighted to hear that half of New York is walking around in yarmelkehs these days, even the goyim. Attendance at our shuls is going up sharply for a change."

"My father was worried that football was a pagan ritual—a force from the Other Side."

"We argued about that," the Rebbe admitted. "I told him that he was probably overstating the point. But he would not soften his views on the game. He was a very strong-minded and forthright man, as you know. But that's what made him a great rabbi as well—his deep convictions, his total commitment to the faith."

"He refused to see me or even speak to me in recent weeks," Ziggy said unhappily. "That's what hurts so, that my actions completely alienated us. We were no longer father and son, we were strangers. And now he's dead and it's my fault."

Ziggy put his head down, hit with pain and remorse again.

The Rebbe gave a sigh and said compassionately, "You musn't punish yourself like this, Ezekiel. Your father fought with a lot of people, myself included. He wasn't an easy man, but neither am I. My wife is always telling me how impossible I am to live with. We Jews fight a lot at the best of times— how else could we have stayed alive in a hostile world? If your father hadn't fought you over football, he would've fought you over something else. And the same holds true for you, because you're a fighter at heart, Ezekiel. It shows up on the football field. You're a tiger, a Jewish tiger!"

Ziggy managed to smile at that. The Rebbe smiled back at him before continuing: "Ezekiel, I can only wish you luck in your athletic career, should you wish to pursue it. I think it's wonderful that you have the option of a second livelihood, outside the pale, so to speak. Some of us do not have the luxury—or the desire—to live for ourselves. Our calling is to live for the sake of others. That is always the final measure of a man—how he has lived his life for the Supreme Master and His commandments. It's the only measurement worth anything, for we cannot carry our wealth or fame into the hereafter. We will be judged only by the way we have lived for the sake of heaven."

The Rebbe paused for another sip of tea, eyes trained on Ziggy now, boring deep into the hidden parts of him.

"You spent a good part of your life preparing to follow in your father's footsteps, the footsteps of the rabbis who preceded him as well. You showed the qualities a rabbi must have: leadership, intelligence, sensitivity to others, and of course scholarship.

"That you chose not to follow through on your training was a personal decision I can only respect, difficult as it was for most of us to accept. If you feel your break with the rabbinical tradition is complete and irrevocable, then so be it, you'll make your contribution to heaven in a different way. But if there is any chance you feel a life devoted to Torah and its teachings is still within the realm of possibility, please know that we would be delighted to welcome you back.

"We would like you to take over your father's congregation and most of his duties," The Rebbe continued. "Not immediately, of course, but after the season ends, when you are free of all other obligations and have had time to think things over."

"It's out of the question" was Ziggy's immediate response. "I could never take over for my father. I'm not a good Jew," he explained. "I don't believe the way he did. I'm not the man he was."

"That remains to be seen. I think you're a better Jew than you realize. Not only do the outward signs show it—the beard and *payess* you're growing again—but the inward signs, too. You've been both leader and teacher to the Giants; I've heard all about it."

"We're just kidding around, Rebbe."

"It's having more effect than you think. You've changed the way many gentiles think of us. You've also become a role model for young Jews who've been inspired by your exploits. Your impact on America's spiritual life has been considerable."

"What kind of role model will I be if I don't sit shivah for my father?" Ziggy asked.

He explained to the Rebbe that because of the playoffs he would be obliged to practice every day, leaving him unable to mourn his father in the weeklong traditional way. He would cover his mirrors and wear torn garments, but real shivah was impossible.

The Rebbe reflected on that, stroking his beard reflexively. "That's unfortunate but it's not a crime," he said at last. "You'll be able to say kaddish for him over the next eleven months and to set a tombstone for him. You'll also be able to celebrate his memory in other significant ways."

It was the Rebbe's turn to explain himself.

"I truly do admire you, Ezekiel. I appreciate all you've been through, standing up to the pressures of the game, the attacks of the anti-Semites. I see in your courage and strength of character qualities of distinction. In time you could become a great rabbi—as great a rabbi as your father was or as I myself am. In fact, right this moment I feel inferior to you. I feel myself an old man who is incomplete, who knows some things of the spirit but very little of the flesh, the real world.

"You have that knowledge, Ezekiel, and if you can combine it with love and zeal for Israel's sacred treasure, the Torah, I am certain that you will become a remarkable and inspirational leader of your people."

Ziggy stared down at the floor. The Rebbe got to his feet.

"I've said enough. Please know that there are many among us who love you and will continue to love you, no matter what. I give you my blessings, Ezekiel Cantor, son of the late Reb David Saul Cantor, the lion."

He again took Ziggy's hands in his own warm, strong hands and said, "Good night. May you have a long life of Torah and the Commandments . . . and beat the damn Bears in two weeks."

IN THE DAYS THAT FOLLOWED, DAYS OF INTENSE PREPARATION FOR
the semifinal game against the Atlanta Falcons, Ziggy's teammates tried their best to pull him out of his depression.
Cannonball Murphy took him aside and talked at length about
the death of his own father, who had passed when he was sixteen and dearly in need of guidance. Feeling low and lost, he
had turned to the Church, finding solace and strength not
only in the sacred aspects of Catholicism but in its more
homely functions, the doing of good works, the participating
in fraternal affairs. He urged Ziggy to do the same, to take part
in as many group activities as he could at some Manhattan
congregation.

Jesus Maria Gonzalez tried a different tack. He offered to
take Ziggy up to Spanish Harlem, to meet his witch doctor
who would do her best with *santeria* spells and fetishes to lift
his spirits.

Coach Schimpf suggested that Ziggy have a bash or two in
his padded cell, as an alternate means of achieving inner
peace.

Robespierre was of the opinion that a hit or two of laughing gas would do the trick.

Ziggy was touched at his teammates' concern, especially when most of them showed up at the memorial service for his father. They crowded into the small, packed Bronx shul, forty-odd bruisers, men with shoulders like hillsides, necks like tree stumps, their hair hanging in ringlets, their beards growing wild. Wearing the skullcaps and prayer shawls they'd bought on the Lower East Side, they provided camaraderie and moral support for Ziggy as he said kaddish for his father.

Because it was an Orthodox ceremony, the press had been barred from entering, but that didn't stop Dora Glick, who gained entrance by dressing up like her grandmother in an old babushka and overcoat and walking stooped over with the aid of a cane. She registered shock when she was told she couldn't sit downstairs with the men.

Cursing under her breath, Dora made her way up to the women's section and forced her way into the first row, where she began shooting snapshots of the service with a mini camera. The woman sitting next to her, the tyrannical Mrs. Karp, turned and hissed, "You shouldn't be doing that! It's forbidden and sacreligious."

Dora reached up and plucked a long, lethal hatpin out of her babushka, leveling it at Mrs. Karp. "One more word out of you and I'll cut your *kishkas* out, you old yenta!"

Dora fired off a couple of rolls of film, getting some good stuff that her readers would eat up, but she hit real paydirt when she noticed, sitting in the last row of the bleachers, Ziggy's old flame, Rachel.

This had the makings of a story every woman's page in the country would buy: return of the "other" woman . . . Ziggy's love triangle . . . jealous catfight interrupts prayer for the dead. . . .

Dora hadn't had a scoop in weeks, not since that fucking Lieutenant Friedman had pulled the listening devices out of Ziggy's penthouse. Now she was so happy she almost smiled. The surprise factor was working out in her favor, too. Not even Ziggy knew that Rachel, hidden behind a veil and cloche hat, was here. That much was obvious from the way he concentrated on his prayers, mouthing the Hebrew mumbo-jumbo without even so much as a glance up at Rachel.

Dora took photos of all the important people in the joint: Ziggy, Rachel, Darcy, Bubbe sitting over in the far left upstairs corner, Hogarth and Homer wrapped like Egyptian mummies in their long white prayer shawls. Even Gus Schimpf, who'd let his hair and beard grow long in recent weeks, was making like a Jew.

All those misguided gentiles should be driven from the temple and horsewhipped as hypocrites and Pharisees, Dora decided. She'd gladly do the job, flaying those mock-religious bastards for the way they'd treated her all season long, calling her a jock-sniffer and peeping tom.

Bunch of bozos, she'd shown them a thing or two, though, having made it all the way up to the *Today Show* and looking good on it too, thanks to the forty pounds she'd shed. NBC had even asked her back to do additional segments on the upcoming Super Bowl; there was even talk of her being hired as one of the show's permanent hosts, at a seven-figure price.

Once the service ended, Dora made a beeline for the stairs. Outside, Lieutenant Friedman made a grab for her as she shed her Orthodox *shmattes* and took off for her limo. "Naughty, naughty, Dora, you weren't supposed to be in there," the cop said.

She tried to kick him in the nuts, but he dodged the blow and managed to hold on to her at the same time. As they scuffled, Mrs. Karp rushed up and shrieked something about the pictures she'd been taking. The tumult brought Ziggy out of the shul, still in his yarmelkeh and tallis.

He stopped short when Dora broke free and went to the nearby Rachel, snatching the veil from her face and crying, "Guess what, Ziggy—your main squeeze is back from Holland!"

Ziggy, startled, stared at Rachel. She stared back.

As they stood locking eyeballs like that, Darcy came over. One look at Rachel and she pivoted and took off, heading to the nearest cab, driven by Shlomo Volokh.

Ziggy started after her, calling, "Darcy, wait—" But she was gone.

As the other photographers on the scene shot up a storm, Dora leapt into her limo and, while the driver hightailed it out of the Bronx, began dictating over the phone an account of the Ziggy-Darcy-Rachel spat to her city editor.

Life was such a ball these days!

It wasn't much of a spat and Darcy knew it, even to the extent of apologizing later that night for the way she'd over-reacted. It was a silly, schoolgirlish thing to have done, she admitted when Ziggy called her at home. But still in all she declined his invitation to come over and meet Rachel.

"I don't think I could handle that," she said. "Anyway, I'd only be in the way. I'm sure you two have lots of things to talk about."

She was right about that. Ziggy and Rachel stayed up most of the night in Ziggy's apartment, drinking wine, listening to music, talking about Ziggy's father, the fact that he was an orphan now at twenty-four. She also brought him up to date on her own affairs.

"I've become a reporter for a Dutch paper, *De Telegraph*," she said. "I'm on assignment right now, covering the Super Bowl."

"You're kidding. They're that interested in the NFL?"

"Ziggymania's hit Holland, too," she explained. "They consider you one of their own. I'm supposed to write fifteen inches a day about you."

"The Dutch Dora Glick," he laughed. "At least I assume you write in Dutch."

"I'm completely bilingual."

"I thought you were dead set against returning to New York."

She missed a beat or two before answering. "It's different now. I've got a job at the paper . . . and a fiancé."

"Oh?" Ziggy found his face prickling hotly with jealousy. "So you're planning to marry that jazzman?"

"Rudi is yesterday's news. My hubby-to-be is a man named Karel. He's a doctor, an orthopedic surgeon actually, who specializes in sports medicine. Operates on knees, that kind of thing."

She paused a bit, averting her eyes as she took a sip of

wine.

"Aren't you going to congratulate me?"

"Of course. It's just that . . . well, I find myself upset by the news," he allowed. "I guess some part of me still loves you."

"Same here," she said, also with difficulty. "But I think I've done the right thing. I'm happy in Amsterdam, with Karel, with my job, leading a new life—a non-Orthodox life."

"By that I gather Karel is not Jewish."

"Nah. He's a real blond, blue-eyed Aryan. I'm free," she exulted. "I'm finally and forever free of the whole Jewish trip!"

"It seems to me you're paying a big price for that freedom, giving up your country, your language, everything."

"It's what I want, Ziggy. I know you find it hard to understand, but that's because you're still a good Jew at heart. You even look like one these days. You look like a big, overgrown Yeshiveh *bocher* with all that hair on your head."

"It's just cosmetic. The team treats Judaism as a good-luck charm."

"Nah, it goes deeper than that. You're just being yourself, answering the call of your DNA."

"That sounds familiar."

He told her about his meeting with the Rebbe and about the offer that had been put to him.

"I'm not surprised that the rabbinate wants you back. You're an awfully good catch."

"I wish they'd leave me alone. I've got enough to do trying to cope with the Falcon game."

"I'll bet, but how fantastic, Ziggy, that you've come this far. The last time I saw you you were content to be a substitute kicker."

"It's been quite a season," he allowed. "I'm just sorry you weren't here to share in all the excitement."

"I'm sorry too. But I'm still glad I met Karel."

He held out his glass.

"To your new life."

"To the Falcon game and then the Super Bowl," she said.

They clinked glasses.

"L'Chayim," he offered.

"Proost" she replied, adding, *"Daar ga je."* (Bottoms up.)

He tried to dredge up the little Dutch he remembered: *"Hoe gaat het er ermee?"* (Are you really okay?)

"Oh, z'n gangetje," she replied. (Not bad.)

He looked into her dark, mysterious eyes whose depths had never failed to bewitch him.

"You're really sure about him? You're really sure you're in love and not just thumbing your nose at Judaism?"

"Who knows? Perhaps that's the deep-down, secret reason. But I prefer to believe I know what I'm doing. Karel's nice, Ziggy—intelligent, capable, successful, and good-looking. He speaks five languages and helps me with my Dutch."

"In bed, of course."

"Ziggy, that's not fair."

Her anger was justified, but what could he do; against his will, jealousy had seized hold of him and was squeezing him to the point of pain.

"I'm sorry. I had no right to say that. It's just that . . . I still want you."

She turned her face from him.

"Please, Ziggy," she pleaded. "Don't make it any more difficult than it has to be. Let's just be friends. It's better that way."

"Stay with me tonight, just one night," he begged. "Let's have what we had in Amsterdam."

"What about Darcy?"

"One night, that's all I'm asking. Darcy I'll deal with later."

"Amsterdam is over," Rachel said. "Ditto the girl you loved there. I'm a different person and so are you. You're a big football star and you've got a beautiful young model for a girlfriend—a gentile, same as Karel."

"They're our substitute lovers, imitations of the real thing."

"I can't speak for you, Ziggy. But for me Karel is the real thing—or at least I think he is."

"You don't know yourself, either," he insisted. "You're as confused as I am."

"I'm sorry if I've done this to you. I shouldn't have come here tonight. I just thought we'd have a nice civilized chat."

She got up to go but he grabbed at her arm.

"Stay," he begged again. "If not with me, then in the next room. The Hook's not here."

"Who's he shacked up with tonight?"

"He's trying to seduce a girl named Michelle, the last of his cheerleaders. But he's met his match in her. No matter what he does, she won't come across."

"What's the matter, is he losing his touch?"

"He's afraid of that. It's driving him crazy."

"Men!" she cried. "Why do you always let the little head rule the big one?"

"With Hook it's the other way around—the little head is the one on his shoulders."

Rachel laughed and gave Ziggy a hug, holding him close for several long moments. Then she let go of him, picked up her bag, and said softly but firmly, "Good night, Ziggy. Night."

ZIGGY FOUND THE FALCON GAME A BLESSED RELIEF FROM HIS problems. He was able to put all thoughts of his father, Rebbe Kohut, Rachel, and Darcy behind him on Sunday in Atlanta, leading his team to a surprisingly easy 27-10 victory.

With the Bears edging the Laredo Lariats in a spirited 29-28 battle, it meant that Ziggy was going to have to go up against Mad Dog Marlboro once again, this time with the eyes of the world on them in the big one, the Super Bowl.

Schimpf gave everyone a few days off, but by the time they all reported back to work, the media juggernaut was beginning to build to maxiumum force. Ziggy found himself with little time for introspection. If he wasn't working out with the team, he was giving interviews or posing for pictures or being transported to a television studio. His life didn't belong to him now, it belonged to the public.

In a way, he was glad for all the distraction and hoopla. It kept him continually busy and focused on football. All he cared about now was not stinking things up on the ballfield with millions of eyes watching. Apprehension squeezed out the depression in his psyche. It would be awful beyond description if he had a bad game, not just for himself and the team, but the Jews as a whole.

Like it or not, his Jewishness had become a factor in this championship match. The anti-Semites around the country were after him again, with renewed fury and spite. They couldn't bear the idea that a Jewish quarterback was getting all this attention and threatening to become a champion. What also made them mad was the way he and his teammates were flaunting their Jewishness—wearing those Old World skullcaps and shawls, muttering these weird prayers, eating that Jew food all the time. Such tribal behavior was intolerable to the bigots, who fired off e-mail and faxes filled with hate and violence to Ziggy and Bubbe and even to Homer and Cannonball Murphy and the other gentiles on the team.

It got so bad that Ziggy began to fear that someone might make another attempt on his life. Lieutenant Friedman tried to reassure him, pointing out that he, Darcy, and Bubbe were being guarded by the NYPD around the clock and that Hogarth had beefed up private security arrangements for the rest of the team.

"The situation is well in hand, Ziggy," said the detective. "I'd say that you have more to fear from Mad Dog Marlboro than you do from some nutso Jew-hater out there."

Mad Dog, the designated pass rusher and chief headhunter of the Bears, had been spending his pre–Super Bowl days boasting how he was going to take Ziggy out in the big game. It sickened Ziggy to read such threats, not because he was afraid of Marlboro but because of what he symbolized. Here

was a player who for ten years or more had terrorized the
league, pulling every dirty trick in the book to dominate the
men he faced on the field. Marlboro thought nothing of spitting in a man's eyes to blind him, or clipping him from behind
to hurt him. If he wasn't holding or tripping, he was spearing
with his helmet, kicking below the belt.

By all rights, he should have been banned from pro ball and
sent back to the mental institution from which he'd come.
Instead, thanks to media buildup and fan idolatry, Mad Dog
had become a hero of sorts—the man you love to hate. The
Bears paid him three and a half million dollars a year, beer
companies put him in their commercials, kids hung his poster
in their rooms. There was something sick about the whole
thing, that someone who made a mockery of what the game
was about—sportsmanship and fair play—should be rewarded
like this and allowed to play as dirtily and brutally as he liked.

The other Giants came to Ziggy and vowed to keep Mad
Dog off his back. "I'm going to give that *bovan* a couple of *zet-
zes* that he'll never forget," is how Siffie put it. But Ziggy
knew how hard it was to contain Mad Dog, especially when
he was cranked up on speed, which gave that 350-pound
psychotic the feeling that he was invincible, the Prince of
Darkness himself.

Ziggy tried not to show it, but he was beginning to dread
the Super Bowl and wish it were behind him. He'd never felt
that way about a football game before. All his life he'd looked
forward to playing, to competing, especially in a big match
that promised to be hard-fought and close. He used to wake
up on Sundays at five or six in the morning, too eager to get

out to the park and start banging heads to get back to sleep.

Now that feeling of keen anticipation, of childlike excitement, was gone, replaced by a feeling of antipathy. He went to the park every day, but dutifully, glumly, like a factory worker dragging himself to work on the assembly line.

He did his best to hide his real feelings. He was the quarterback, the man who was supposed to lead his team and inspire it. He tried to show the world a bright face and act as if nothing were bothering him, neither the Reb's death nor Mad Dog's threats nor the swastikas in the mail. He pretended to be Etoain Shrdlu again, the mad Albino placekicker. I keek, I keek.

Normally The Hook would have sensed right away that something was wrong with him, but these days his old buddy was preoccupied with Michelle Bradford. Scoring with her was far more important than scoring a touchdown in the Super Bowl. The Hook spent every possible moment working on her, trying to persuade her not to spoil his perfect record by holding out on him. But the harder he hit on her, the more she laughed at him.

The Hook nearly blew a fuse. "I could understand her stubbornness if she were a virgin or found me repulsive," he complained to Ziggy. "But this is a girl who says she likes me. And she admits that she once balled her whole high school basketball team, on a dare. I'm morally outraged that she won't let me put a finger on her."

"What's her explanation?"

"She's just being perverse: 'If everyone else has balled you, I won't. What an ego she has."

"Give her some credit, Hook. She's not your ordinary bimbo. She's very intelligent and talented."

"Hey, whose side are you on?"

"Give the idea up. Eleven out of twelve is not too shabby an achievement."

"Speak for yourself. I've had every single woman I ever wanted."

"Now whose ego is showing? You've met your match, Hook. She's every bit as proud as you are."

"I'm going to shtup her," he swore. "She can't resist me forever."

The Hook went home and brooded on it. Only one thing left to do, he decided finally—invite Michelle up to the Bronx for a family dinner, one that he himself would cook.

It was the ultimate weapon in his arsenal, the last but most important card in his hand.

He got things going with a phone call to his parents, to make sure they were up for a Saturday night dinner. Sal, The Hook's father, now retired, was responsible for buying the wine and contacting all the guests. Josephine, his mother, was responsible for selecting the menu and assisting him in its preparation. Normally, she did all the cooking in her own house, but in light of what was at stake for The Hook, an exception was made.

The foundation in place, The Hook devoted all his spare time to the buying of the fresh ingredients for Michelle's last supper. He drove down to the Village to buy sausage from Fiacco's, picking up the mozzarella and other cheese from Joe's on Thompson Street. The bread he bought at Palermo's on Thirteenth, the pastry down at Veniero's, the pasta from Raffetto's on Houston Street (pausing to wolf down a couple of kasha knishes from nearby Yana Shimmel's).

In all, The Hook spent nearly twelve hours putting together a feast that he believed would be a guaranteed leg-opener. On Saturday he passed up the chance to earn a quick ten thousand bucks by making a personal appearance at a new Fifth Avenue tanning and exercise salon. Instead, he went back up to the Bronx and helped his mom get the elaborate, four-course dinner together. The antipasto was to be simple and light, fresh figs topped with a curl of prosciutto. Zuppa Florentina followed, then a pasta with eggplant, with The Hook's specialty, *Braciolette Ripiene,* topping the bill.

Aided by Jo, a tall, gray, but still-handsome woman in her seventies, The Hook lavished care and love on his cutlets, soaking the yellow raisins in warm water, mincing and chopping the Italian parsley and pine nuts, pounding the veal until it was thin enough to dissolve on contact in Michelle's sweet mouth. He spread the cutlets gently, fingering them as he would her loins, tamping down the stuffing and rolling them up in the shape of a tube. Tying them off, he then sprinkled them with salt and freshly ground black pepper. If that wasn't an aphrodisiac, he didn't know what was.

The old man came into the kitchen an hour before company began arriving, a case of wine from Santarpia's liquor store in East Harlem on his shoulder. It was easy to see that The Hook took his looks from him, a tall, supple man with deep, wavy hair that he dyed black, and piercing brown eyes and a full, sensual mouth that had driven many a Sugar Mama wild. He

also possessed a sexual tool that rivaled The Hook's, though it
was beginning to shrivel from age and disuse. Not even Extra-
Strength Viagra could help him any more.

While The Hook and Jo worked, Sal brought out his musical instruments—mandolin and ukelele—and tuned them up.
He warmed up his own voice as well, a voice that had been
first trained back in his Catholic school days. Not that he had
lasted long in the Church. The priest had kicked him out for
seducing a choir girl in the chapel.

By seven the dinner was simmering, the candles were lit,
and the guests had begun to arrive. The Hook had arranged
for a limo to pick Michelle up and bring her up to the Bronx,
with a nice bottle of champagne to help take the pain out of
crossing the river.

When she stepped into the small, redbrick house just off
Eastchester Road, she was greeted by a burst of laughter and
good cheer. All five of The Hook's brothers and sisters were
here, with their spouses and children. Half a dozen old neighborhood friends had come as well, along with Ziggy and
Darcy.

Michelle, knowing she'd be on show, had worked almost as
hard on herself as The Hook had worked on dinner. She'd
spent the whole day at a health and beauty spa, letting a horde
of attendants bathe and perfume her, pluck her eyebrows, cut
and highlight her tresses, massage her spine, do her finger-
nails, apply hundreds of dollars' worth of lotions and makeup.

Wearing a new dress, a classic, heart-shaped off-the-shoul-
der black thing with gold chains for straps, Michelle stopped
all conversation when she sauntered in, her long blond hair

and pink skin like an explosion of sunlight in that roomful of swarthy Mediterraneans.

The Hook's throat caught when he saw her. *Madonna,* what a woman she was with that tall, tapered body and bursting breasts and that sly, wicked look in her eyes. He found himself responding to her in a way he never had before.

He stayed by her side for the next hour, keeping her glass filled, introducing her all around, keeping the jokes going, trying to make her feel comfortable. It wasn't a chore; she seemed to love the warm, earthy family atmosphere and feel at ease with everyone she met. And when the food came, she tucked in to it lustily, packing away huge amounts of pasta, practically licking her plate clean of the *Braciolette,* and matching even the hard-drinking Sal when it came to knocking back the jug wine.

It was all going to plan, The Hook noted with satisfaction. She was reacting to the Gemutlichkeit Gambit just as he had hoped she would, raving about the food, being warmed by the wine, made giggly by the badinage. She was softening before his eyes, opening to him like a flower, shedding defenses like petals.

Then came the *pièce de résistance,* the musical part of the evening. Sal, cup of espresso and a grappa by his side, sat cradling his mandolin, joined by The Hook on ukelele, his brother Chuck on guitar, his cousin Vinnie on piano, and Ziggy playing spoons and brushes. Everyone else gathered around and started singing along with Sal on an old Irving Berlin favorite of his, the "International Rag":

London dropped its dignity,
So did France and Germany
All hands are dancing to that raggedy melody
Full of originality . . .

Michelle had memorized it by the time they went around for a second time:

The folks that live in sunny Spain dance
to the strain of the Spanish fandango
Dukes and Lords and Russian Tzars,
folks who own their motor cars,
all hands are dancing to that raggedy melody
full of originality
Italian opera singers have learned to snap their fingers,
the world goes round to the sound
of the international rag . . .

It went on like that for the next few hours, with lots of passing around of instruments and changing of personnel, but with the music and songs flowing non-stop, reverberating round the DiVecchio living room like celestial thunder, lifting spirits and unleashing affection and enveloping them in a warm glow of homeliness and love. As soon as one song ended, someone called out the name of another or simply sang the first line of the lyrics, triggering immediate recognition and response.

When Uncle Joe plays the rag on the old banjo
Everybody starts a-swingin' to and fro
People gather all around the dancin' floor

Screamin' "Uncle Joe, gimme more, gimme more!" . . .

The wine and cognac continued to slide down throats and heat up temperatures and libidos. Collars were pulled open, high heels were kicked off, men and women began to grab at each other and press tight on the dance floor.

Michelle, her arms draped around The Hook's neck, body pushing hard against his (and feeling the full, blood-hardened length of his legendary organ), murmured, "I'm having such a good time. I love your family, the food, the music, everything."

The Hook, smiling inwardly, confident of her now, replied, "We can have lots more of these parties in the months to come, if—"

"If what, Hook?"

"C'mon, you know what I'm talking about. Stop being a tease."

"I'm not saying anything I don't mean," she said earnestly. "I really do like it here. You see, I didn't have much of a childhood. I spent my first twelve years in an orphanage. A family is what I want most out of life."

"What about your cheerleading and modeling and all the rest?"

"I'd give it up in a flash if I could have a home life."

"I find that hard to believe. You seem so driven."

"Couldn't care less. Give me a nice hubby and a gang of kids and a party like this every Saturday night."

The Hook pulled back, suspiciously. "Wait a minute. What are you trying to tell me—that you won't ball me unless I marry you?"

"I wouldn't put it so crudely, but I guess that's the bottom line. You see, at heart I'm a very traditional girl. I could love you, Hook. I learned that tonight, that I could really and truly love you. But only if we had this to share, a real family, a normal life."

The Hook was rendered speechless by this. It was not where the evening was supposed to lead. He'd had bedroom on his mind, but all she was talking about was kitchen. Or even worse, the nursery.

He could not believe it. This blond, blue-eyed bombshell with the thin, water-free ankles of a nymphomaniac, was talking like a *baleboosteh*, a prosaic little homemaker. The two things just didn't fit together. Yet when he looked at her, really looked in her eyes, he knew she meant it.

He felt his breath grow short, his heart begin to pound in his chest. By all rights, he should break off dancing with her, lest this anxiety attack get worse. But his nostrils were too full of her entrancing smell and she was pressing too tightly against him, so tightly that he could feel the place where her thighs met, and how hot that place was, how burning hot and sweet and. . . .

That's when The Hook suddenly heard himself saying, "You know what, Michelle. I feel the same way, too. I'm tired of chasing around, worrying about knocking somebody up, catching a disease. So let's do it, goddammit—let's get married."

Michelle let out a shriek of joy and spun around, crying out to his family, eyes full of tears, "Guess what, everyone. The Hook has just proposed to me!"

In the uproar that followed, The Hook immediately had

second thoughts. But then everyone in the room came rushing over to congratulate them and there was his mother, also with tears in her eyes, crossing herself and thanking God for this unexpected blessing. Even the old man, drunken rogue that he was, pronounced it a good idea and kissed Michelle and The Hook on the cheeks. So what could he do but accept their best wishes and give Michelle a hug, whispering into her ear, "Now can we go to bed?"

Through her tears of joy she whispered back, "Not until the license is signed!"

"Come on," he pleaded as they began a slow dance, "don't do this to me. I'm burning up alive."

"I want to do things the traditional way."

"Next thing you know, you'll be telling me you want to get married in church."

"Not in church," she corrected. "Shul."

"What?" He stopped short and looked at her, this standard-issue WASP princess of his.

"The family that adopted me was Jewish," she explained. "I was so grateful for the way they treated me that I took their religion when I grew up."

"Are you really a Hebe?"

"Yes. Isn't it a hoot?" she giggled.

"How come you never said a word about this before, with all the Jewish stuff going on?"

"I didn't have a need to go public with the news. But now that I'm going to be married, the time is right. Is that okay with you?"

"That you're Jewish? Hell, yes—Ziggy's my best friend."

"I don't mean that. I mean about getting married in shul."

"Anywhere you want, dammit, as long as I can get into your pants."

"Hookie, I'm talking about going the whole nine yards."

"Meaning what?"

"Meaning you'll have to convert. And. . . . "

She looked at him, apprehensively.

"You mean. . . . ?" His jaws locked tight on the rest of the words.

She nodded. "Yes, I'm afraid so."

Suddenly The Hook had to sit down.

"I'm asking a lot, I know," Michelle said. "But look what you're going to get in return . . . a sex machine who'll also be a good Jewish wife to you. There hasn't been a combination like that since Marilyn Monroe."

"But . . . but," The Hook said feebly.

"Poor Hookie," she sighed compassionately. "I don't envy you. But on the other hand, if you go through with this for me, I'll know you really love me."

He looked searchingly at her.

"Are you really a sex machine?"

"I'm the best," she swore. "The very best you'll ever have. You won't ever be sorry you married me, that much I can promise you."

"You're very beautiful, Michelle. You're just about the most beautiful girl I've ever met."

"And the most loving. You'll see."

To prove it, she leaned over and placed the sweetest kiss he'd ever had on his lips.

Everyone in the room cheered the lovers again.
So what could he do but kiss her back.

THE NEXT DAY, SUNDAY, THE GIANTS FLEW DOWN TO TEXAS TO take up residence for Super Bowl Week. Home of the Laredo Lariats, the NFL's newest expansion team, the domed coliseum where the game would take place seated 150,000 people and stood in the center of a twenty-mile-square theme park built by the Mitsubishi Corporation, owners of the team and of Laredo itself, which had been acquired by the Japanese conglomerate in a NAFTA-related distress sale in the early part of the twenty-first century. The theme park had video game arcades and virtual reality chambers that allowed you to pilot the Mitsubishi blimp or have sushi served by a geisha girl.

To make visitors from Texas and Mexico feel at home, Mitsubishi had turned part of the theme park into a mock desert town complete with trailers, RVs, and wrecked cars littering front yards.

The plexiglas-enclosed Tex-Mex Coliseum itself, designed by a leading Dallas architectural firm, resembled a giant bowl of chile with grated processed cheese on top. It had three decks of luxury suites crowned by a layer of individual seats, each of which came equipped with a wide-screen Mitsubishi allowing those who couldn't see the field to either watch the game on closed-circuit TV, cruise the net, or play DVDs.

The Tex-Mex Coliseum had an air-conditioning plant the size of Harrisburg, Pennsylvania, artificial turf the color of dog vomit, and a press box with its own bar, wine cellar, and Alcoholics Anonymous meeting room. The concession stands sold food prepared by El Pollo Loco, music was provided by a home-grown mariachi band that strolled from luxury suite to luxury suite playing the one and only song it knew, "Cielito Lindo." Occasionally the mariachis went upstairs to serenade the Mexican nationals who had bought season seats (at a hundred thousand dollars each) in a segregated section called The Golden Barrio.

When the Giants reported to the coliseum on Monday morning for their first practice session, two vans came roaring up and made a screeching stop in the parking lot, spilling out a mob of wild-eyed, fist-shaking, cross-waving people. These followers of a militant Pentecostal sect called the Army of Christ believed that these were the last years before the Second Coming of Christ but that He would not come until a final battle of Armaggedon was fought with the forces of Zion. Once their saints were triumphant, they would rule and reign with Jesus for all eternity.

The police, taken by surprise, were unable to keep the mob from attacking the yarmelkeh-wearing, religiously bearded Giants' football players. Using their wooden crucifixes as clubs, the zealots went after Ziggy in a concentrated way. Immediately, the players around him, joined by Russell

Hogarth, Homer, and Lieutenant Friedman, tried to defend him. A brawl followed, with hard blows being landed and blood being spilled.

Hogarth found himself squared off against a man in a silver Lone Ranger mask. As they wrestled with each other, he got a hand up and yanked the mask off, only to recoil at what was revealed, a sunken-cheeked man with angry, glittering eyes. "Daddy!" he cried. "What in hell are you doing here? I thought you were running the KKK!"

"I'm just lending a little moral support," his father said. He made a sour face at Russell. "Look at you—you look like a goddamn Jew!"

"I am a goddamn Jew!" Hogarth replied, drawing back his fist and letting the old man have a shot in the chops that knocked him cold.

Meanwhile, Ziggy was grappling with two hysterical women who were trying to sink their teeth into his infidel flesh. He was able to repel them, but before he could make a run for it, a teenager in a T-shirt reading JESUS HITS LIKE A HEAVYWEIGHT CHAMP, threw a rock that split his mouth open, covering him with blood.

That was too much for Darcy, who freaked and ran for a taxi, screaming all the way. She went right to the airport and caught the first flight back to the safety and peace of Los Angeles.

As Lieutenant Friedman, Homer and Cannonball—followed by Dora and Bubbe—carried Ziggy into the coliseum, the press people on the scene went into a feeding frenzy. Camera teams ran this way and that, shooting from the shoulder, anchorpersons brandished their microphones like swords, reporters whipped out their cellular phones, photographers lit up the gray morning sky with their rapid-fire flashbulbs.

In the Giants' locker room, Schimpf flipped for the first time in weeks when he saw his meal ticket lying dazed and bleeding on a training table. The longhaired coach (who had come to resemble an unemployed Hungarian zither player) ripped his yarmelkeh off, flew out of the room, and ran through the catacombs of the coliseum searching for a padded cell. The closest thing he could find was a men's room decorated in color-coordinated earth tones, where he threw himself headlong at the nearest partition, hitting it so hard that he broke it into pieces and knocked himself unconscious.

When Schimpf came to later, he found himself lying on the cold tile floor with his head cradled in someone's lap: Dora Glick, messenger of mercy.

"Gus, why do you keep doing this to yourself?" she inquired solicitously.

"Never mind me, I'm fine," he said. "How's Ziggy?"

"No major damage, but he does need stitches. What a terrible thing: Now I won't be able to interview him for my *Today Show* spot."

He groaned a little, more in protest than pain.

"Our lives are tied to Ziggy's. His fate is our fate. It's not a healthy situation."

"You're right. We need something else to fall back on—something more secure than stupid-ass football. Any ideas?"

"Lots," she said, "but this isn't the time and place to discuss them."

"I'm glad you're here," Schimpf said, peering up at Dora from between the crook of her surgically altered breasts.

She bent over and kissed him.

When their tongues met and mated, Schimpf found himself becoming aroused.

Dora made a feral noise and wrestled with him until she had the commanding position.

"Now," she said. "Now we can fuck."

Schimpf had no choice but to obey.

That day set the stage for the Super Bowl game itself, which turned out to be the bloodiest, most unforgettable game in the history of the sport. The ex-CIA men who owned the Bears encouraged the team to play as dirty as it liked. That was just what Mad Dog Marlboro wanted to hear. He arrived at the park early that morning and prowled the sidelines, kicking and pawing at the turf and making whinnying noises in his throat. The only time he shut up was when someone stuck a pot of raw meat under his nose.

When the game began Mad Dog went after Ziggy every time he could, the hate pouring off him like red-hot lava. The first cheap shot he got in was right after Ziggy tried to run a draw. Mad Dog earholed him by chopping him on both sides of the helmet with his fists, making Ziggy's head ring and his hearing go temporarily dead.

Whenever Ziggy went down under a pile of players, Mad Dog would grab his throwing arm and squeeze it with all his might, numbing it.

With his arm and head hurting and his split, swollen lips making it hard for him to call signals, Ziggy wasn't himself in the first quarter. He pressed too hard and tried to force a couple of passes when he shouldn't have, leading to interceptions that cost the Giants dearly.

The Bears kept up the pressure on him, going after him time and time again. Mad Dog caught him late in the first quarter with a forearm smash to the jaw that stunned him and dropped him to his knees.

"Howdja like it?" Mad Dog shouted with glee. "Got any good Jewish jokes for us now?"

Ziggy was so woozy that Schimpf had to yank him and send Walston in as quarterback.

Walston knew a moment of elation as he took over, thinking that maybe he wouldn't have to pull a number after all to neutralize Ziggy; the Bears had done it for him.

But Ziggy's condition was diagnosed as a mild concussion and he soon recovered enough of his wits to return to the front lines. Walston realized that time was running out for him. The Bears hadn't helped him any more than Jake did. His fate was his own to decide.

Walston knew that Lieutenant Friedman had been dogging him. The cop had even searched his locker earlier, looking for some kind of weapon. Dumb-assed cop, who did he think he was dealing with, a first-timer? When he made his move it was going to be slick as diamond dust.

He had to be careful though: The attack by the Army of Christ had made Friedman paranoid. He'd stationed hundreds of Texas Rangers and plainclothesmen everywhere around the coliseum, to look out for snipers. Police dogs had sniffed the Giants' bench for explosives, helicopters were hovering overhead ready to intercept airborne marauders.

Holding a walkie-talkie to his ear, binoculars draped round his neck, Friedman himself was pacing around behind the Giants' bench, nervous as a junkyard dog. But he was no longer focusing on Walston.

Time, then, the number two quarterback thought. Time to do your thing.

What Walston didn't realize, though, was that someone was watching out for Ziggy who'd been doing it a lot longer than Lieutenant Friedman and all the Texas Rangers put together. It was none other than his sweet-faced old grannie, Rose "Bubbe" Diamond.

This was one factor Walston hadn't taken into account—the force and power of a Jewish matriarch. Not for nothing had she helped birth Ziggy, raise him, feed him, and educate him. She wasn't about to let anything happen to him while she was around, not her beloved *chukkeleh.*

Her eyes never left Ziggy while he was on the sidelines. The game she could do without. Football was rough enough to begin with, but today it more resembled a battleground, a bloodbath. She knew all too well that the Bears were after Ziggy's head, but she couldn't do anything about that other than hope for the best. But when he came off the field, that was another story, that's when she watched over him like a mother hen.

She was doing just that when Walston sidled over and picked up the cup of chicken soup she'd left for Ziggy and slipped something into it before setting it down again. Quickly, she got to the cup before Ziggy did and ran with it to Lieutenant. Friedman, Walston chasing her all the way, yelling, "Give me that!"

Friedman took one sniff with his educated nose and said, "Naughty, naughty," to Walston, who then made a grab for the cup. But the cop was too quick for him.

Backing off, he poured a finger into another cup and handed it to Walston. "Drink this down or I'll be obliged to arrest you."

"If you know what's good for you, you'll do what he says," Bubbe advised him. "He means business, buster."

Walston scowled down at the cup, but in the end took an unwilling sip from it.

When he keeled over a few moments later no one noticed it because of the excitement on the field, Ziggy finally connecting on a long bomb to The Hook for the Giants' first touchdown. Ziggy converted for the extra point, making the score at the end of the first quarter Bears 14, Giants 7.

When the paralytic Walston was driven by Lieutenant Friedman and two Texas Rangers to the locker room on a motorized cart, only Bubbe knew what was wrong with him, and she wasn't telling. Too much to do now anyway, like ladling out another batch of soup and replenishing the supplies of boiled *flanken* on the Giants' bench. The boys needed lots of strength and energy to keep standing up to the Bears, who pounded and slugged away at them mercilessly, pulling every underhanded trick in the book.

Leader of the cutthroats continued to be Mad Dog Marlboro, who came after Ziggy on every play, using his knees, elbows and fists to get past the blockers in a fanatical attempt to sack him. And whenever he succeeded, he danced around maniacally, waving his fists in the air, baring his missing teeth in a vulpine leer. "I'm gonna kill you, Jewboy," he swore. "I'm gonna bury you before the day is over!"

Ziggy tried his best to ignore Mad Dog's ravings. He tried to concentrate on the game, play it the way he liked to play it, loose and free, like a Jerry Garcia solo. Once in a while he managed it, managed to rise above the hate and madness, leading his team to a relatively easy score with his improvised and puckish calls, his polyglot Hebrew, English, and Yiddish audibles, his breathtakingly precise passes to The Hook.

But every time the Giants scored, tying the count, the Bears would come roaring back, not only going ahead again but pursuing their vendetta against Ziggy even more vengefully. Finally, the violence and evil got to him and he did something he had never done before on a football field—or anywhere else, for that matter. He tried to do another man intentional harm. Malicious harm.

The object of his ire was Mad Dog Marlboro. Ziggy waited until it was third down and long, an obvious passing down, watching out of the corner of his eye as Mad Dog charged from his defensive end position with arms upraised to try and block the ball. When he came close, Ziggy cut loose with his pass, aiming it not downfield but right at Mad Dog's exposed Adam's apple.

The ball hit with a sickening *thwack* and Mad Dog went down with a howl that was more canine than human. He too had to be helped to the infirmary by the medics, who in turn sent him off by ambulance to Laredo's main hospital, where he was operated on for massive damage to the trachea.

Without Mad Dog leading the charge, the Bears weren't the same team. The other linemen, fearing Ziggy might dish out similar medicine to them, became wary of the Giants' quarterback and began playing by the rules for a change, roughly but cleanly.

In that kind of game, the Giants had a chance to catch up, doing so on a long pass from Ziggy to Amen Armstrong sneaking out from his backfield position and spearing the ball with a graceful one-handed swipe.

The Bears came right back, punching out yardage on straight-ahead ground plays but scoring ultimately on a trick play—an end around that surprised the Giants and cost them six big ones and the point-after.

Ziggy, able to take his five-yard drop without finding Mad Dog in his face, rallied the Giants with a series of well-thrown passes that brought cries of appreciation from the enthralled crowd.

His last one, a twenty-three-yard bullet to Cannonball in the endzone, put the Giants ahead 31-28, only to have the Bears immediately regain the lead with a ninety-yard kickoff return.

At this point the Bears' fans, spurred on by local evangelists, taunted the yarmelkeh-wearing Giants' supporters by making signs of the cross and shouting things like, "The end is in sight . . . renounce your sinful ways, accept Christ as your savior!"

In return, the Giant fans sent up their now-famous cry of:

Give 'em a *zetz*, give 'em a *whisk*
Give 'em a *frosk in pisk!*
Giants, Giants, Giants!

The last ten minutes of the fourth quarter saw a magnificent display of hard-fought football worth every bit of the thousand-dollar price of admission. Both teams slugged it out valiantly and evenly, holding each other to short gains only. Ziggy tried and failed on some long heaves to The Hook, the last of which resulted in an interception down on the Bears' ten-yard line.

Fortunately for the Giants, a mistimed handoff resulted in a fumble, which the Bears recovered in the end zone. The two-point safety made the score 35-33, Bears' favor.

It stayed that way until the last five seconds of the game, when the Giants drove down to the Bears' forty-eight-yard-line.

Timeout.

The stupendous crowd in the Tex-Mex Coliseum, sloshed on tequila and beer, guts aboil with tacos and frijoles, was up on its feet for the whole interlude, which lasted for six minutes so that all remaining TV commercials could be shown during the break not once but twice each.

High up in the Giants' coaching box, Homer Bloetcher, draped in his king-sized prayer shawl and Second Avenue skullcap, stood facing east and davening compulsively, sending Hebrew prayers up to the All-Holy one, thanking Him for the blessing of life and importuning Him to pull this one out for the Giants.

In the Giants' executive suite, a split-level four-room condo complete with a fifty-foot bar, exercise room, His and Hers marble bathrooms, Russell Hogarth, also in yarmelkeh and tallis (with the Gucci trademarks showing), was pacing around with a telephone pasted to his ear as he described to the Gnomes in a mixture of German, Yiddish, and English all that was at stake in these last fateful seconds.

Out in Pasadena, Darcy Dalton, the "Jailbait" girl, sat in her parents' house eating fistfuls of popcorn as she stared at the TV, rooting with all her might for Ziggy.

In the Tex-Mex press box, crowded with three thousand inebriated reporters from around the world, the glamorous-looking Dora Glick glanced up from the story she was poised to transmit to the *Post* and trained her binoculars on Ziggy, standing before the Giants' bench, his helmet off, as he conferred with Coach Schimpf.

Dora could read Schimpf's lips as he looked at Ziggy and asked, "What do you think? Can you kick it that far?"''

"I keek, I keek," was Ziggy's reply.

When he reached the huddle Ziggy told his team, "Field goal on three, hold 'em guys, keep 'em off me, you *momzers*."

"*A glick ahf dir!*" Cannonball said. "Good luck to you, Reb."

"Yeah, *zol zein mit glick!*" the rest of the team chorused.

They lined up for the long field-goal attempt, The Hook going to one knee ready to hold for Ziggy. When the snap came, though, it was a bad one, sailing over The Hook's outstretched hands and into Ziggy's grasp. Startled, he didn't know whether he should run with it or throw it.

Meanwhile, he started moving sideways, trying to make up his mind.

From this point on things happened in unexpected fashion. Later some said that it was only blind luck that enabled the Giants to pull off what they did. Other observers disagreed, attributing the success of the broken play to the team's ability to improvise on the field, play the game in unfettered, free-wheeling fashion. Still others (Homer Bloetcher and Russell Hogarth included) gave credit to the Master of the Universe for having answered their prayers with a bona fide miracle.

The touchdown sequence went like this. Ziggy, trapped by pursuing Bears, stopped near the far sideline and threw a desperation pass over the middle to the quickly scrambling Hook.

The Hook, about to be tackled, flipped the ball behind him to Amen Armstrong, who had come barreling downfield to help out. The startled Amen took off in turn and went another ten yards before getting trapped and lateraling to Cannonball Murphy.

The latter went as far as he could and looked around for a friendly face.

Surprise. Here came Ziggy, who had picked himself up from where the Bears had decked him and taken off, going on instinct alone.

Catching the backward pass from Cannonball, he got down to the Bears' twenty-yard line and was just about to be gang-tackled when he heard a familiar voice:

"Gieben ahair!"

It was The Hook, racing up behind him at full speed.

Ziggy dished off, only to have The Hook dish it back. Together they zigzagged down the field, tossing the ball back and forth like a hot knish and giggling gleefully as they ducked and dodged one tackler after another, causing the Bears to take headers and pratfalls.

Gone was the Super Bowl and any awareness of what was at stake in this huge hothouse stadium with its TV cameras and screaming fans. They were thirteen-year-olds again, back in French Charlie's and goofing around as they careened down the field like errant pinballs, Ziggy finally crazy-legging it across the goal line with the upthrust ball for the winning touchdown.

Even then, as he was picked up and carried to the locker room by his delirious teammates and splattered with champagne and congratulated by the President of the United States, nothing was (or ever would be) as good as that feeling of being thirteen again, back in Bronx Park playing football for the pure, sweet hell of it.

T WO DAYS LATER, BACK IN NEW YORK, ZIGGY GOT THE NEWS just before he was about to join the Giants' ticker-tape parade up Broadway. It was Dora Glick who called him with it, from her office at the *Post*.

"Guess what," she said. "Mad Dog Marlboro just died on the operating table."

Dora and the rest of the press were all over him after that, trying to get him to comment on Mad Dog's death. Was it an accident, they wanted to know, or had he aimed the ball at his throat with intent to maim or kill? Ziggy mumbled something about it being an accident, but inside he knew it wasn't true.

Over the next few days he thought mightily about the rage that had seized him and made him do such an evil thing. He could only conclude that it had come from the *sitra achra*.

So his father had been right after all. There was something about football, at least the professional version of the game, that could bring out the worst in a man. Ziggy felt humbled, chastened, and disgusted with himself. He hadn't wanted to murder a man, just hurt him badly, punish him for being such a dirty, vicious son of a bitch. But in the end he had gone too far. He had become as evil and cruel as Mad Dog. He had taken pleasure in drilling him, in seeing him collapse like that. It had felt good to kill. All too good.

In the days that followed Ziggy stayed holed up in his penthouse, refusing to take part in any of the Super Bowl celebrations, the dinners and parties, the bawdy nights out in the bars and discos. He also refused to take any calls, whether they came from Dora Glick and the other press, or from Russell Hogarth and Darcy Dalton.

Instead he remained at home, reading the Torah and the Talmud and Spinoza as well. In the latter's work he found a passage that seemed particularly appropriate: "In so far as men are tormented by anger, envy, or any passion implying hatred, they are drawn asunder and made contrary one to another, and therefore are so much the more to be feared, as they are more powerful, crafty and cunning than the other animals. And because men are in the highest degree liable to these passions, therefore men are naturally enemies. For he is my greatest enemy, whom I most fear and be on my guard against."

The only thing that brought him out of his funk was a call from Mrs. Karp, up in the Bronx, who reported that she had discovered a couple of trunks in the basement belonging to his father. "You need to go through his things and decide what should be kept and what should be given away to charity."

Ziggy drove up and spent a long day sorting through the

Reb's papers and possessions, finding pictures of his mother that he hadn't seen in years, shots of her and Bubbe in New Brunswick, others showing her as a young bride and looking radiant and happy in those early years of marriage. Looking at her brought back the love he felt for her and the pain, the indescribable sorrow, that had descended on him when she died.

When his tears dried, he began poking around further in another of his father's trunks. In sorting out some clothing, he found the Reb's formal Orthodox garb, the round black fur-trimmed hat and long caftan and black pants and white shirt that he wore on ceremonial occasions. Ziggy tried them on and was startled when he looked in the mirror and noticed that, with his black, blossoming, curly beard and earlocks, he was a dead ringer for his father as a young man.

As he stood staring at himself, comparing himself to a photo of the Reb at twenty-five, the skin on the back of his neck prickled, so uncanny was the resemblance. He also felt strangely comfortable in this garb, cheered up and strengthened somehow. He felt connected to the Reb as never before and even to the other rabbis in his family, the whole long line of them. They too had once worn *shtreimls* and caftans like these, big powerful men with luxuriant beards and ringlets and dark, probing eyes that had pondered the deepest questions and contradictions of existence. They'd tried to understand the split between good and evil in man, tried to find a reason why the righteous suffer and the wicked prosper, struggled to maintain their belief in an all-seeing, all-powerful God.

He found it hard to take off his father's garments. It pleased and comforted him to see himself like this, the likeness of a good, pious, and compassionate Jew. He liked himself for the first time since the Super Bowl, if only because he was pretending to be someone else, someone better than himself.

Finally, after changing, he went outside to start loading his car up and was surprised to discover a mob of people; somehow the news had got out in the neighborhood that he was here. The groupies, autograph hounds, and just plain friends sent up a cry and pressed forward, shouting his name.

Quickly, he went back inside, put the caftan and *shtreimel* back on, slipped out a back door and walked to the Pelham Parkway subway station. Nobody recognized or bothered him at any point during the long ride downtown. A young Yeshiveh *bocher* even beckoned to him and said, "Take my seat, Reb."

The most noteworthy event of the ensuing two months was the dual circumcision ceremony of Homer and The Hook. They had joined forces in order to provide each other with moral support.

The *bris* took place in Bubbe's apartment and had to be adapted to suit the circumstance of the subjects being adults. The *mohel,* who had never circumcised a grown man in his life, required four shots of shnapps to calm his nerves and steady his hand. Even then, the thought of doing his job in front of a roomful of football players, great hulking brutes in New York Giants' skullcaps, gave him the shakes. Normally, he performed his services in front of a baby's family. Normal people, normal circumcision.

Today, though, everything was *farkuckt*. Ziggy acted as the *sandek* or godfather, putting his arms around Homer and The Hook and reciting a Hebrew greeting: "Blessed be that cometh."

Then, instead of placing the baby on his lap, Ziggy led Homer and The Hook into the bedroom, where they stretched out on twin beds. More prayers were pronounced. Then it was time for the *mohel* to do his thing.

Apprehensively, he approached Homer first. The big-bellied, red-faced Oklahoman lay flat, a Hilton towel draped over his bare loins. A nurse and doctor stood by. The MD could have done the circumcision, but Homer had insisted on a religious functionary. "Let's do it the right way, the Orthodox way."

He kept his eyes closed as the *mohel* approached him. The Hook shut his eyes as well. Off to one side, Bubbe and Michelle, the brides-to-be, stood clutching each other, staring down in horror at the blade in the *mohel's* hand.

Homer, tanked on Jack Daniels, turned white as the *mohel* stood over him, breathing in irregular gasps. Others in the room who also held their breath included Russell Hogarth, Gus Schimpf, Dora Glick, Darcy Dalton, Cannonball Murphy, and Buford "Siffie" Sifton. The *mohel* pulled Homer's towel away and raised his knife. Bubbe had to be lowered into a seat.

Surprisingly, the rest was anticlimactic. Thanks to the anesthetic the nurse had delivered earlier, Homer felt nothing when the blade fell. Also, the *mohel* was quick and expert. Homer's only suffering came much later, when the anesthetic wore off. Ready to howl, he swallowed the rest of the bottle of J.D. and managed to pass out in Bubbe's arms.

The *mohel* had been warned what to expect when facing The

Hook. Otherwise, old man that he was, the shock might have been too much for his nervous system. But even so, his eyes widened and he cried out *"Oy, Gottenyu!"* when the towel came off and The Hook's infamous sex organ was exposed.

Unable to move, eyes goggling out, the *mohel* stood staring down at it, transfixed. Seconds like minutes went by.

Finally, the irate Hook snarled, "Come on, already. Do it!"

As the mohel raised a trembling hand, Michelle was heard to whisper, "Don't take off too much!"

The mohel, knowing this was his finest moment, the crowning achievement in a long and otherwise uneventful career, brought his blade down emphatically.

That's when Gus Schimpf and Darcy Dalton gave a scream, Cannonball and Siffie, too. Michelle caved in, falling into Ziggy's arms. Even the *mohel* had to sit down when he was done, trembling and weeping with relief.

The only person who didn't crack was Dora Glick who later, over sponge cake and wine, reminded everyone that the prophet Abraham, a man after her own heart, had circumcised himself. She also remarked that it had been a most successful joint ceremony.

Several weeks later, Homer and The Hook once again took part in a combined religious ceremony, this one their marriages to Rose "Bubbe" Diamond and Michelle Bradford.

Another soon-to-be-wed couple was in attendance, Gus Schimpf and Dora Glick. They had scheduled a civil ceremony in the state of Delaware, which is where their company had been incorporated, the one they'd set up to test-market the first commercial padded cell ever built in America, in Westport, Connecticut, an affluent, hard-drinking commuter town with a big need for instant family therapy.

The prototype was so successful that they had been able to sell their idea to the Gnomes of Zurich, who planned to franchise the idea internationally under the name of "Tantrums Anonymous."

Overnight multimillionaires, both Gus and Dora resigned their jobs and made plans to return to college to get their degrees in clinical psychology.

The dual wedding went off relatively smoothly, the only hitch coming when The Hook suddenly got cold feet over becoming a married man. "It's an unnatural way to live," he told Cannonball Murphy and Buford Sifton in the waiting room. "No man can possibly fuck the same woman for the rest of his life."

He tried to bolt, but they were ready and held him in place. Cannonball guided him down the aisle, using a half nelson to keep him from getting away. And when The Hook was asked if he took this woman to be his lawfully wedded wife and opened his mouth to protest, Cannonball kept applying the pressure until The Hook's cry of "No" was transformed into "Nnnooo . . . aagggh . . . dooo!"

In all, it was a moving and inspiring ceremony. Michelle in her long, sweeping, white gown made a ravishing bride. Bubbe, in a Ralph Lauren suit, was fetching and bewitching. Homer, resplendent in a white *kittel*, smiled his way through the whole Hebrew ritual. Even The Hook managed to cheer up by the time it ended.

Officiating at the nuptials in the newly opened "Temple of the Stars" in Giants Stadium was the first chaplain-quarterback in pro football history, Rabbi Ezekiel "Ziggy" Cantor.

Six months later Ziggy returned to the chapel to give thanks to the Supreme Master for the seven-year, quarter-of-a-billion-dollar contract he had signed with the Gnomes of Zurich, and to ask for blessings on his forthcoming marriage to the "Jailbait Girl," Darcy Dalton, who was pregnant with their first child—a boy, of course.

WILLARD MANUS is the author of *Mott the Hoople,* among other books. His plays have been produced in London, Paris, Vienna, Berlin, Los Angeles, Washington, and New Orleans. He is a member of the American Theater Critics Association, and writes on blues and jazz for several magazines. He lives in Los Angeles.

THE PIGSKIN RABBI, by Willard Manus.
PERFECT SILENCE, by Jeff Hutton. A novel of baseball and the Civil War.
TOWARD THE SUN: The Collected Sports Stories of Kent Nelson.
CHANCE by Steve Shilstone. A baseball novel, a literary riddle.
LOW AND INSIDE: Baseball Anecdotes, Oddities, and Curiosities (1850-1915)
THREE MEN ON THIRD: Baseball Anecdotes, Oddities, and Curiosities (1915-1950)
GOLF WITHOUT TEARS: Stories of Golfers an Lovers, by P. G. Wodehouse.
THE ENCHANTED GOLF CLUBS, by Robert Marshall.
TENNIS AND THE MEANING OF LIFE: A Literary Anthology of the Game.
          Edited by Jay Jennings.
FULL COURT: Stories & Poems for Hoop Fans. Edited by Dennis Trudell.
HOCKEY SUR GLACE   Stories by Peter LaSalle.
CAVEMAN POLITICS, by Jay Atkinson. (rugby novel)
METAL COWBOY: Tales from the Road Less Pedaled, by Joe Kurmaskie.
THE QUOTABLE CYCLIST: Great Moments of Bicycling Wisdom,
          Inspiration, and Humor. Edited by Bill Strickland.
NORTH WIND IN YOUR SPOKES: A novel of the Tour de France,
          by Hans Blickensdorfer.
SPOKESONGS: Bicycle Adventures on Three Continents, by Willie Weir.
THE LITERARY CYCLIST: Great Bicycling Scenes in Literature
          Edited by James E. Starrs.
THE WHEELS OF CHANCE, by H. G. Wells. (cycling novel)
THE YELLOW JERSEY, by Ralph Hurne. (cycling novel)
THE QUOTABLE WALKER: Great Moments of WisDom and Inspiration for Walkers
          and Hikers, edited by Roger Gilbert, Jeffrey Robinson, and Anne Wallace.
THE WALKER'S LITERARY COMPANION, by Gilbert, Robinson, & Wallace.
THE RUNNER'S LITERARY COMPANION: Great Stories and Poems about
          Running. Edited by Garth Battista
THE QUOTABLE RUNNER: Great Moments of Wisdom, Inspiration,
          Wronghead-edness and Humor. Edited by Mark Will-Weber.
THE ELEMENTS OF EFFORT: Reflections on the Art and Science of
          Running. By John Jerome.
FIRST MARATHONS: Personal Encounters with the 26.2-Mile Monster.
          Edited by Gail Kislevitz.
MY FIRST IRONMAN, edited by Kara Douglass Thom
WOMEN RUNNERS: Stories of Transformation, edited by Irene Reti and Shoney Sien.
IT'S NEVER TOO LATE: Personal Stories of Staying Young Through Sports.
          Edited by Gail Kislevitz.
THE OTHER KINGDOM, by Victor Price.
BONE GAMES: Extreme Sports, Shamanism, Zen, and the Search for
          Transcendence, by Rob Schultheis.
WIND, WAVES, AND SUNBURN: A Brief History of Marathon Swimming,
          by Conrad Wennerberg
THE QUOTABLE RUNNER TRAINING LOG. Mark Will-Weber
THE PENGUIN BRIGADE TRAINING LOG John Bingham
THE SWEET SPOT IN TIME: The Search for Athletic Perfection
STAYING WITH IT: On Becoming an Athlete, by John Jerome
STAYING SUPPLE: The Bountiful Pleasures of Stretching, by John Jerome.
THE ATHLETIC CLASSICS OF JOHN JEROME
EYE ON THE SEA: Reflections on the Boating Life, by Mary Jane Hayes.

BREAKAWAY BOOKS
IN BOOKSTORES EVERYWHERE
1-800-548-4348   **www.breakawaybooks.com**